Jonas Hassen Khemiri, born in Sweden in 1978, is the internationally acclaimed author of four novels and six plays, and his work has been translated into more than twenty languages. His first two novels, *One Eye Red* and *Montecore*, were awarded several prizes in Sweden, including best literary debut and the Swedish Radio Award for best novel. His fourth novel, *Everything I Don't Remember*, was awarded Sweden's prestigious August Prize and was a top ten bestseller. He lives in Stockholm with his family.

Praise for *Everything I Don't Remember*

'Jonas Hassen Khemiri's wry, sharply observed tales of post-9/11 Swedish life have a huge following in Sweden, giving him a status something like that of Zadie Smith. *Everything I Don't Remember* is heartbreakingly sad and laugh-out-loud funny. Its chorus of young drifters, romantics and cynics stick in the memory, each competing to tell their own truth about Samuel and his tragic death' Hari Kunzru, author of *Gods Without Men*

'Unforgettable. In this non-putdownable puzzle of a story, Khemiri manages to both thrill and break your heart' Gary Shteyngart, author of *Super Sad True Love Story*

'A wonderful and mysterious book. Close to a journalistic or criminal investigation, every sentence trembles with Khemiri's electrifying prose. A very original tour de force that still vibrated in my mind long after I had read the last page' Herman Koch, author of *The Dinner*

'My books of the year [include] Jonas Hassen Khemiri's enigmatic novel' Joyce Carol Oates

'With its energetic prose and innovative structure, *Everything I Don't Remember* confirms that Jonas Hassen Khemiri is not only one of Sweden's best authors, but a great talent of our time' Vendela Vida, author of *The Diver's Clothes Lie Empty*

'*Everything I Don't Remember* is a wonderful exploration of human motivation – why we love, hate, crave and reject each other. Khemiri writes with an acute sense of perspective and his clean, conceptual prose is gripping from start to finish' Nikita Lalwani, author of *Gifted*

'[An] intelligent, sensitive book' *Big Issue*

'Jonas Hassen Khemiri's audacious and richly drawn new novel pushes the boundaries of literary fiction ... Beneath [the] structural pyrotechnics lies a broader story of imposition, appropriation and lack of individual agency: that of the immigrant experience' Lucy Scholes, *The National*, UAE

'Compelling ... [A] painful novel about youthful optimism gone hopelessly wrong' *Publishers Weekly*

'Jonas Hassen Khemiri has crafted an enthralling jigsaw puzzle of a book. Part love story, part reflection on loss, on memory, *Everything I Don't Remember* is a smart, one-of-a-kind literary novel that is both beautiful and heart-breaking. This is story-telling at its best' Jennifer McMahon, author of *The Night Sister*

Everything I Don't Remember

JONAS HASSEN KHEMIRI

Translated from Swedish by Rachel Willson-Broyles

SCRIBNER

LONDON NEW YORK TORONTO SYDNEY NEW DELHI

First published in Sweden with the title *Allt Jag Inte Minns* by Albert Bonniers, 2015
First published in Great Britain by Scribner, an imprint of Simon & Schuster UK Ltd, 2016
This paperback edition published by Scribner, an imprint of Simon & Schuster UK Ltd, 2017
A CBS COMPANY

Copyright © Jonas Hassen Khemiri, 2015
English translation copyright © Rachel Willson-Broyles, 2016

This book is copyright under the Berne Convention.
No reproduction without permission.
® and © 1997 Simon & Schuster Inc. All rights reserved.

SCRIBNER and design are registered trademarks of The Gale Group, Inc.,
used under licence by Simon & Schuster Inc.

The right of Jonas Hassen Khemiri to be identified as author of this
work has been asserted in accordance with sections 77 and
78 of the Copyright, Designs and Patents Act, 1988.

Published by agreement with Ahlander Agency.

'What's My Name', Rihanna feat. Drake, written by Tor Erik Hermansen,
Aubrey Drake Graham, Traci Colleen Hale, Mikkel Storleer Eriksen,
Esther Dean. Copyright © EMI Music Publishing Ltd.

1 3 5 7 9 10 8 6 4 2

Simon & Schuster UK Ltd
1st Floor
222 Gray's Inn Road
London WC1X 8HB

www.simonandschuster.co.uk

Simon & Schuster Australia, Sydney
Simon & Schuster India, New Delhi

A CIP catalogue record for this book
is available from the British Library

Paperback ISBN: 978-1-4711-5510-9
eBook ISBN: 978-1-4711-5509-3

*This book is a work of fiction. Names, characters, places and
incidents are either a product of the author's imagination or are
used fictitiously. Any resemblance to actual people living or
dead, events or locales is entirely coincidental.*

Typeset in the UK by M Rules
Printed and bound by CPI Group (UK) Ltd, Croydon, CR0 4YY

Simon & Schuster UK Ltd are committed to sourcing paper
that is made from wood grown in sustainable forests and support the Forest
Stewardship Council, the leading international forest certification organisation.
Our books displaying the FSC logo are printed on FSC certified paper.

Oh na na, what's my name?

RIHANNA

PART I: AM

PART II: LAIDE

PART III: PM

PART I

AM

THE HOUSE

The neighbor sticks his head up over the hedge and asks who I am and what I'm doing here.

*

Welcome. Have a seat. Relax. There's nothing to worry about, I promise. One click of the panic button and they'll be here in thirty seconds.

*

The neighbor says he's sorry; he explains that after everything that happened they can't be blamed for being suspicious of anyone they don't recognize.

*

I had definitely pictured what it would be like in here, too. You know, more like in the movies. Thick iron bars, a disgusting toilet in the corner, bunk beds, and steamy showers where you have to be careful not to drop the soap. I thought I would have to walk around with a razor blade in my mouth twenty-four-seven to be prepared. But you can see for yourself. This is more like a hostel. The people here are chill. The toilets are clean. There's even a workshop where you can make stuff out of wood. I was lucky to end up here.

*

The neighbor invites me in for coffee; we walk up the gravel slope together; he closes the door to the study and turns on the coffeemaker in the kitchen. Tragic, he says, shaking his head. It's so incredibly tragic, what happened.

*

Two months and three days left. But it's okay. I don't think about it too much. I'm pretty happy here. Okay. It's a long time. But then again, I don't have to worry about how I'll make rent. What do you want to know? Should I start with how I met Samuel? Do you want the long version or the short one? You decide. I have all the time in the world.

*

The neighbor sets out small white cups and places Ballerina cookies on a saucer. Who else have you talked to? he asks. So many rumors are going around the neighborhood. Some people say that Samuel was depressed and had been planning it for a long time. Others say that it was just an accident. Some people blame that girl he was dating, what was her name?

Laida? Saida? That's right, Laide. Others say that it was Samuel's big friend's fault, that guy who's in jail, the one who would do anything for money.

*

The first time we met was in February, two thousand nine. I was making rounds with Hamza. He had received a tip that a certain person was at a house party in Liljeholmen. We went over there and rang the doorbell; Hamza stuck his foot in the door before the girl who had opened it had time to close it, and he did his spiel about how we knew someone who knew someone and we were here to celebrate her new apartment. At last she let us in from the cold.

*

The neighbor pours coffee into the cups, holds out the saucer of cookies, and says that he didn't know Samuel particularly well. His grandmother, though, I knew her. When you've been neighbors for over twenty years, you get to know each other, it's inevitable. We used to say hi when we ran into each other down by the mailboxes. We asked how things were going; we remarked upon the weather. One time, we had a longer conversation about the pros and cons of installing geothermal heating. She was a great woman. Honest and straightforward, stubborn and strong-willed. It's really too bad everything ended the way it did.

*

I followed Hamza into the fancy apartment. We walked from room to room, we nodded at people who looked down at the parquet instead of saying hello. I wondered what we were doing there, because the people at the party didn't look like people who would have business with Hamza. The guys were wearing suit jackets and the girls were wearing special indoor shoes; the fridge had a digital display and an icemaker. I thought, this will be quick, Hamza just has to find the right person, do what needs to be done, and I'll stand there next to him to make it clear that this is no time for discussion.

*

The neighbor takes a sip of coffee and turns his face toward the ceiling to swallow it. The last time I saw Samuel? It was when he was here to pick up the car. I remember it like it was yesterday. It was a Thursday morning, it had rained overnight but the weather had cleared. I was sitting here listening to the radio when I saw someone sneaking around down by the mailboxes. I stood up and went over to the window to get a better look.

*

There was music in the living room. People were dancing politely, like shop mannequins. They had these smiles on them like Lego men. But in there among them was Samuel. And my first thought was that he was having an epileptic fit. He was, like, vibrating in time with the low-volume music. Then he got down on his knees and bounced like a guitar player.

6

Then he shook his head side to side like he was pretending to be a church bell. It was two hours before midnight and Samuel was dancing like it was the world's last-slash-best song.

*

The neighbor rises and goes to stand by the window. This is where I was standing. Right here. It was twenty minutes to nine. I stared at the mailboxes. I was holding the phone. I had a certain number to call in the event it was someone I didn't recognize. But I quickly realized that it was Samuel. He was coming up the slope with the local paper and a few advertising flyers in his hand. He was wearing a shirt and jacket under his unbuttoned coat. He was walking slowly, looking at the ground.

*

Hamza kept going. I followed him. We found the right person, we had a short conversation, bills changed hands, everything went nice and smooth. When we were done, Hamza was thirsty and wanted a drink. We went to the kitchen. Hamza poured two drinks for himself and one for me. He chugged the first drink and did this big cartoon shudder. Then we stood there in silence. No one talked to us. We didn't say anything to anyone. Now and then the girl whose party it was peeked into the kitchen to make sure we didn't swipe anything.

*

The neighbor extends a crooked index finger. Do you see that birch? That's where he stopped. He stared up at the charred

7

treetops and the burned house. I remember thinking that he looked paler than usual. He raised one hand and patted himself on the cheek, as if he wanted to wake himself up or maybe comfort himself.

*

After a few minutes, Samuel and a girl with a downy mustache came into the kitchen. Samuel had dark circles under the arms of his T-shirt; the girl was wearing a red blanket without holes for her arms. She was talking evening plans, there was a club night at Reisen and a DJ had put them on the guest list at Grodan and later someone called "Horny Hanna" was having a party in Midsommarkransen. Samuel nodded and filled up his glass. I was thinking that he was about as muscular as a bow and arrow. Hamza went to the bathroom. I stayed put. This was a good time to say something. At this point you could stick out your hand and introduce yourself the way people do when they meet at parties. How's it going? I could say. What's up? How do you know the girl whose party this is? Which DJ is playing at Reisen? What is Horny Hanna's exact address? But I didn't say anything. I just stood there thinking that I should say something. Because there and then I wasn't as used to hearing my own voice as I am now.

*

The neighbor sits down again and pours more coffee. Then about fifteen minutes must have passed. When Samuel came out of the house he was carrying a plastic bag that was so full it looked like the handles would break. He stuffed the bag in the backseat and was just about to get behind the wheel when he caught sight of me. He raised his hand to wave.

*

Samuel's friend went out for a smoke. Samuel started opening and closing the kitchen drawers.

"You don't happen to know where I can find a knife, do you?" he asked me.

I pointed at the knife block.

"Thanks."

Samuel took a watermelon from the fruit bowl, split it in half, and asked if I wanted a piece. I nodded. Then he cruised through the kitchen, handing out pieces of watermelon to anyone who wanted one.

"Lame party," he said when he came back.

I nodded.

"Are you guys going somewhere else later?"

I shrugged.

"Do you want to try something cool? Here—stick your hand in here."

Samuel held out the watermelon half. I wondered if he was entirely sane.

"Seriously—do it."

"Why?" I asked.

"It will be memorable."

And without really knowing why, I put out my hand and stuck it into the melon.

"How does it feel? Weird, right? Awesome? Now it's my turn."

It didn't feel like anything special. Wet. And crisp. I pulled my hand out of the watermelon and Samuel stuck his own in. The other people in the kitchen looked at us like we were pissing in the sink. But Samuel just smiled and asked if they wanted to try it.

"You'll regret it," he said when they shook their heads.

*

The neighbor sighs. He stood there. Next to his grandma's Opel. With his hand raised in greeting. And I was close to waving back. But then I saw the soot-covered yard, the remains of what had been his grandma's attic, the black burn marks on the roof of my garage. I remembered how badly it might have ended if the wind had been blowing in a different direction. I looked away. But it was harder than I would have expected. I nearly had to do this so my hand wouldn't wave all on its own [pushing his right hand down with his left]. Some things are so deeply ingrained that it's impossible to stop yourself. You've done them all your life and they're just automatic. It's like with sexuality.

*

Samuel wiped his hand and introduced himself. I didn't know which name I should use because when I was out doing rounds with Hamza I never gave my real name. One time I called myself "Örjan." Another time I introduced myself as "Travolta."

Once when we slipped into a private party in Jakobsberg, on the hunt for twin sisters who had borrowed money to keep their hair salon afloat, I called myself "Hoobastank." I could say anything I wanted, because when you look a certain way no one would dare to tell you that your name is not your name. But when Samuel introduced himself I told him my real name. I braced myself for the inevitable questions. "What did you say? Vamdad? Vanbab? Van Damme? Oh, Vandad. What kind of name is that? What does it mean? Where are your parents from? Did they come here as political refugees? Were you born here? Are you whole or half? Do you feel Swedish? How Swedish do you feel? Do you eat pork? By the way, do you feel Swedish? Can you go back? Have you gone back? How does it feel to go back? Do you maybe feel foreign when you're here and Swedish when you're there?" When people realized I didn't want to talk origins they would ask about working out, whether I liked protein drinks, or what I thought about MMA.

*

The neighbor pushes away his coffee cup and clears his throat. In retrospect, I think I might as well have waved back. What difference could it have made? Maybe none at all. Samuel's day would have started out a bit more pleasantly. He would have been in a slightly better mood when he pulled out into traffic. But there was no way I could know that it would be the last time I saw him.

*

Samuel was different. Samuel didn't try to talk origins or working out. Samuel just said:

"Vandad? Like the shah who battled Genghis Khan? Rad."

Then he devoted ten minutes to talking about Mongols. He said that point-five percent of the men in the world share DNA with Genghis Khan solely because he had sex with-slash-raped so many girls. He said that Genghis Khan's empire was the largest in world history and that the Mongols killed like forty million people. He said that the Mongols punished cheapskate village chieftains by pouring freshly melted, red-hot gold into their bodily orifices until they were fried. I had no clue why this scrawny little dude was talking to me about Mongols, and I had no clue why I was listening. But there was something different about the way we were chatting. We never brought up jobs, addresses, or backgrounds. We only talked about Mongol weaponry, their battle techniques, their loyalty, their horses. Or. Mostly Samuel was the one doing the talking, and I listened. But when the girl whose party it was came into the kitchen and saw us standing there, super deep in conversation, it was as if she started seeing me in a different light. I liked the way she was looking at me.

"How do you know all of this?" I asked, thinking that maybe he was a history teacher.

"I don't know," Samuel said, and smiled. "I think it comes from some computer game. My memory is fucking weird. Some things just stick."

"But mostly they just vanish," said his red-blanket-clad

friend, as she came back in from the balcony in a cloud of smoke.

*

The neighbor brushes a few crumbs from the vinyl tablecloth and says that he certainly isn't like *some* people in the neighborhood. I don't have any prejudices against people from other countries. I have never understood the point of different cultures isolating themselves from each other. I love to travel. Ever since I retired I've spent the winter abroad. Indian food is very good. There's a guy who works at the fish counter at Konsum who's from Eritrea and he is very nice. I had no problem at all when new people started moving into Samuel's grandmother's house. It didn't bother me that some of the women had veils. On the other hand, I didn't like it that they used the grill out on the roof terrace and threw their garbage bags in my garbage can. But that had nothing to do with their background.

*

When Hamza came back, the mood in the kitchen was transformed. People held their glasses closer to their bodies.

"Ready?" I asked.

"Do fags fuck in the woods?" he said.

"Why do fags fuck in the woods?" Samuel asked.

"Aw, it's a fucking figure of speech," Hamza said. "Read a book and maybe you won't have to broadcast your ignorance."

Hamza and I took off; I noticed that he was in a mood, something had gotten into him, it was going to be a long night. I was right, before the night was over some stuff had happened, I can't get into exactly what, but I backed him up, I didn't let him down, I'd said that I would be with him all the way and I was, I had his back, loyal as a Mongol. But on the way home I promised myself I'd scale back and try to find a new way to pay the rent.

*

The neighbor shakes my hand and wishes me good luck in reconstructing Samuel's last day. If I were to give you one piece of advice, it would be to keep it simple. Just tell what happened—no frills. I've read parts of your other books, and it seemed like you were making things unnecessarily difficult for yourself.

THE HOME

The nurses' aide on the first floor says that she doesn't want her real name to appear in the book. Call me "Mikaela" instead. I've always wanted to be "Mikaela." I had a friend in daycare with that name, and I was always so jealous that she could say it and no one would ask her any questions about where she was from and what her name meant. She looked pretty much like me but because of her name she was treated differently. Put that I didn't really know Samuel. I had only met him a few times at work; all I did was open the door for him when he visited his grandma. The last time he was here I heard a rapping sound at the door, a sharp noise that hurt my ears, and when I came out Samuel was standing there knocking on the glass with a car key. I had given him the code before and once I had even given him my mnemonic, the one I used to remember the code at first, but now there he was again, knocking and looking kind of ashamed when he saw me. He looked like he'd just woken up. He was holding a plastic bag that was full to bursting and a round ring of vapor had formed in front of his mouth and I recall wondering how long he had been standing there trying to remember the code.

*

Nothing in particular. Believe me. If it was crucial to the story I would tell you. Some crap. Shenanigans. Hamza was meeting a guy who owed him money, and the guy and Hamza were not in complete agreement about how big the loan was. We had to take him to the bathroom and remind him of the amount. Nothing serious, I don't think he even reported it. It was just a normal night that ended with us calling our taxi-driver contact, who took us home nice and quick with no receipt. Hamza was giggling in the backseat, he was happy with the night's profits, he counted out bills for me and as usual he said that we ought to join forces, strike out on our own, not just slave for other people. But I had decided I was done with all that.

*

"Mikaela" smiles when I ask about her mnemonic. I mean, it sounds super nerdy when you say it, but that's the thing about mnemonics, the nerdier they are the better they work, and back then the code was fourteen seventy-two and I always thought that the job was like a mix between entering a world war—fourteen—and being kidnapped by terrorists in an Olympic village—seventy-two. I shared my rule with Samuel twice because I was tired of opening the door for him, and here I had to do it again, I opened it and said hi and asked him, didn't he remember the mnemonic?

"Mnemonic?" he said.

And I thought: Okay, it's one thing not to remember the code, and another to not remember the mnemonic. But it is pretty weird if you can't even remember that you ever heard a mnemonic. I might even have been thinking: Okay, it's a family trait, see you here in a few years.

*

Later that same week I contacted a moving company. I knew some people who had gotten jobs there on short notice. Blomberg was sitting there with his yellow baseball cap and his headset and his binders and when I came in and introduced myself his eyes wandered from one of my shoulders to the other.

"Do you have a driver's license?"

I nodded.

"Are you a Swedish citizen?"

I nodded.

"When can you start?"

*

The nurses' aide on the second floor has no problem at all having his real name in the book. My name is Gurpal but everyone calls me Guppe. Do you want my last name too? Write that I'm thirty-eight years young and single, I like long walks, space movies, and R. Kelly, but not his dirtiest songs. I've been working here for two years, almost three, but it's just temporary, I'm actually a musician, I have a small studio at home, built it myself, a converted closet where I record my own songs, it's modern soul but in Swedish, lots of strings and a piano, seasoned with bhangra influences, hip-hop beats, and melodic refrains. A buddy described it as up-tempo trip-hop pressed through a filter of jazzy soul, it's urban pop music marinated in classic bebop, with a jungle streak. Oh, it sounds wack when I describe it but I'd be happy to send you a few songs if you want to take a listen?

*

Before we get back to what happened then, I want to know a little more about you. How did you come up with this idea? Why do you want to tell Samuel's story? Who else have you talked to?

*

Guppe says it was the end of his shift when Samuel came out of the elevator. It was nine thirty but his grandmother had been up since seven and was asking about him every ten minutes. By the time he finally arrived, she had fallen asleep.

"How is she?" Samuel asked, stifling a yawn.

"It seems to be a good day today," I said. "Are you moving in?"

Samuel smiled and looked down at the plastic bag, which was as full as a trash bag.

"No, no, just a few things from her house. Nostalgia stuff. Thought it might be nice to have."

"For you or for her?"

18

"Both. Have you heard this classic?"

Samuel dug a CD out of the bag. On the cover was a transparent toy piano full of candies.

"*Ear Candy Seven?*"

Samuel nodded.

"By Lars Roos. Also famous for the masterpieces *Ear Candy One* through *Six*. Grandma listened to him all the time when I was little."

Samuel walked over to his grandma, who was sitting in the TV room and napping. She was wearing white shoes, a thin beige jacket, and a skirt whose color I don't remember. Her suitcase stood next to her. I had tried to explain that she didn't need it, that she was only going to the hospital and then she would come back. But she contradicted me; she said she had to bring it along and if there was anything I'd learned in my time here it was that you couldn't change her mind once she had made it up. "I'm not stubborn," she liked to say. "But I never give in."

*

Okay. Take it easy. Put your CV away. I don't give a crap which publisher does your books. I don't care what else you've written. I'm just curious as to what about your personal history makes you the right person to tell this story. What made you want to write about *Samuel*?

*

Guppe says that Samuel stood there looking at his grandma for a minute or two before he woke her up. She was snoring.

19

She was sitting there with her mouth like this [he opens his mouth wide as if he's trying to tan the back of his throat by the fluorescent ceiling light]. Her suitcase was beside her and when Samuel opened it, out fell tea-light holders, a cake slice, and two remote controls. Samuel patted her cheek [touches his own cheek twice, closes his eyes] and she gave a start and rubbed her eyes. She looked at her grandson. For a second or two, it was as if she didn't remember him. Then she smiled and cried [makes his arms into airplane wings]:

"At last!"

And then:

"What a surprise!"

They went to her room. When they came back out, Samuel was wearing this mangy brown fur hat. He had the suitcase and plastic bag in one hand, and he was using his other arm to steady his grandmother.

"We're off!" she cried with a wave. "It was nice running into you."

She looked happy, happy in a way she never was otherwise [looks sad].

*

Okay. I understand. I'm sorry. I don't really know what to say.

*

Guppe says that the first thing Samuel's grandma did when she moved in was accuse all the dark-skinned men who worked at the home of theft. She was convinced that we snuck

20

in at night and took her pearl necklaces, no matter how many times her children and grandchildren tried to tell her that her pearl necklaces were safe and sound in the safe deposit box at the bank. I don't know if she even had any pearls, but she would hide her jewelry box under her bed and two hours later she would ring the call button and say that she was the victim of another robbery. Her family apologized, they said she had never been like this before, they told stories about how she'd worked as a teacher in a poverty-stricken area and started a club in her congregation to raise hundreds of thousands of kronor to build schools in African countries. She sold things at flea markets and ripped up sheets so they could be used as bandages in Romanian hospitals, and once when her contact at an orphanage in Latvia couldn't find a driver to bring over a busload of winter clothes, she got her eldest son to do it and she went along; the two of them drove to Latvia and dropped the boxes of clothes at the orphanage.

After a while it was almost strange to listen to her relatives list all of these facts, I heard the same stories over and over again from different family members, it was as if they wanted to compensate for something, as if they didn't understand that we were professionals. We were used to it. We have our routines. There's a confused old man or woman in every room, and when they press the call button and say that there's a scary person in the bathroom, we hang a sheet over the mirror. When they say that an old person is spying on them through the window, we pull the curtains. None of the old men are allowed to shave by themselves, because if they do they might show up to morning coffee without eyebrows. We can't leave bottles of rubbing alcohol unattended, because someone will drink them up. Samuel's grandmother was far from the worst. Although she was one of the ones whose mood was the most changeable.

*

When did it happen? Were you close? Are you still in touch with the family?

*

Guppe says that once when Samuel's grandma was in an extra bad mood, Samuel's mother tried to give him a tip. She held out a hundred-krona bill and said she was sorry for all the things I had to listen to. I looked her in the eye and said, in a friendly but firm voice:

"Put that away."

Because, okay, it was one thing to be called "sand-nigger" or "towelhead," but somehow that felt better than standing there like an idiot and being given charity for a job well done. When I came home and told my wife about what had happened she called me an idiot for refusing the money. We had just bought a terrace house and the twins were eighteen months old and diapers and pacifiers and wet wipes didn't come free. When I went to bed I lay there for a long time, wondering whether I should have accepted the money. But I would do the same thing today. Did I say wife? I meant ex-wife.

*

I understand. I'm just wondering why you've wasted so much time. Why didn't you come here earlier? Why did you talk to Laide and Panther and Samuel's old school friends before you met me? How did you expect the staff at Samuel's grandma's dementia home to help you understand what happened? What does Samuel's grandma's neighbor have to do with it? If I'm going to be part of this, I want to be there all the way from beginning to end, because no one knew Samuel better than I did.

*

Guppe says that he prepared the morning coffee and rang the bell. Then I looked out the window and saw that Samuel and his grandma hadn't left yet. They were walking toward the car. She was holding his arm. She hobbled toward the driver's side to get behind the wheel. Samuel led her to the passenger side. Then he helped her buckle herself in and once he'd closed the door and put the suitcase and the plastic bag in the backseat he stopped to catch his breath in a way I know I sometimes do. He, like, stood there for a second to muster his strength for the next half of the game. I would do the same thing after a long day at work. He did it after twenty minutes with his own grandma. Then he took off the fur hat, patted his own cheeks lightly, and got behind the wheel.

*

Which neighbor was it, by the way? That guy in number thirty-two? He goes to Thailand to fuck whores every winter.

I swear it. Young whores, too, like on the verge of being legal. Whores he can pay to say they're twelve so he can get his sad little retired-guy cock hard. He goes there every winter, he boards up his house and puts timers on all the lights and is gone for two or three months and then he comes home with new photos of whores he's fucked and he prints out the photos and puts them up on the bulletin board in his office, like postcards. It's true; we saw it through the window. Samuel used to call it his "wall of shame." I suspect it was the neighbor who set the fire. He hated everyone who lived there. And he didn't seem surprised at all when the fire department showed up.

*

Guppe says that the car started and moved back and forth, back and forth. On like the fifth try, Samuel managed to drive out of the parking spot and turn the car around to head for the bridge. Then he revved the engine and whizzed down the hill. Going way too fast. Would I remember that if I hadn't heard about what happened the very next day? I don't know. I don't think so. It was the last time I saw him [looking oddly upset, given that he hardly knew him]. If you want to talk to Samuel's grandma, you'll have to come back once she's feeling better. But unfortunately, I don't think she'll be much help. She's drifting further and further into the fog.

CORRESPONDENCE

In her first email, his mom apologizes for taking so long to respond. After careful consideration, in the end, after many "buts" and "what ifs," I have decided not to take part. I don't live my life in the public eye. I'm not used to being interviewed. I have never liked being documented; in fact, I feel uncomfortable even when my daughter pulls out her phone to take videos of me with my grandchild. So I hope you respect our wish not to participate. And I use the word "our" because this decision goes for both me and Samuel's sister, whom I know you have contacted. We are trying to move on. We want to put this all behind us. Good luck with the book. Warm wishes.

*

Then three months went by and I didn't see Samuel in all that time. I'd broken off contact with Hamza. Or, well, not broken off, but I had stopped going on rounds with him. I avoided his calls. I made up excuses for why I couldn't come. Instead I set the alarm on my phone and went to Blomberg's office early on weekday mornings to be paired up with someone on the team and spend the day moving dressers and Murphy beds and kitchen benches. The moving boxes first, then secure them behind double beds, and then in with the flowerpots and rugs and TVs wrapped up in blankets.

*

In her second email, his mom writes that she appreciates my tenacity. Stubbornness is a virtue. We always said that when I was growing up. Everyone but my mom, who stubbornly maintained that she was not stubborn at all. But I will tell you once again that I do not wish to be interviewed. Don't take it personally. It's not because I'm "anxious about the memories that might be dredged up." And it has nothing to do with your qualities as an author. Even if the things you write are very different from the sort of literature I enjoy, that's not the reason I (once again) choose to decline. It makes no difference that I wouldn't be filmed. Just knowing that someone is going to record my voice is enough to bother me and make me stumble over my words. I have always been able to speak much better when no one is listening. Or when someone who knows me is listening. So I'm saying no. Again. If there are any concrete points of fact you want to double check, perhaps I can help over email. All my best.

*

My life went on. I changed up a few habits. I adjusted to my new salary. Instead of going into town I found Spicy House. Instead of buying new clothes I took care of the ones I already owned. One day we were sent to Nacka to move everything in one house to another one that was only fifty meters away.

"Why are you moving?" Luciano asked.

"Well, it's not for tax reasons, anyway," replied the man who signed the hours-worked contract and smiled as if he had just told a joke.

We emptied the home of someone who had died on Lilla Essingen. We helped a guy who had divorced his wife pack everything that was his and move it to a cramped one-room apartment on Thorildsplan.

*

In her third email, his mom writes that she has chosen to respond to my questions in list form:

1. Twenty-six. He was about to turn twenty-seven.
2. Pretty often. About once or twice a day. Usually I was the one who called, but sometimes he did.
3. No, I wouldn't say I knew Vandad. But I knew of him. We met a few times. It was clear that life hadn't been entirely kind to him.
4. Yes, of course he had other friends too. But they were probably more like acquaintances. Samuel had a tendency to have intense friendships and spend most of his time with one or two people at a time. And that made him vulnerable.

*

An old woman wanted to move from Östermalm to Södermalm and she lived in an apartment the size of a museum. She was the sort of customer who wanted double blankets and bubble wrap on everything. The dusty mirrors were antiques and the shabby dresser had to be handled as if it was pure gold. At first we did as she said, but after a while it was impossible; if we were going to finish before the day turned into a week we had to speed up the process. So we did, we packed everything in boxes but at the same time we tried to do it as fast as possible because time was getting away from us and when we got to the new place, the elevator, which had been described as "large" in the booking, was one meter square max and it had an iron gate, and neither the display cabinet nor the bed nor the old-fashioned sofa with carved wooden flowers on the armrests would fit.

*

His mom continues:

5. Laide was the first girlfriend Samuel ever introduced me to. They were together for about a year. It was a turbulent relationship. They fought a lot. Laide looked for flaws in Samuel. Samuel felt suffocated. I think both of them were pretty relieved when it ended.

6. No, I wouldn't describe him as "secretive." Doesn't everyone have secrets? No one tells everyone everything, do they? I would be more inclined to

describe him as curious. Enthusiastic. And maybe a little restless.

7. Yes. Without a doubt. Who said otherwise?

8. No, it started back when he was little. When he was seven he would come home from a birthday party and be absolutely amazed that he couldn't recall what flavor of ice cream he had eaten that afternoon. To him, that made it seem like the ice cream was worth less. Maybe now that I write this down it seems rather precocious and more philosophical than it really was. At the time, I mostly thought it was a strategy to get more ice cream.

9. Not on my side. Samuel's dad did have a melancholy streak. But I wouldn't go so far as to call him "depressive."

10. Samuel was nine and Sara was eleven. It was a complicated divorce. Their dad was very hurt, and for several years he only saw the children occasionally. Then he severed contact completely.

11. Yes. Samuel and I talked to each other that last day. But if you want to know more about what I remember, you'll need to ask more specific questions.

Best wishes.

*

Three o'clock went by, and four, five, six. We fought to get everything in place and by nine o'clock we were done. The floor lamps and picture frames and a small stool made of brown wood came with the last load. I was the one who took the stool; I put it in the hall and brought out the contract where the client was supposed to write down how many people had been working and tally up the hours. The old lady was just about to sign her name on the contract when she caught sight of the stool and made a sound as if someone had thrust a knife into her stomach. She lifted up the stool and then I realized that it wasn't a stool but a child's chair that had lost its backrest. Marre ran down to the truck to see if anything had been left behind, but all he found were a few flat slats that might have been a backrest, and the client sat there with her little chair and the broken slats and she petted the stool as if it were a cat. Bogdan and Luciano tried to keep from laughing and made gestures in the air to show she was crazy. I just wanted her signature, and at last I got it, she signed and we hopped into our fifteen-footer and drove back to the office. Later that night I thought of her sitting all by herself in an apartment with that stool that had until so recently been a chair. I don't know why I remember her in particular.

*

In her fourth email, his mom writes that she is bewildered to hear about my goal of understanding what happened by mapping out Samuel's last day. Do you seriously mean that you want to know exactly what we said to each other? Okay, this is how I remember our last phone call. I called his phone, Samuel answered, it was quarter past ten, they were on their way to the hospital.

"How's it going?" I asked.

"Good."

"Did you pick her up?"

"Mmhmm."

"Where are you now?"

"Almost there."

"And it's going okay?"

"Mmhmm."

"Is she asleep?"

"No, she's sitting here."

He was using an impatient voice, as if I had asked if he had brushed his teeth that morning. In the background I could hear a piano melody that I recognized but couldn't place.

"How is she?"

"Fine."

"And you?"

"Fiiiine."

He sounded incredibly irritated when he said that last word, as if I had been dragging our conversation out for hours.

"We'll talk soon, then," I said.

"Bye."

That was the whole conversation. It took maybe a minute. Max. And after each monosyllabic response he was quiet, as though he wanted to make it clear that there was nothing more to say. We hung up. Fifteen minutes later I called back.

"Are you there yet?"

"Looking for a parking spot."

"Do you have the department number or should I text it to you?"

"Got it, thanks."

"Did you get gas?"

"Didn't need to."

"How does she seem?"

"Fine."

"Nervous?"

"Sort of."

We were silent for a few seconds.

"Can we talk later?" Samuel said.

Our call lasted no longer than that. I asked him to call after the doctor's appointment and then we hung up. That was the last time I heard his voice.

Yours truly.

*

One Tuesday we were at the university, loading boxes of books and swag candy and projectors and a big yellow plastic sofa into the fifteen-footer. There had been some sort of fair there. The customer had said that it should only take a few hours, but it was past lunch and we still weren't done. The sun was shining, students were lying on the grass, and in the distance I saw a slim figure with a loosely hanging backpack walking toward the subway. It was Samuel. I was sure of it. I never forget a face.

*

In her fifth email, his mom writes that she doesn't agree with my simplistic description of Samuel. He was so much more than a person who "spent his money on experiences but didn't care about food." If you want to get to know him, you have to understand what a great child he was, how lonely he was as a teenager, how much he wanted to change the world when he started studying political science. You have to understand how difficult it was for him to get his degree and then be unemployed for eleven months, only to end up working at the Migration Board. It was so far removed from his dream. How many details do you need in order to understand him? Is it important to know that he had a stuffed toy lizard named Mushimushi that we lost on a vacation in Crete? That he was scared of sirens when he was little? That he started crying when he heard sad music and said that it "hurt him inside"? That he collected those plastic PEZ dispensers until he started middle school? That he loved the last few years of compulsory school but hated upper secondary? That he stopped calling his dad "Dad" after the divorce and started using his first name? Who decides what is important and what is superfluous? All I know is that the more details I give you the more details it seems like I'm leaving out. That makes me doubt this entire project.

Regards.

*

I jumped down from the truck and went over to say hi. Samuel was wearing headphones, green ones, the kind with a headband, and when he didn't hear me I tapped him lightly on the shoulder. He jumped like I had tried to force him off the path. Then he smiled and nodded.

"Sorry, I didn't hear you."

"That's okay."

We stood in silence for a few seconds. He looked at me with knitted brows. His brain was working overtime to try to remember.

"Are you Felix's friend?"

I shook my head.

"Oh, right—we played basketball together, didn't we? Or wait, were you in Sara's grade?"

"We met in Liljeholmen. At a pretty lame party."

"That's right! At Tessan's."

Samuel nodded and it looked like he remembered for real. I put out my right hand.

"Vandad," I said.

"Samuel," said Samuel.

"So how's it going?"

I said it the way I had practiced at home in front of the mirror. The way I had heard hundreds of people say it, at parties, at movies, on buses when they ran into old classmates. But somehow it always sounded wrong when I was the one saying it.

"Oh, I'm doing fine," Samuel replied. "Although it's also not great because I just gave a lecture and you know how it is, you're standing there in front of a bunch of people who could be you a few years ago and the teacher wants you to talk about an average day at work and how you use your theoretical background in your job, and you do it, you say that you sit in your office and convince them that it's worth throwing away four years on a worthless education and then they applaud and the teacher thanks you and then you leave and feel like a giant fucking fraud. That's pretty much how things are going. How about you?"

"Fine," I said, nodding.

Not that I knew exactly how he was feeling, but I understood him, I got what he was trying to say.

"That's kinda how I felt at my brother's funeral," I said. "When my mom wanted me to give a speech and say something positive."

Samuel looked at me. I looked at him. He didn't ask any questions. I didn't say any more. We didn't know each other. But something had happened. Something arose when we spoke to each other. Both of us could feel it. It was clear that we ought to be friends. We exchanged numbers on the university's gravelly paths; we said we would be in touch, both of us knew that this was something special.

*

In her sixth email, his mom writes that she certainly understands that an author can take poetic license. But there's a difference between the truth and extreme exaggeration. I would never dream of calling Samuel ten times a day. I'm not a "control freak." Who told you that? Was it Panther? I don't have a "tendency to be clingy," especially not compared to my mom. But I did enjoy talking to my son. And there were a lot of practical matters we had to go through after the fire. But sometimes two or three days would go by and we didn't speak at all. One time, several years ago, I was sitting at the cafe in Kulturhuset, the one on the top floor, with a view of the Hötorget high-rises and the roundabout and the crowds of people. Suddenly I caught sight of my ex-husband crossing the open square at Plattan. Which was strange, because he left Sweden after the divorce and swore he would never return. It took a few seconds for me to realize that it was Samuel. When he was little he looked like me, but with each year that passed he looked more and more like his dad. It was something about his posture. One shoulder a bit lower than the other. The way they swung their arms as they walked. I reached for my phone and called him. I didn't want anything in particular, I just wanted to say hi. His phone rang. I saw Samuel stop. He took out his phone. He looked at the screen. Then he stuck the phone back in his pocket again. But that wasn't so strange. Maybe he was waiting for another call. Maybe he was in a hurry. That evening I called and he answered and we talked just like we usually did. Is this perfectly everyday memory one worth keeping? Maybe not. But either way, it's true. Unlike the rumors you seem to believe.

Sincerely.

*

On the way back to the moving truck I thought of how I had known Hamza for twelve years and Niko for fourteen. After the funeral we didn't talk about what had happened. They tried a few times at first, mostly Niko, but Hamza too. Every time they did, I protested in a way that kept them from trying again. It was different with Samuel. I don't know why.

Luciano watched Samuel go.

"Who's the fag?"

"You're the fag," I said.

"Both of you are fags," said Bogdan.

"Whoever doesn't get back to work and make sure we're done by five is the fag," said Marre. "I have to pick up the kids from daycare."

Bogdan closed the rear door and Marre hopped up behind the wheel. All I had to do was go up to the driver's side and look at him for him to apologize and shove over next to the others. He knew the drill, and soon we were on the highway and had dumped the goods at a warehouse and then we drove back to Vasastan to drop off our belts and gloves and joke with Blomberg that this was our last day of work ever.

*

In her seventh and final email, his mom writes that nagging won't change anything. Neither I nor my daughter wishes to meet with you. Not even over "a quick cup of coffee." What we want most of all is to ask you to drop all of this. But if you do persist in moving forward, it's important for you to change all the names and specify that in no way did I stay "in the background" after the fire. I did not have a "sudden rush of bitterness" toward either Samuel or my mother. My siblings and I simply chose to divide up the responsibilities. My eldest brother took care of the practical matters surrounding the house—contacting the authorities, the insurance company, the firefighters, and the police. My younger brother was responsible for making sure Mom felt secure at the home, he informed the staff about what had happened and tried to stop by to see Mom as often as he could to keep her calm. On the doctors' recommendation we decided not to tell her what had happened to the house. They said it would be best if she was allowed to believe that it was still there and that she could go back if she wanted to. I was responsible for Mom's documents. I looked for missing receipts and contracts of sale and blueprints and organized them all in carefully labeled binders. But as usual, my efforts ended up being overshadowed. They always do. When Mom first got sick I spent a week canceling her newspaper subscriptions, paying her bills, and doing her taxes. At the same time, my youngest brother stopped by and replaced a bulb in an Advent star lamp. Then he hung it up in the dining-room window and Mom talked about that star for several weeks.

"It hangs so perfectly in the window and it gives just the right amount of light and your brother even said he can install a timer on it! He's quite the little electrician. I never saw the like. What would I do without him?"

At the same time, I was taking care of all her financial matters and I hardly got a thank you in return. Apparently that was nothing compared to the time my brothers came by the home and took her to Kista to eat at a drive-in McDonald's. They had banana milkshakes! And ate apple pie! To hear her tell it, her beloved sons had invented milkshakes, drive-in restaurants, the road, the sky, and the air around them as they sat there munching in the car. There are some things you're just expected to do as a daughter.

Those things always take more time. Toward the end I didn't have as much time to visit her as my brothers did, so it was nice that Samuel had offered to take time off and drive to the hospital. I don't feel guilty. I don't regret anything. It was my brothers' responsibility to keep the car in good shape. They ought to have told Samuel that the brakes were bad and the tires were worn down. If they had done that, everything would have turned out differently.

*

I waited a few days before I contacted Samuel. I thought there was no rush. I knew he was a special person because he talked to people he didn't know as if he thought they were ace and he listened to people like he really was curious about what they had to say. And it wasn't until later on that I got that what was special about Samuel wasn't that he was a good or a bad listener, it was that he was an unusual listener. Because he listened without listening. Or, how about this. He listened without wanting to understand. Or he listened without caring. The most important thing for him was that he never wanted it to be quiet and there were many times I told him stuff that he didn't seem to remember three weeks later. Other people might have gotten angry and said that he didn't listen well enough. I thought his way of listening was perfect. You could say anything you wanted and if you told a story and it got a good reaction all you had to do was wait like six months because then you could tell it again and get almost as good a reaction the second time.

*

His mom ends her final email with a simple request: Thanks in advance for not contacting me again. [Her name.]

BERLIN

Panther sets out Turkish lentil soup, warms pita bread in the microwave, and says that it's nice to see me. Was your trip okay? How long are you staying? Does it feel nostalgic to be back? The stairwell is weirdly quiet without your music. I, like, never thought I would miss a Rihanna instrumental on repeat [hums "What's My Name?"]. How did it go with the book? It was never published, right? Does it suck to have worked on something for four years without finishing it? Here in Berlin everything is the same. The pierced bouncer with the fisting-depth ruler tattooed on his forearm still stands there outside Berghain. The little döner stand over by the zoo is still the best. That bitchy transvestite still works at Luzia. A couple new hipster places have opened in Neukölln, a few squatter apartments in Prenzlauer Berg have been shut down by the police. But how are you? Have you gotten through the worst of it? How was the funeral?

*

I suggested the place, Samuel said it sounded perfect, it was only a few stops from the apartment he was subletting in Hornstull. On the way to Spicy House I thought of all the nights I had sat there. It was the perfect place. No one ever bothered you. No one asked any questions. Everyone came in, ordered, was left alone. I still didn't know the names of some of the bartenders. I opened the door, walked past the drunks by the gambling machines, ignored the biker gang in the corner and slid onto a barstool next to Samuel.

*

Panther says she knows the feeling. I still have Samuel in my phone. I know, it's a little weird, but I can't bear to delete it. There wouldn't be any trace left of him if I did. The name after his would just jump up a spot. Now I see his name every time I look at my favorites [scrolling on an invisible cell phone]. And I still think about how sick it is that he no longer exists. Did you know he only came to visit me once? He was always coming up with new reasons why it wouldn't work out for him to come down here. First he had no cash because it was expensive to sublet, and then he moved in with Vandad and all his money went to going out with him, and then he met Laide and there were all kinds of things to fix up around the house. And when he did come, I had the feeling that Vandad had, like, forced him to leave Stockholm. I don't know what he was afraid of.

*

For a second we weren't sure how to greet each other. Handshake? Fist bump? I went with the nod and Samuel reciprocated the nod and I said:

"What are you drinking?"

"I waited to order."

"Beer?"

"Great."

I motioned two beers to the bartender and seasoned the bar with my hand to show him we wanted some nuts. We started by talking about how things were going (fine). Then we talked about our weekend plans (maybe going out, or staying home). Then Samuel started talking about fish parasites.

"Sorry?" I said.

"Fish parasites. There are some really disgusting fish parasites. Have you ever heard of isopods, for example?"

*

Panther says of course she remembers how they met. It was through basketball. We played in the same league; he was on the boys' B team, which was totally worthless, and I was on the girls' team, which won the national championship twice and got silver once. Once we got to know each other, the joke was that I should move over to their team so they could finally win a game, because at the time I looked pretty much like a boy. Probably no one would have noticed, and my real name works for boys and girls. But I've never liked it, which is why I started telling my teammates that people at school called me Panther and at school I said that people from basketball called me Panther, and soon people started calling me that, the name spread, and now even my sister calls me that. She played basketball too, and even she was better than Samuel, people called Samuel "Chickadee" because he was so scared of the ball and he was way too small to get rebounds. The first few times we saw each other outside of basketball we went to the Water Festival or hung around for hours at the twenty-four-hour McDonald's on Hamngatan. And I remember thinking that Samuel was different from other guys because it was like he talked because he liked talking and not because he wanted to fuck. He felt non-sexual somehow. We became brother and sister; when things were rough at home I could crash at his place, his mom became my second mom, she understood without needing to know too much, she never asked why I needed to run away, I was welcomed into his family and I will always be grateful for that. They saved me when I needed it the most and I— I'm sorry. Sorry. I'll pull myself together.

*

I signaled to the bartender again and soon we had two new beers in front of us. Samuel hardly seemed to notice. He was in the midst of his description of the isopod parasite. He described how it likes to live in certain kinds of water and when a particular type of fish approaches it gets inside the fish's mouth and eats up its tongue.

"Okay," I said, checking over my shoulder to make sure no one was listening to our conversation.

"Neat, huh?"

"I don't know."

"It eats up the fish's whole tongue."

"Oh."

"And then—do you know what the best part is?"

"Even better than eating up the tongue?"

"Mmhmm. When the tongue is gone the parasite turns around and its body takes the place of the tongue. The fish starts using the parasite as a tongue, for crushing up food and stuff. Pretty cool, huh?"

"I hardly even knew that fish have tongues," I said.

"Me neither."

We took a few sips of the beer, the glasses were foggy, the drunks mechanically hit the buttons that made the symbols on the screen spin round and round. The biker gang pointed at the darts game on the TV and seemed upset.

"Do you come here often?" Samuel asked.

"Pretty often. I live nearby."

"Big place?"

"A one-bedroom."

"Rent or own?"

"Rent stabilized."

"Wow. Congratulations."

"Thanks."

*

Panther blows her nose and says that after upper secondary school she started the art school foundation course and

Samuel studied political science at the university. We didn't
have as much contact for a few years. I hung out with people
in art circles and Samuel was surrounded by a bunch of people
who wanted to study international relations and get jobs at the
Ministry for Foreign Affairs and work for the UN and save
the world and that had definitely been Samuel's thing at
school. I thought he would feel one hundred percent at home.
Instead he pulled away from it. He took his exams and went
to the required seminars, but in his free time he kept going on
about how life is short and you have to fill up with new
experiences so you won't die unhappy. He sounded like a
fifteen-year-old version of me. One night he called to ask if I
wanted to go to Tumba with him to watch an innebandy
game.

"Innebandy?" I said.

"Yes! It's the final of a tournament called Capri-Sonne."

"Do you know anyone who's playing?"

"No."

"So why would we—"

"Aw, come on. It'll be fun. Something to remember!"

I said no. The same way I said no when he suggested we go
to the Police Museum, take part in a medical study on insom-
nia at Karolinska, watch the horse races at Solvalla, or go to
Hellasgården to try ice fishing.

"I'm a vegetarian," I reminded him.

"So? We can throw the fish back. Come on. It will be fun.
Live a little!"

And maybe in retrospect it sounds spontaneous and

exciting. But it wasn't. There was something desperate about the whole thing. Samuel actively tried to seek out new experiences, but he was completely incapable of enjoying anything. The more he talked about depositing things in his Experience Bank, the emptier he seemed. I remember feeling sorry for him. He seemed lonely. Especially when he texted me on the way home from the innebandy tournament in Tumba to say that two of the three matches had been "hella exciting." Out of some sort of desperation and fear of . . . I don't know what. Sorry, here I go again, I really don't mean to. Can you grab me some toilet paper?

*

Then we sat there in silence. But it wasn't uncomfortable silence, the kind that makes you want to overturn the bar and run for the door. We sat there, me thinking about the fish parasite, Samuel answering a text from Panther—the girl who had been with him at the party in Liljeholmen.

"Have you been friends for a long time?" I asked.

The question came perfectly naturally. It wasn't like I had to think to come up with it. I was curious and I asked it, and Samuel replied that they had known each other since the end of compulsory school. They were in the same basketball league and later her family kicked her out because she didn't want to live the same way they lived and then she stayed at his mom's place for about six months.

"Where did you grow up?"

Again: the question just came out. I don't know how or

from where, but I sat there at the bar asking questions like I was some hot-shot TV journalist. Samuel told me about his childhood, that he and Panther were from the same neighborhood, an inner-city housing project.

"It was a nice place. Pretty mixed. There were homies and Swediots, alcoholics and pensioners. We liked it there. What about you?"

I told him briefly about my background, moving around Sweden, my childhood in Halmstad, my teen years in Gothenburg.

"Oh, I get it," said Samuel.

"What?"

"Your dialect. I was having trouble placing it."

He didn't ask anything about my brother. He didn't try to get to know me by digging for anything historical. And that was why we got to know each other. We gave each other time. Even though we didn't talk the whole time, we knew on that first night at Spicy House that we belonged together. Erase that. Just put that we didn't have to talk the whole time to know we were going to be best friends.

*

Panther collects herself, nods, and says that if anything came up repeatedly, it was Samuel's concerns about his memory. He would jot down little notes in notebooks to remember his experiences. He was paranoid about never remembering faces. Sometimes I wondered if his memory was getting worse *because* he was working so hard to improve it. In the spring of 2007 he initiated Project Memory Phase. Has anyone mentioned it? It was a totally bizarre idea. His plan was to divide up the year in memory sections. When January started he put on a particular pair of jeans, a certain cologne, and a special cap. Then he wore those things every day for a whole month. Then came February and he switched to a different pair of pants, dabbed on a new kind of cologne, and wore a beret. And he also realized he could use sound, so he listened to nothing but Tupac, all February. Then came March and he put on a pair of chinos and a new kind of cologne and went with no hat and only listened to Bob Marley. Then came April and he did the same thing again, new pants, new cologne, new music, and an old-man hat on his head. He hoped that all this would make connections in his brain and life would feel longer somehow. But as so often happened with him, it was a better plan in theory than in reality. He had given up the whole project by summer. When I asked why, he said it wasn't having the right effect. Instead of remembering his experiences, he remembered the music and the pants and the cologne. But his actual daily life as it went by, he was remembering even less of that. And when he told me this, it was a Sunday afternoon, we were waiting for the Metro at Mariatorget, we had just played basketball, our fingers were sore after all the dunking on the kid-high baskets, our fingertips were rough and smudged gray, and he shook his head and looked toward the train that was about to roll in, the rails crackling like a bonfire.

"I don't know how you all do it."

I assumed he was talking about memory and I told him that I had a shitty memory too.

"I hardly remember what I did last week," I said.

Samuel looked at me, his face lighting up with a grateful smile.

"Really?"

Maybe it wasn't completely true, but I said it to make him feel better, I felt sorry for him, he worked so hard to try to understand and control something that came perfectly naturally to so many people.

*

After three rounds it was last call and then last last call and we got the bill. I paid. Samuel hardly seemed to notice. But as we were standing on the square, about to say goodbye, he said:

"Thanks for the beer. Next time, it's on me."

"No problem," I said, putting out my hand to say goodbye.

He took my hand, pulled it up toward his chest, and leaned in for a hug. I let him do it, I didn't hug him back, but I didn't shove him away either, I didn't head-butt him, I hardly thought about how it would look to the people on the Stairmasters inside the twenty-four-hour gym. It would have been an unnecessary thought anyway, because the gym was empty, I noticed once we'd said goodbye and I was walking home.

*

Panther says that she would be happy to share her memories from the last day. Samuel and I talked to each other at quarter to eleven. I was the one who called. He picked up and said he was in the car but he would call back soon. We hung up and I thought: "in the car?" Whose car? And where is he going? And why did it sound like there was freaking elevator music in the background?

*

Nothing in particular happened on the second night, and not the third or fourth either. We met at different places (twice at Spicy House, once at a bar in Gamla Stan). We ordered drinks, we drank, we talked. About normal stuff. About the kind of things people talk about to seem not totally bizarre. But in the midst of all the regular stuff, unusual things would pop up. Like when Samuel suddenly asked if I had tried putting saffron on pears.

"It's wicked good."

Or when he told me about the kayak stand by Norrtull where you could borrow boats without being a member.

"Want to try it sometime?"

Or when he asked if I'd been north of the polar circle.

"No," I replied. "Have you?"

"I went up to Jukkasjärvi a few years ago to check out the northern lights."

"By yourself?"

51

"Mmhmm. But I was only there for one night. I stayed at a hostel and trudged through snow up to my thighs for several hours, on the hunt for the northern lights. But the sky was totally pitch black. Then I got it in my head that I had to do something to make them show up. I started making snowballs and I thought, if I hit the same tree with three snowballs in a row I'll get to see the northern lights. It was harder than I thought. It took me like fifteen minutes to do it."

"Did you see them?"

"No. The sky was just as black as it had been before. But on the way back to the hostel I got lost in the woods. Then I looked up at the sky and saw the light. It was a yellowish round circle in the middle of all that black. It looked incredibly alien, a lot more amazing than in pictures."

"Nice."

"But the next day the girl at the desk in the hostel said I had probably just seen the lights from the sports arena nearby."

*

Panther says that when Samuel called back, it was a bit past eleven. I answered on my German phone, we agreed to call each other on Skype, we logged in and called. Samuel apologized for sounding so irritated when I first called, he thought it was his mom calling to talk money.

"The house?" I said.

"Mmhmm. That fucking house."

"What's going on?"

"Not much. Sitting in the waiting room at Huddinge hospital."

"Everything all right?"

"Yeah. I'm here with Grandma. She's trying to get her driver's license back. She's getting her vision checked right now. Then she's going to drive in a simulator."

"What are the chances she'll succeed?"

"On what scale?"

"One to ten."

"Minus twelve."

*

One night we were talking names and Samuel said that his dad wanted him to be named Samuel because he had started to figure out the reaction a foreign name would get you from employers and landlords. His dad didn't want his son to run into the same problems.

"What would your name have been otherwise?" I asked.

Samuel smiled and gave examples of names that required two throat-clearings, names that started with h-sounds deep down in his stomach, names that sounded like a sneeze or rhymed with two insults, and as we sat there at the bar talking names and drinking beer I heard myself saying that my brother had hated his name.

"Once he said that his greatest wish was for his name to be Patrik, and I teased him because I thought Patrik sounded so fucking lame."

Samuel nodded, he didn't ask any further questions, and in

his silence I started telling him things about my brother. There was no logic to what I said, I just told him that my brother had always wanted a video-game console, but he had to settle for a Gameboy, and his favorite turtle had been Leonardo at first and Raphael later, and his turquoise pajama bottoms had a bad waistband and they were constantly crooked because he always hiked them up on one side, and once when we were eating chicken he said that it was good but it was too bad about all the cute little chickens who had to die so we could eat them up, and the whole family paused their forks and looked down at their plates but my brother kept happily eating and his hair wasn't as kinky as mine and when he was little he teased me about my hair but when he was older he asked me if there was some way to make his hair kinkier and as revenge for his teasing I made up that bananas are good for kinking hair and he ate bananas nonstop until Mom noticed that the weekly fruit bill had sky-rocketed and I revealed my joke and once when it was New Year's Eve and the city was rumbling with firecrackers my brother woke up and came rushing out of his room in his crooked pajama bottoms with two toy pistols, shouting that he had to shoot back. I sat there for an hour saying things I remembered but had never told anyone. Samuel listened and nodded and ordered more beer. He didn't say: Is your brother the one who died? Or: How did it happen? He just sat there looking at me. And when he didn't ask any probing questions it somehow made it easier to keep talking.

*

I said he had been twelve years old when it happened. And that we were relatively new to Stockholm.

"Mom had gotten a job in sales at a company that manufactured kitchen fans, my brother was with two friends and the big sister of one of the friends, they were going to go bowling, they were crossing a parking lot by Kungens Kurva, there was a lot of snow, they got run over side-on by a tanker truck, the friends survived, the sister too, but my brother died."

Samuel looked at me. He didn't tilt his head to the side. He didn't look sorry for me.

"Did they catch him?"

"The driver? Mmhmm. There were witnesses and everything. But they let him go. He said he didn't notice that he had run them over. He said he thought he had hit a shopping cart."

I thought, here come the questions, he's going to ask me how it felt and what happened to our family, if the divorce was because of my brother, if that was why Mom decided to quit her job and move back. But no. Instead he said:

"You're lucky you have such an awesome memory."

"Why?"

"Because it means you still have him. He's not dead. He lives on. Thanks to you."

We sat there in silence. When the bill came, we never split it. One of us covered it all. Sometimes it was him. Pretty often it was me.

*

Panther says that Samuel insisted on calling his grandma's dementia "confusion." He told her about all the things his family had done so she wouldn't have to move out of her home. They printed out pieces of paper with clear instructions for how to turn the burglar alarm on and off. They put colorful sticky notes on the remote so she could remember how to change the channel. They bought a landline phone with buttons the size of sugar cubes because she always forgot to hang up the cordless phones and it made everyone worry when the busy signal beeped for over two hours, and someone had to hop in a taxi and go out to the house only to find her sound asleep in front of the TV. One time Samuel told me that he had called her home phone and when she answered the TV was so loud that she said "wait a second." Then the TV went off and his grandma tried to continue her conversation with Samuel via the remote. I laughed when he told me that, and Samuel laughed too, but then he added:

"It would be funny if it weren't so fucking tragic."

I never understood why he was so upset by his grandma's illness. For me, aging was a natural part of life, you get old, you forget, you need other people to help you. But Samuel seemed to have a hard time accepting it.

*

One evening Panther stopped by. Or. First came Panther. And then her hair. And last, her perfume-slash-cigarette smell.

"Christ, what a lively bunch," she said when she saw us sitting there in silence.

She was wearing a pair of army pants and a jacket with a purple peacock pattern that made her look like a drowned pom-pom (it was raining out—her jacket was dripping dark thready patterns on the floor). This time we said hi to each other. I thought, Panther? Why Panther? If there was any animal this person did not resemble, it was a panther. Drowned Turkish hamster, maybe. Kurdish marmot, definitely. Oversized Syrian meerkat, possibly. Stoned Persian peacock, yes, but only because of the jacket. Instead of asking why she was called Panther I asked what she wanted to drink and went to the bar to order.

*

Panther said that Samuel sat there in the waiting room at the hospital and told her that he had taken a bunch of nostalgic things from his grandma's house. Photo albums and CDs, perfumes and Christmas cards and old clothes his grandfather had worn. All to try to bring back his grandma's memories.

"Is it working?" I asked.

"Don't know. It comes in waves. Sometimes she's perfectly lucid. She sat there in the car humming along with the music and asked how Vandad was. Then three minutes later she thought I had kidnapped her. It's so fucking bizarre."

He said it in a gravelly voice. Then he cleared his throat.

"When she doesn't recognize me I usually put on my grandpa's old fur cap. That makes her cooperative. But you have to keep your distance because sometimes she wants to lean in for a kiss."

As we spoke he stood up and walked around in the

hallways, twice I heard him ask about a coffee machine, and then a nurse said he could find one "over there" and then he walked over and poured a cup. When I asked how Vandad was he was quiet for a few seconds before he responded.

"Vandad's fine," he said. "I think."

"What, did something happen?"

"No, not really. He's fine. I'm fine. Everyone's fine."

"Okay."

As usual, Samuel was very bad at lying. All I had to do to find out the truth was not say anything [making her hand into devil's horns and listening to her index finger].

"No, I mean, we haven't talked for a while."

Short pause.

"And we don't live together anymore."

Pause.

"I'm subletting again. By Gullmarsplan."

Long pause.

"But it's good, it really is, I like it. I'm thinking of buying a place of my own soon."

I'm not sure what happened between Samuel and Vandad. Do you know? Did it have something to do with Laide? Was it something about the house? You'll have to ask Laide if you get hold of her because I have no idea.

*

From the moment Panther entered the room, it was like Samuel was transformed. I thought that Samuel with Panther meant Samuel became less Samuel, because he stopped talking and started nodding and looked at Panther like she was his idol and asked questions with the efficiency of a tennis machine spitting out balls. Panther was talking ninety miles a minute. She told us about some schoolfriends who had started up a project about "diversified recruiting" and I never figured out whether she thought it was a good idea or a bad one because she told us about the project and dissed everyone who was part of it and then she said:

"But it is a good thing that it's being done because all the art schools—including ours—are so segregated it's sick. It's not exactly Berlin."

Then she talked about all the awesome things she'd found at an art bookstore in Söder that was having a liquidation sale.

"It was so incredibly cheap—like, Berlin prices."

Then she told us about a Norwegian curator who kept calling her twenty-four-seven and wanted to do an exhibition of her stuff in Oslo.

"It's super cool," she said. "Even if Oslo isn't exactly Berlin."

I felt like I ought to say something, I had been quiet far too long, here was my chance.

"It sounds a little sketchy," I said.

"What does?"

"Why would a curator want to do an exhibition?"

"Maybe because it's his job?"

We looked at each other. A quick smile fluttered across her face. I had misunderstood something. I didn't quite get what.

I prepared myself for the mockery and laughter and being told I was an imbecile. I could picture how Samuel would high five and pinch me on my side and call me "Mr. Curator" for the rest of the night. But it didn't happen. Instead Samuel asked what the theme of the exhibition would be and whether it was *Time Pieces* or maybe *Notre Dame* that he was interested in showing, and Panther seemed grateful that she could finally turn the focus of the discussion back onto herself. I didn't say much more that night. Samuel didn't either. But I remember thinking about it afterwards, that in front of a friend he had known for more than ten years, Samuel took my side. Instead of mocking and demeaning he smoothed things over and had my back. That was a sign that our relationship— Erase that. A sign that our friendship was real.

Then we went out and one of us owned the dance floor (Samuel) and one of us bought cocaine (Panther) and one of us sat in a corner keeping an eye on the drinks (me). On the way home, after we said goodbye to Panther and it was just me and Samuel in the taxi, I said things I'd never said to anyone. I talked about my nightmares, I described the pillow when I woke up and the sound of screaming that somehow lingered in the room after I woke up, as if the air molecules had changed and were still vibrating when I opened my eyes. I said all of this in a taxi even though the driver was in the front seat and I wasn't even worried that Samuel would start laughing and use it against me. Instead he said:

"I know the feeling."

And even though he didn't explain it any more and even though he didn't have a dead brother, I believed him when he said it.

*

Panther says that before they hung up they talked about her for a bit. Samuel asked a few questions and I answered them. I gave him a short summary of everything that had happened since last time we talked, though since so much had happened the summary took a pretty long time. But I want to make it clear that we didn't spend our entire last conversation talking about me. We were interrupted by a nurse. A female voice said something in the background.

"Okay," Samuel replied. "She's done now. I have to go."

We hung up. Our last conversation was over. It had lasted forty-five minutes. It was a few minutes before noon. I thought about how quickly the time had passed. Far too quickly. I'm sorry, it's starting again, I don't know what to do about this, how many tears can a body hold, anyway? I don't even feel all that sad right now, you know, this is just a physical reaction [reaching for the roll of toilet paper].

*

We had been friends for a few months when Samuel said that Panther was moving to Berlin.

"When?" I asked, and I felt happy.

"In a few weeks. She's just going to take off. Leave me here."

We didn't say anything for a few minutes. I didn't quite

understand why he looked so sad. He drained his glass, signaled for a refill, and asked if I wanted to go somewhere else.

"There's an end-of-term party at her art school tonight. I was planning to go. Want to come?"

I wasn't sure, I liked it better at Spicy House.

"Come on. It'll be fun. Think of the Experience Bank!"

"Experience Bank?"

"No matter how boring it is, we'll still remember it. And that makes it all worth it, don't you think?"

One hour later we were standing in front of an old building that looked like a boat factory. Bouncers were checking names against the list, Samuel had RSVPed for him plus one. But the bouncers were no typical bouncers. They greeted everyone with a smile and instead of black flak jackets and headsets they were wearing terrycloth playsuits—I mean like the kind that babies wear, but adult-sized, and one of them had a giant lollipop in his front pocket.

"What the fuck was that?" I whispered to Samuel as we were on our way in.

"Oh, I'm sure it was part of the art."

But he wasn't sure, and I wasn't either, because at that party, absolutely anything could be art. We went from room to room and Samuel nodded at guys that looked like girls and girls that looked like little boys. Everyone's clothes were either really colorful or entirely black. Some of them gave me sideways glances, they noticed that I didn't fit in, my skin wasn't pale enough, my muscles were too big, my leather jacket too black, and I smelled like cologne instead of sweat and rolling tobacco.

*

Panther ponders the question for a long time before she answers. Do I regret anything? Of course I regret some things. Everyone does. Anyone who says they don't is lying. Everyone walks around with feelings of loss and sadness and shame. It's perfectly normal. And I get that his family is trying to convince themselves that it was an accident. After all, they were the ones who were on him like bloodhounds at the end, with a thousand calls about insurance clauses and renovation money and loan qualifications and inheritance distributions. In the end he couldn't take it anymore. He made up his mind. He was ready. He made the decision. We're the ones who have to live with it.

*

Panther's room was full of people and the art was hanging on the walls, it was mirrors painted over with different texts and headlines. Panther herself was wearing an American flag like a toga, with a knot over one shoulder, she hugged me and Samuel, she said that she had been waiting all night for us and then she disappeared to say hi to some other people.

"What do you think?" Samuel asked as we stood in front of a piece of art, each with a plastic glass of red box wine in hand.

"I don't know," I said.

Because I didn't know. We went from room to room, look-ing at art that was sometimes art and sometimes turned out to be an ashtray that someone had left behind from an after-party. The girls looked rich, or they must have been rich, because only rich girls can go to a party with so little make-up and such unshaved armpits and such dirty canvas bags with-out being ashamed. The only room we stopped for a little bit extra in was at the far end of the building. Someone had made a work of art with a glowing warm furnace.

"I like this," I said.

"Me too," said Samuel.

We stayed in the room, the warmth warmed us, the fire crackled. Suddenly Samuel put out his hand and rested it on the furnace. He held it there until I swatted it away.

"What the hell are you doing?" I asked.

"Just wanted to check how hot it was."

I looked at him and wondered if there was something ser-iously wrong with him. Then I looked at the fire and thought that if good art was *this* good I could definitely learn to like art.

*

Panther sighs and throws up her hands. But at the same time it's really hard to know what you could have done differently. I don't think it's possible to save someone who doesn't want to be saved. There's something self-centered about the whole idea that it's up to you to take care of everyone around you. People live their own lives and when they don't want to do that anymore there's not much you can do. I'm convinced that this would have happened even if I hadn't moved to Berlin. Even if I had been a little better at keeping in touch. What about you—do you feel guilty? Do you wish you had done something different?

*

We were interrupted by two students from the school. Samuel nodded their way and asked who had made this awesome piece of art. The students laughed.

"This furnace belongs to the glassmaking workshop."

I swallowed and braced myself. But there was no attack. No scornful smiles. No sense of standing there naked. Samuel didn't deflect the blame, he didn't say that I was the one who'd come up with such an idiotic thought. He just blew on his hand, laughed, and asked if there was an after-party. When the students moved on, Samuel and I stayed in the room, the fire crackled, it smelled faintly of something I thought might be burned hair or sulfur.

"This is still the best thing here," Samuel said, and I nodded.

He had my back. He didn't let me fall. I thought, I will always do the same for him.

*

Panther looks surprised and maybe a little disgusted. Are you joking? What do you mean, "relieved"? I was totally crushed. Part of me died along with Samuel. There is nothing, not the tiniest atom in my body, that felt "relieved" when I heard what had happened. No offense, but anyone who comes up with an idea like that must be pretty disturbed.

*

After the art party we went into town. There was a line to get into East, but Ibbe from the gym was manning the door and I mimicked Hamza, I tried putting two fingers up in the air, and Ibbe waved us in.

"Wow," Samuel said after we found a table in the corner. "Did I just see two blackheads get into East at one thirty in the morning on the Saturday after payday?"

"Should we call the Guinness Book of World Records?"

We had a toast, we drank, we ordered more, we moved toward the dance floor.

"Baller culo."

"Check out her booty."

"Look at that sweet ass."

"Damn, baby's got back!"

"Nice humps."

But we said it more to ourselves than to the girls. When a song Samuel liked came on, he vanished onto the dance floor. He was dancing in that way that made people point and shake their heads. He transformed his arms into a sunset and roared along with the chorus. He crouched down and whispered secrets to the broken glass on the floor. He shook his ribcage side to side like maracas. When he came back to have a drink I could smell his hardworking deodorant.

*

Panther shook her head. I don't know. I don't have a good answer for that. Maybe he forgot to take it off? It's not impossible. Or he could have been driving so fast that he knew the speed would be enough and that no seatbelt in the world could save him.

*

We had drunk more than usual. The sink in the bathroom was rocking like a rowboat. I had to max out my concentration in order to grab the door handle. When I came back I found Samuel leaning into a corner, his legs planted wide as a tripod. The music stopped and the bouncers drove people out with arms like side-boom trucks.

"Home?" I said.

"Soon," said Samuel.

It was chaos at McDonald's. Two drunk Stureplan brats were lying on the floor and pointing at the spitballs on the ceiling as if they were comets. A teenage girl had thrown up on the window. A homeless guy with a raincoat and plastic bags on his feet was sitting at a table and reading a newspaper and looking like the most normal person there. An old lady in a gray coat was in front of us in line. She was swaying, she was taking a long time, there was some problem with her card. Samuel looked at his wrist (even though he didn't have a watch) and said:

"How about this weather?"

Then the old lady turned around and gave him a surly look. We discovered that she wasn't an old lady at all; she was a girl about our age or a little older. She had a strangely bell-shaped coat and some gray streaks in her hair. She muttered something and walked toward the street. I saw that she was wearing a gold brooch shaped like an owl on her coat. The girl was Laide. And as I walked up and ordered for myself and Samuel, we can establish that this was the first time Laide and Samuel saw each other. There were no strings playing from the loudspeakers. No choirs of angels. No random car went by on the street with its windows down, blasting D'Angelo's "Lady." The sky outside did not fill with nighttime fireworks. Samuel and Laide were at the same McDonald's. He saw her. She saw him. It was late at night or early morning, and life just went on. As if nothing had happened. This was their first meeting. Even if I seem to be the only one who remembers it.

*

Panther says that after the phone call she got a text from Samuel. He wrote that the streets of Sweden were safe because his grandma hadn't passed the test and now they were going to eat lunch and go back to the home. Then he wrote: *Thanks for calling. It meant everything to hear your voice. Fuck everyone else.* I don't know exactly what he meant by "everyone else." I had a hectic afternoon, I had a working lunch and then a studio visit and to be completely honest I forgot about his text. I never responded. I didn't really know how to answer so I just didn't and then it was too late.

*

We stood on Kungsgatan. Empty cabs zoomed by us, one, two, four, six, ten of them. We just laughed.

"Hi, Guinness Book of World Records," Samuel said. "It's us again."

"Don't bother sending anyone over."

"Stockholm is the same as ever."

We walked up toward Sveavägen to test our luck there. There were two beggars lying under the bridge. Samuel stopped and read their signs. Then he placed two gold ten-krona coins in one's mug and put a fifty-krona bill in the other's. He just did it, without checking whether anyone was looking, without seeming proud. I looked at him and thought that he was a very unusual person. Not because he gave money to beggars, but because he did it there and then, in the middle of the night, when no one was looking. Except for me.

*

Panther is quiet, thinking back. Just so you know, that last text sounds more dramatic now that I'm telling you about it. But I definitely should have responded. I could have written, like, *Take it easy bro, I'm here for you, you're not alone, everyone has felt the way you're feeling at one point and you'll make it, don't worry, don't let go, hold on.* But of course I didn't [pausing, looking out the window]. Okay, damn it, that's enough, would you stop looking at me like I'm so guilty? [Standing up, walking to the bathroom.] What the hell is with you, what the hell do you want, I didn't have time [slamming the bathroom door].

*

Twenty minutes later. Still no taxi. Or—an awful lot of taxis zoomed past us with their signs lit and picked up other customers further on. In the end we decided to go for a solo wave. I went to stand near a shop window with my phone to my ear, Samuel stood alone on the sidewalk. A taxi stopped, Samuel opened the door and said where we were going and when the taxi driver accepted, I pretended to end my call and jumped into the backseat. The driver saw me and swallowed and moved the passenger seat forward so I would have room for my legs. We drove south in silence. Samuel was low on cash and I said it was fine.

"I'll get it."

"Thanks, I'll get the next one," he said, as usual, and clapped his hand to his wallet-slash-heart.

I shook my head to say it didn't matter and I would never let money come between us. The taxi drove on. We dropped Samuel off in Hornstull and continued toward Örnsberg. When we turned off Hägerstensvägen I leaned forward and showed my cash to the driver.

"Don't worry," I said. "I have money. I'm not going to rob you."

The driver gave a nervous smile, he tried to hold the wheel a bit more loosely but I noticed how relieved he was when I unfolded my body from his backseat and the car recovered its usual center of gravity.

*

Panther calms down and comes back. She says that later that same day, at four or five in the afternoon, a stranger called from Samuel's phone. He said that there had been an accident, he said that it probably wasn't that serious, he had worked in Cambodia and had seen things that were considerably worse. But I called Vandad anyway, I told him what had happened and I thought that if it was serious someone would contact me. When I didn't hear anything I assumed that everything was fine. I went out that night, a few drinks at Möbel-Olfe and then a party in a courtyard near Görlitzer Bahnhof.

*

Okay. I realize we don't have "all the time in the world." And of course I can "fast-forward to Laide and Samuel's next encounter." As long as you agree that everything I've told you up to now plays an important role in what happens later on. The rest of the year flies by. Panther moves to Berlin to concentrate on her career in art. Samuel and I go from being acquaintances to being friends to moving in together. By day he works at the Migration Board and I stack moving boxes in fifteen-footers. On the weekends we do all those things Samuel gets it into his head we have to do so as not to miss out on life. And I tag along; I never say no. Even if there are times when his ideas make me want to shake my head and ask why. Why take an airport bus to Arlanda and back to watch planes landing and eat dinner at a buffet place that according to Samuel's cousin is "every pilot's best-kept secret"? Why swing by the shooting range in Årsta to check out the recoil in a Glock? Why buy a used Sega Genesis online to see if NBA Jam is still as fun as it was when we were little? I don't know. Samuel doesn't either. But we do it all anyway and we share everything equally and if one of us is low on cash the other one pays and when Samuel finds out that his sublet won't be renewed the obvious choice is for him to move in with me. I help him with the move, get him free boxes from work and borrow a cargo van. He takes the living room, I keep the bedroom. Once Samuel says that he's never had a friendship that was so "wonderfully undemanding" and I'm not a hundred percent sure what he means but I nod and agree.

Sometimes when I walk into the bathroom in the morning and see his toothbrush beside mine I think that we have grown awfully close in an awfully short amount of time. That this closeness is— Delete that. Delete all of that. Just write that the rest of the year is like a stroboscopic slideshow of rumbling basslines, clinking glasses, nods at people we don't know but recognize, sticky dance floors, rubber coat-check tags in my back pocket, steamy smoke-machine smell, cigarette butts in overflowing toilets, cigarette packs smushed into empty glasses, conversations in front of speakers where the only way to make yourself heard is to cup the listener's ear. Then home in a taxi with ears ringing and waking up the next day with wrists full of stamps and pockets full of crumpled bills and forgotten beer tickets and sweaty gum and involuntarily stolen lighters and brown flakes of tobacco and receipts from places you hardly remember being at. But then you remember, of course, and smile at the memory. In short: it was a happy time. Maybe the happiest of my life.

*

Panther sighs and shakes her head. It hurts to think about this. The next day was a Friday. I was standing at the market in Kreuzberg, I was just about to buy two artichokes, I had them in a thin blue plastic bag, I had my change purse out, my phone rang, I answered. Vandad told me, he just said it and then he hung up. I know I collapsed, I remember that the guy selling vegetables seemed to think at first that I was trying to steal the artichokes, then he realized what was up and he ran out and stood near me so no one would accidentally step on me, it was crowded, the cobblestone street was full of vegetable bits and black water, there was a sound, it wasn't crying, it was an animal, a mewling primeval animal, I squatted there, I don't know how long, the vegetable seller stood there waiting for me to get up, he borrowed a bottle of water from a colleague, he handed it to me, I took it but couldn't drink, shoes and unshaven shins walked by me, two German guys with guitars were talking loudly about pineapple tomatoes which were apparently like regular tomatoes but in the shape of a pineapple, they tasted the same as other tomatoes but the shape was totally different, and one guy said "then what's the point of them" and the other answered something I didn't hear because they had walked past me, they were already gone, after a while I could get up, the man with the artichokes wanted to give them to me but I paid, I didn't want anything

for free, I took the plastic bag and walked home, fifteen minutes later I realized I was going in the wrong direction, I
turned around and walked home, I had bought artichokes,
the sun was shining, German guys were talking about pineapple tomatoes, a truck was unloading lamps and dressers
outside a furniture store, beer was glittering in plastic glasses
at an outdoor restaurant, it was a nice day, people were happy,
bikes wobbled by, taxis honked, cats meowed, the city was
alive, but Samuel was dead.

PART II

LAIDE

THE LIVING ROOM

Did you come straight from the airport? Was it hard to find? You've lived in Paris, right? This neighborhood was probably pretty different back then. These days it's super quiet. Or almost super quiet. But it's lucky you didn't come last Tuesday because the RER drivers and Air Traffic Control went on strike. I thought we could sit in here, will that work, sound-wise? Do you want tea or coffee? Milk? Hot or iced? Foam or no foam? Why don't you tell me a little more about what you want to know while I get it ready?

*

Then came the autumn when Laide and Samuel met for real. And that's probably what some people (like you, for example) would call the beginning of the story. And others (like me, for example) would call the beginning of the end.

*

Should I just start talking? Okay. But I'm going to trust that you'll turn what I say into something that works as a text. I mean, like, take out when I say like "like" and "um," because I know how spoken language looks when it's written down word for word, it's totally bizarre, you seem like an idiot and I don't want to seem like an idiot, I want to seem like me.

*

In the spring of two thousand ten, I noticed that Samuel was changing. At first it was little things. Like when we did a toast together, more and more often he would say:

"To love."

Even though both of us were single. He talked about Panther more and more often, he was annoyed that she wouldn't answer his emails, he said we should go down to Berlin and visit her.

"We were as close as you can be without being together, and now suddenly she's gone."

But every time I wanted to book a trip, he put it off.

*

I moved home to Sweden in the spring of two thousand ten. I had gone back and forth like fifty times. Weekend visits, friends' wedding, Dad's sixtieth birthday. All the trips were the same. When I was little I loved to fly. Mom used to sit next to me and say that I was steering the plane, that it was up to me to take care of all the technology. When we backed out of the gate I was the one who did it by twisting the knob that held up the tray, and when we started the engines I was the one who gave them fuel by pushing on the recline button and to take off I had to push the recline button and turn the tray knob at exactly the same time. Then the plane would get up to cruising speed and then we could turn on the autopilot and retract the landing gear by turning the tray knob and pushing on the recline button.

*

Mostly, of course, we hung out together. But sometimes Samuel got the idea that he should go on a date. He met girls with names like Malin-slash-Esmeralda-slash-Zakia. They exchanged numbers, they went for coffee, they went out to eat. They were heading in a certain direction. Then a few weeks later I would ask how it was going with Malin-slash-Esmeralda-slash-Zakia.

"Oh, nothing came of that," Samuel would say.

"What happened?"

"Malin and I went to the movies and the way she breathed was totally disgusting, it was like the air whistled when it went through her nose. At first I didn't notice, but once I heard it, it was impossible to stop thinking about it."

Or:

"Esmeralda was nice but her parents are conservatives, I mean like they're on the city council, and that's not going to work. Plus she lives in Gärdet."

"So?"

"It's kind of far to go all the time."

Or:

"I don't know, Zakia and I never clicked. Yeah, we hung out a little but I was never quite there. Something wasn't quite right, I don't know what. Maybe it was the age difference."

"Wasn't she just two years younger than you?"

"Mmhmm. But it felt like more. Plus she had an ugly purse."

*

By now traveling was a boring routine, a tiresome waiting game. I hardly remember my trip home. But I remember that it felt weird to bring less luggage home with me than I had had when I moved down. I had left most of my books behind, and a lot of clothes too. My belongings felt sullied somehow, they were part of a relationship that was over, they were a shell I had worn for five years and now I was free.

*

At the same time, Samuel started sliding up to strangers at bars to ask about their definitions of love. People would be sitting there talking about the kinds of things people talk about in Stockholm (how hard it is to find good skilled labor, good realtors, bad realtors, who earned what on a rental turned co-op-slash-sale-slash-bid) and without any sort of lead-in Samuel would approach them and force whatever he wanted to talk about into the conversation. Like this:

"A good tradesman can make you fall in love a little, and by the way, how would you define love?"

Or:

"I assume you end up with an intimate relationship with your realtor, almost as intimate as with a romantic partner. And how would you define ..."

I saw him do the same thing time and again. And the strange thing was that people answered him, everyone had their own definition. One taxi driver said that for him, love was a relationship that always yields increased returns.

"Like a bank account?" said Samuel.

"Yes, but a damn good bank account. With amazing interest. And guarantee of deposits. Not one of these fucking huge banks, you know. A small, specialized niche bank."

"But there aren't any guarantees with love," I said.

"No, you might be right about that," the taxi driver said with a sigh. "So I guess it's probably a pretty crappy bank account."

Another time we were at an after-party and some girl claimed that love is when someone else is the main character in the movie of your life and you yourself become a supporting role and everyone else is an extra. After a trip to the movies Samuel and I were sitting at a cafe and when I came back from the bathroom I heard the lady next to us say to Samuel and her husband:

"No, no, no. You two just don't get it. Love isn't about 'being happy and content.' Love is suffering and pain and feeling sick and still being prepared to give up everything for the other person—everything!"

Her husband shook his head. Samuel nodded and looked like he understood. But even then I thought that he didn't get it and never would.

*

The only piece of clothing I missed was an orange scarf I wore on my second date with my ex-husband. I thought that would ruin the scarf forever, but in fact I sometimes yearned for it. And every time, that yearning made me happy. It felt, like, nice that a scarf could win out over that long-as-intestines, painful mess of a relationship.

*

When Samuel brought up the definition of love for the hundredth time, I was a little irritated.

"Love is love," I said. "What more do you want to know?"

"But there has to be a better definition than that."

"Okay, here's the definition of love. The definitive one. Love is when things that are chill get extra chill because the person you're with is so chill."

Samuel laughed and told me I sounded poetic.

"That's right, I'm a poet. Now let's call a taxi."

*

Sometimes I actually toyed with the thought of calling my ex-husband, just calling him and asking him to send the scarf. As if we were distant colleagues who had never lived together, been married, gone at each other so hard that I sometimes doubted we would come out of it alive. But we did, and of course I will never call him. It's over, it's finished, I hardly think about him anymore. But that scarf, on the other hand.

*

The spring grew warmer, Stockholm's outdoor cafes opened, and ... Yes! Take it easy! Chill out ... It seriously stresses me out when you do that ... They meet soon, I promise. Laide moved home to Sweden and we were sitting at that cheap beer place by Fridhemsplan. People were talking soccer, horse-racing, or which rappers have the finest honeys in their videos (someone said the southern ones, someone said West Coast, no one said East Coast). Samuel and I were talking about who we were back in upper secondary school. I said I was about the same as I was now, a regular old invisible person who people knew they shouldn't start something with. Samuel said he hadn't been bullied, but there were people at his school who thought he was a little weird. He hadn't had any problems in compulsory school because he went to one near his neighborhood and people knew who he was, but in upper secondary he ended up in a school that was farther away and the atmosphere was different there. The guys were supposed to be a certain way and the girls were supposed to be another way and at first he got respect because people could tell that at the least he wasn't totally Swedish. But then a rumor went around that he was gay and Valentin who did Thai boxing and was the terror of the school grabbed Samuel's headphones in the common room and even though Samuel mostly listened to hip-hop, Biggie and Tupac and Snoop, this particular time he happened to be listening to a classical piano piece, and Valentin laughed and started calling him Chopin, which turned into chicken, which turned into chickadee because of course Samuel was brown but white at the same time. They took his cap and spit gobs of snot into it, they graffitied his locker, in the shower after gym everyone left when he came in, and in the lunchroom Valentin liked to trip with his glass of milk and drop it in his food or onto his neck and if it got in his face he said sorry without holding back his laughter because the milk looked like cum. Samuel told me all of this in a voice that said it was nothing to worry about. But when I heard it I wanted to look up Valentin's address and pay him a visit at home, ring his bell, stick my foot in the crack, and explain a thing or two. Samuel smiled and said that was nice of me, but it wasn't as bad as it sounded.

"It's not like I was bullied."

When the bill came, one of us picked it up, it didn't matter who, because we shared everything equally.

*

I landed at Arlanda. In the midst of feeling sort of free because I was alive. Freed from my ex-husband's sticky web. The colors seemed bolder, my body lighter, and everything seemed possible as I stood there by the baggage carousel waiting for my bags. "Welcome to my hometown," said all the famous faces, blown up huge on the walls. Then I jumped on the train into town. It was classic Swedish spring sun, cold and clear light that gave the illusion that it was warm out if you were sitting behind a pane of glass. I looked out at the ancient-forest landscape that still surrounds Stockholm and felt all my enthusiasm vanish. What the hell am I doing? I thought. How can I voluntarily be on my way back to this fucking backwater town? Am I really going to waste my life in this nowhereland when there is a whole world out there? And at that point I wasn't thinking about Brussels, I was thinking bigger than that, I was thinking São Paulo, I was thinking New York, I was thinking Beirut. I was thinking about anything that wasn't an adorable little city center with a few buildings from the Middle Ages and a castle that looks like a barracks and three measly little Metro lines and an inner city surrounded by industrial areas while everyone talks about how the city can't grow any bigger and then and there, before I had even arrived, I felt like I had to get away, that this was a trial period. I promised myself I would stay for only six months, a year at the max.

*

Spring became summer. Time passed. Samuel continued to ask people about definitions of love and when he encountered people who seemed content in their relationships he would always ask how they met. I stood next to him, thinking that everyone had a tale and that tale grew taller and taller every year.

"How did we meet? Oh, that's actually an amazing story."

And even though no one but Samuel cared, they would start telling it. They were in the same class in elementary school and hadn't seen each other for fifteen years when, by "huuuuge coincidence," they ran into each other at a market. In Italy. At sunset. They were at a conference and ended up next to each other in line for the breakfast buffet. They sat there until lunch. Until dinner. They didn't leave the dining room for several days. They stood next to each other at ICA in Bredäng in two cash register lines that were exactly the same length, and after the line had stood still for thirty seconds, five minutes, fifteen minutes, they started talking to each other. The conversation never ended and "that's how it happened" they said, smiling their liar smiles. I suppose they wanted our eyes to light up, wanted us to share their joy. But in fact, both Samuel and I thought that they ought to keep their joy to themselves, because they didn't get that there were people out there who hadn't experienced that, who were still waiting.

*

I refused to become one of those people who gets stuck in a place just because it's comfortable, who meets someone and takes out loans and buys an apartment and imagines that this shithole of a city with its nervous baristas and bartenders who drool over celebrities and racist bouncers and narrow-minded politicians and redneck police force is the norm; who forget that Stockholm is an anomaly, a tiny goddamn backwater populated by peasants, as far north as you can get, a city that completely lacks purpose and is so afraid of its own shadow that people don't talk to each other even when the Metro stands still in a tunnel for fifteen minutes. It's the only city in the world where newborns learn how to avoid eye contact. You see it in children who grew up somewhere else, they come here and think that people will fawn over them on the Metro, they flutter their eyelashes, they offer pacifiers to dogs, but their fellow passengers quickly let them know the score, not a single glance up from the phone, not a single smile from anyone in return, like mummies, like pillars of salt they go back and forth, to work, home from work, each fellow human is treated like a beggar, and if there's only one thing I must remember it is that this is not everything. There is a way out, there is always a way out, I thought as the train approached the city.

*

My theory is that Samuel had waited so long that in the end he was ready for it to happen, no matter where, no matter who with. And when it happened, it happened later that same year, when the summer was over. The trees had started to turn red and the sidewalks were getting slippery. The place was no Italian vegetable market, no flashy conference dining room. The place was the parking lot outside the Migration Board's offices in Hallonbergen.

*

Then I arrived and everything shifted. My sister was standing there at Cityterminalen. Around her: Ylva, Santiago, Shahin, Tamara, and several friends from interpreter school, plus a few people from my syndicalist years whose names I don't want to use. They had made a laughably ugly banner that said WELCOME HOME LAIDE! (with glitter around my name) and they had put on party hats. Shahin had brought her saxophone, but since she had forgotten the mouthpiece it just hung around her neck, all shiny. They caught sight of me and everyone rushed up and screamed and clapped their hands and there were group hugs and pictures and I was so overwhelmed that I hardly knew what was going on, you can tell in the pictures from that day, I don't even look happy, my mouth is just open like a fish and I'm looking around in confusion, as if I have just found out that the world is one big set and my friends are actors. Only afterwards, once we were in the car on the way home, did it start to sink in that my sister had organized all of this for me. She was sitting in front of me in the passenger seat and checking her phone as if nothing much had happened, as if she put together this sort of surprise once a week.

"I did thank you, right?" I asked.

"You stood there without saying a thing for five minutes."

"Thanks."

"No problem."

She reached her hand back over her seat and I took it.

*

This is more or less the way Samuel described it to me when he came home from work and ran into the kitchen with his shoes still on:

"Oh my fucking holy shit I mean whooooaaaa I think I met her or I mean I don't know but shit I mean shit it was so fucking I don't know oh my God I mean shit I phew hold on a second I'll tell you hold on I just have to calm down a little but holy shit I mean holy shit!!!"

I looked at him, waiting for him to utter a complete sentence. Or at least a third of a sentence.

*

We arrived home at my old apartment, five years had gone by, first a French student from Tours who was doing a Ph.D. in biology had rented it, then a Senegalese couple, and most recently a Hungarian family with two children. Five years and so many people ought to have changed the smell of the apartment. But as I stood there in the hall, breathing and looking at myself in the hall mirror, it was like no time had passed.

*

After about half an hour the story of what had happened came out. Samuel had gone to work. Same as always. He took the red line to T-Centralen. Got on the escalator, the moving walkway, the escalator. Transferred to the blue line toward Akalla. Got off. Walked by Hallonbergen Centrum, wondered whether he should buy a lunch now or go with the

Thai takeout. Settled on Thai. He walked toward his building. He swiped his access card. He sat in his ergonomic chair. He glanced through his cases, he contacted a few embassies, he booked a few trips, he wrote a few reports. None of what he was doing demanded his concentration. His thoughts wandered freely and presumably he was thinking what he usually did at work: here I am with my degree in political science, sorting papers like a mailman and booking trips like a secretary and writing reports like a report-writer. Or maybe he was thinking about something else.

*

When I left Sweden I was pretty new as an interpreter. I had my degree and I'd been working for one and a half years when I received my special-project assignment in Brussels, which soon turned into a permanent position. For five years I sat at meetings that lasted an eternity, I translated phrases like *trade-barrier speculation clause* or *EU subsidy reform supplements* from French to Swedish; from English to French. Only when I went to restaurants did I get to use my Arabic. I knew more than I wanted to about the UN convention on maritime law, ocean-sonics studies in international waters, and the precarious situation of the bluefin tuna. Back in Stockholm, I had no trouble finding a job. Everyone wanted a licensed interpreter with my experience. But I felt like I wanted to do something different. Something that really affected people's lives.

The girl at the agency said I would have no problem at all finding work as a phone interpreter.

"All you have to decide is whether you want to take daytime or nighttime calls."

"What's the difference?"

"Well, we have a lot of different clients. But in general, the nighttime calls tend to be a bit more emotionally demanding. There are more calls from the police and the emergency room at night. And during the day, there are calls from the Social Security Agency and the Employment Agency."

I said I would get back to her with which type of calls I wanted. I went into the city and bought a new phone that I would use for work and then I called up the interpreter agency again.

"Here's my new number, and by the way: I'd be happy to take calls both day and night."

She laughed like she thought I was joking.

"When are you going to sleep?"

"It's no big deal. I don't sleep much anyway."

*

It was a perfectly normal day. To avoid small talk with his colleagues, Samuel took a late lunch. He left the office at one. He walked out into the bright autumn sun. He sat in the biting wind down at the Thai place, which was a small food cart with colorful lanterns in the parking lot behind the Migration Board building. He bought the daily special for sixty-five kronor, he thought of the friend who had ordered scampi at the Thai stand at Zinkensdamm and found a syringe in his food, he made sure his food was syringe-free, ate it up, looked at the bare trees swaying in the wind. Perhaps he was thinking that time passed slowly even when he was on break.

*

When I told my friends from interpreter school that I was going to go with nighttime calls, I was advised to prepare myself.

"Study body parts and medical terms," said one friend.

"Brush up on your weapons," said another.

"But you can hold off on different dialects," said a third. "That will come later on, once you've been working for a while. That's the hardest part."

I followed their advice. I studied body parts and made sure I knew how to say norovirus and rheumatism, fly-kick and head-butt. I freshened up on the nuances that differentiate cudgels, pokers, and clubs.

"Some calls can be really hard," said one friend.

I nodded and thought I understood what she meant.

*

After a little more than an hour, Samuel walked back to the office, that big chunk of concrete that looked like a parking garage. Activists had left stickers on the stairs; they said things like *LEO, age 8, taken away in the night by police and sent to Iraq. Migration Board: as usual, everything went smoothly* or

ALL DEPORTATION MUST STOP. The stickers were half ripped off, but it was still possible to read the black text, tattooed on the concrete like a shadow.

*

I had been working for a month when I had my first call with Nihad. It was eleven o'clock on a Sunday morning, the police officer introduced himself and said he was calling from the emergency rape clinic at Södra hospital.

"I'm sitting here with a woman who needs your assistance as an interpreter."

And I remember thinking, didn't he need it as much as she did?

The woman introduced herself, her voice was quiet and dogged, I started translating her story from Arabic to Swedish. She said that she was twenty-nine years old, she had started talking with a guy at the bar, they met at Golden Hits on Kungsgatan, they sang karaoke together, first "Winds of Change" and then a Brian Ferry song she didn't remember the name of. Then he added her on Facebook, he called himself Bill, they started a relationship, they went out a few times, he bought her dinner, twice she slept at his place but nothing happened. He was nice, he took care of her, when they went on dates he always paid, he said he had contacts that could help her get a permanent residence permit.

The policeman's voice: So she's here without authorization?

Me: Do you have a residency permit?

Nihad: No. Or, I'm here on my husband's permit.

Me: No. Or. She's here on her husband's permit.

Nihad: But my husband and I are separated.

The policeman: Okay. She knows I'm a police officer, right?

He said it like he was trying to make a joke.

*

Samuel approached the entrance to the Migration Board office. Something was going on. The security guards, who normally stood on the inside and kept an eye on the people taking queue numbers, were standing out in the parking lot. A young woman was holding back an older woman. The older woman was wearing a veil, she was waving her fist and screaming something in Arabic. The young woman translated it into Swedish. Samuel walked by. He heard their voices. They were shouting that this was a scandal, a violation of rights, a disgrace. They would go to the media, there would be consequences, major consequences. One of the guards waved her hand as though she wanted to shoo away an annoying wasp. The other guard looked like he had a toothache.

"Is this what you call a democracy?" the women shouted.

Samuel looked at the younger woman. He stopped. He realized that she was beautiful. Or, in Samuel's own words later that night:

"I mean bro, bro— I like can't sit down when I think about her. I swear, she wasn't just beautiful, she was the foxiest fox, she was foxier than the Fox River, she was Beyoncé times a hundred, we're talking Janet Jackson before the plastic surgery, we're talking that girl from *21 Jump Street*, the big sister on *Cosby*, Hilary from *Fresh Prince* but with brains, she was so beautiful that I DIED—I saw her and I wanted to melt, you know what I mean, I wanted to go up to her and lap up the sweat from her shoes, I mean for serious, what is it Biggie says in that song? She was so beautiful I was ready to suck her dad's dick, you know?"

I felt strange, it was like nausea, I think it was Samuel's story about the syringe in the Thai food.

"Then what did you do?" I asked.

"I. Uh. First I walked past her and into the office. Then I turned around and went back out. I walked up to them, said hi in Arabic, and asked what had happened."

*

Nihad continued her story. The day before yesterday, the guy who called himself Bill came to her place without warning, he was just there in a car outside, and he called her phone and asked if he could come up.

The policeman: So she had given him her phone number?

Me: He wants to know if you had given him your phone number.

Her: Yes.

Me: Yes.

When she said it wasn't a good time for him to come up, he left the car and came up anyway.

"He stood in the stairwell, he had flowers with him, two

different colors of tulips, he wouldn't give up, it smelled like he had been drinking, I asked how he was going to drive home, he said he wasn't going to drive home. Finally I let him in, I didn't know what to do, he was talking so loudly, I didn't want the neighbors to notice, he came in without taking off his shoes, he walked around in the apartment I was living in temporarily, and he acted like he lived there, he sat on the sofa, put his feet up on the table, asked if I had any food in the house, and when I said I wanted him to leave he refused, I lied and said I was expecting someone and he said I was cheating, that I was waiting for another man, he started using ugly words, he asked if it was a black man who was coming, he said it several times, 'is it a black man who's going to fuck you with his big black cock, is that what you want, to be plowed by a big black cock,' and when he said those things I realized he was touching himself, he was sitting there in my borrowed apartment, on my borrowed sofa, touching himself, and then I ran to the kitchen and grabbed a frying pan, I don't know why I didn't grab a knife, I said he had to leave or else I would call my ex-husband, and he said, 'So call him, call that blackhead, what do you think he can do, what do you think will happen if I report him for threatening me? What do you think will happen if I say he came over and assaulted me?'

"While he said that he took something from the pocket of his jacket, at first I thought it was a gold ring, for a brief moment I thought he was going to propose to me, get down on his knee and break into a smile and say that it had all been a joke. But it wasn't a gold ring, it was brass knuckles, he slipped them on and hit himself above his eyebrow, it was so strange, I just stood there with the frying pan in my hand and he sat there on the sofa in his jacket, bleeding from the eyebrow, blood running into his eyes and into his mouth, he smiled when he saw how scared I was, he asked what I was going to do now, now that I had already hurt him, now that there was proof I was unstable. 'What do you think the courts will have to say about your chances of staying here if it comes out that you assault upstanding citizens for no reason?' He was still smiling, his teeth were red, it was dripping on the sofa, I lowered the frying pan. At first I didn't put up a fight, he lifted me toward the bed, I let him do it, I couldn't feel my body, he took off my clothes and forced himself into me, it was difficult, it hurt, I looked away, there was the window, the knickknacks, the curtains I had bought just because my son liked the tree pattern."

The policeman's voice: Her son?

Me: Do you have kids?

Her: One son. But he's with my husband. He has a better life there.

*

Samuel wrote down the woman's case number, went inside, and looked it up on the computer. A few minutes later he was back in the parking lot.

"I think it's her salary that's the problem. In the application it says she will only earn thirteen thousand kronor per month."

"But I'm the one who helped her," Laide said without waiting for her client to respond. "We were told that thirteen thousand was the minimum."

"According to the rules, that's too little if you write that you work full time." Samuel lowered his voice and looked around. "Perhaps Zainab here can work a little less from now on? For example, if she could consider *writing* that she works at eighty percent for the same salary, there is a *very good* chance that her application will go through."

He said it in that slow way you say things when you want it to be clear that what you want to say is different from what you're actually saying. Laide looked at him and smiled.

"Thanks."

"No problem."

They kept standing there in the parking lot. None of them quite knew how to end things.

"Was there anything else?" Laide asked.

"No."

The client thanked Samuel, Samuel thanked the interpreter, everyone shook hands and said goodbye and instead of asking all those questions he'd been hoping to get into (who are you, where do you live, where are you from, what's your favorite tea, what's your personal definition of love, when will we meet again and what is your phone number) Samuel swiped his access card and took the elevator back up to his office.

*

Nihad continued:

"The frying pan was nearby, I could have reached it but I didn't, I could have bitten off his tongue, but I didn't do that either, I let him start, when it didn't work he swore and said cruel things about my body, he said it was too disgusting, that I was too fat, that no one would ever want me. Then he propped himself above me and touched himself until he came, most of it landed on him, only a little got on me, he told me to lick it up but I couldn't reach it with my tongue, then he grabbed my tongue and yanked it, then he kissed me, then he said I was too disgusting to touch, then he left, he walked toward his car, I kept lying there, I heard the elevator as it went down to street level, I heard the beep from his car, the engine when he turned the key, then it idled for a minute or two and then he drove off, he was gone, I kept lying there."

*

The office was exactly as Samuel had left it before lunch. The copy-machine smell. The whiteboard. The desk. The plastic plants. The pale gray computer screen with stickers left behind by the person who worked there before him. And Samuel. Who suddenly, there in his office, felt as natural as a bear on a skateboard. He had a hard time sitting still, he was sweating, he felt like the walls were closing in on him, he wanted to get away, get out, move on. Finally he opened the case again, he saw that the contact person-slash-interpreter was named Laide. He entered her number into his phone.

*

Silence for a few seconds, then the policeman's voice:

"Can you ask her to clarify if the act was consummated?"

"She says it was not consummated."

"Can you ask her to describe in what way she resisted?"

"She says she was too afraid to resist."

"Why didn't she come in right away?"

"She was scared."

"Can you explain to her that I am more than willing to make a report? I definitely think we should report it. But can you tell her there is a risk that this case will not proceed?"

"Do it yourself."

"You're the interpreter."

"But she can understand you."

"Yes, but I don't think she understands me as well as you do."

"I don't think I understand you."

"Please, this is not a judgment on my part. I'm not a lawyer, and you're not a lawyer, and she's not a lawyer, right? So I'm sure we can agree that it's up to the lawyers to determine what happened here, can't we?"

Nihad's voice: "What did he say?"

Me: "That it's going to be difficult."

Her voice: "But I know where he lives, I have his address, although I think he gave me a fake name."

Me: "I understand that, but I'm not sure if he understands that."

Her: "His blood is still on the sofa."

The policeman's voice: "What did she say?"

Her: "What did he say?"

Me: "He's a fucking idiot."

Her: "I know."

Me. "Is there anyone else you can talk to?"

Her: "I don't know, I'm so, I'm so, I don't know what to do."

Him: "What did she say? Can you try to get her to calm down? I know it's hard, but it's no help to anyone for her to act like this."

Me: "Say you want to speak to a female police officer."

Her: [moaning, crying, snuffling]

Him: "What did she say?"

Me: "That she would like to speak with a female police officer."

Him: "She said that?"

Me: "Yes. She wants to speak with a female police officer."

Him: "Are you aware that this conversation is being recorded?"

Me. "She wants to talk to someone else."

The policeman sighs, a chair is pushed back, a door opens.

Her: "What did you say to him?"

Me: "That you want to talk to a female police officer."

Her: "What will happen to me if I file a report?"

Me: "We'll have to ask her. You have to talk to someone else, someone who is on your side."

Her: "Thanks."

Me: "No problem."

Her: "What do we do now?"

Me: "We wait."

*

Later that same night we were sitting in our shared kitchen, talking through what had happened. Samuel described (for the fourth time) what she had said and what he had said and what she had been wearing and how beautiful she was.

"The energy in that parking lot was extremely special. I swear, man, it wasn't just in my head. She must have felt it, I swear she felt it."

"What are you going to do now?"

"Don't know. What do you think?"

"No idea. But I would lie low if I were you."

"Why?"

"I think it would be best that way."

That was the best answer I could come up with, and I don't know why I said it. I just answered with what I felt there and then. It isn't the right time for Samuel to meet someone, I thought. Not now. Not her.

*

While we waited, Nihad said that her husband had accepted her decision to divorce him. He had never hit her. He was a good man who was being trained as a cook in a lunch restaurant in Nacka. But she would never be able to tell him about this. She had left him to be free and she had been allowed to borrow the apartment temporarily because she was desperate and now the sofa was ruined and the man who called himself Bill knew where she lived and . . . She started crying again. I explained to her that since she was here on her husband's permit there was a risk that she would be taken to a detention facility and be sent back now that she had confessed that her relationship with her husband was over.

"But what am I supposed to do?"

"I don't know. But if I were you I would get out of there. Fast."

*

But was Samuel listening? Did he trust his best friend's gut feeling? No, a few days later I came out of the shower and found Samuel at the kitchen table.

"Okay. Okay okay okay," he called, half happy, half panicked. "I just did it. I pressed 'send.' I texted her!"

"Who?"

"Her. The contact person. The interpreter. I went the work route. I said thanks for last time and asked her to contact me if her client needed any more assistance. Best, Samuel, Migration Board."

"You said thanks for last time?"

"Yeah, was that weird or something?"

"That's what you say after you've been to a party. Not when you've had a random encounter in a parking lot."

103

"Oh, but . . . It felt like the right thing to . . . I don't know."

I poured a cup of coffee, I looked out at the courtyard. An empty playground, the swings were moving gently in the wind like absent-minded leaves.

"So has she responded?"

"Not yet. But it was a good text. I wrote lots of drafts. Want me to read it to you?"

"No thanks," I said.

But I didn't say it in a mean way, I just informed him that I wasn't all that curious to learn the exact contents of his text. Then I went to my room to get ready for the workday. Samuel was still sitting at the kitchen table when I came back out. He was still bare-chested, his twig-like arms held the phone, his eyes were focused on the screen.

"But of course it could be taken ironically as well."

"What can?"

"Thanks for last time. Maybe she'll see it and think it was a joke. Was it stupid to sign off with 'best'? Is that too impersonal? I should have written out a whole greeting—'best wishes, Samuel, Migration Board.' Or maybe I should have ended with 'all my best.' Or 'xoxo'? What do you think? Would it have been too much to—"

I closed the front door and pressed the elevator button. If I had been able to put a stop to it all there and then, I would have. I had a bad feeling about it. But the pinball of fate was rolling and nothing could stop it.

*

Of course it was unusual. I had no right to give Nihad legal advice. I had only heard what had happened to other women in similar situations. Maybe it was different for Nihad. I don't know. But I asked for her number and called her right away from my personal phone and we talked as she stood up and left the room. I heard the sound of doors and running steps, elevator dings and two voices talking about a soccer match ("it was like total fucking pyrotechnics!"). Then the rubber-squeaking sound of her shoes against the hallway floor as she ran for the exit, her breathing, the scraping sound of her jacket collar, someone (a taxi driver?) calling out a last name, he said it slowly and tiredly, as if he had been standing there in the hospital entryway calling the same last name since the dawn of time. Then birds chirping and car engines and wind and creaking brakes and the hissing sound of opening bus doors.

"I'm out."

Before we hung up, I promised to help her apply for a work permit.

*

Three days went by. Three days in which Laide didn't respond to Samuel's text. A normal person would have real-ized that it was time to let go and move on. But not Samuel. To him, the fact that he didn't receive an answer was a sign that it was really *her*, she was *the one*. Four days after Samuel's first text he asked if he could come with me to the gym.

"Are you serious?" I asked.

"Yes. I need to get some exercise. It's been a long time."

"How long?"

"Oh. Eight or nine years."

Samuel came down the stairs to the gym changed and ready. I understood. I would have done the same thing if I had arms as strong as spider webs and thighs as thick as candles. He was wearing a pair of purple sweatpants with cuffs, a T-shirt from a music festival, and two sweatbands dangling from his wrists like bracelets.

"Wanna get going?" he asked. "I was thinking of starting with the jump rope."

And there's nothing wrong with warming up by jumping rope, but it all depends on the way you jump with your jump rope. If you have control of your body and mix single jumps with double jumps while dancing like a boxer, it's okay. Samuel jumped rope like he was back in the schoolyard. His feet got caught in the rope, he started over, people stared at him, people shook their heads. But the crazy thing was, I wasn't ashamed. I liked that he was there. And since he was there with me, no one dared to say anything. But Samuel sure was talkative. As I worked through my program, he commented on the brands of kettlebells, he asked if I thought the sounds coming from the stereo were happy or sad, he wondered if I thought Laide would answer his text today or tomorrow or next week. A lot of the time I let his questions hang in the air, I was focused on doing my own thing, it didn't mean I wasn't listening to them, but sometimes there were so many of them that it was enough to respond to every other one.

*

The calls kept coming. I translated for moms who needed help being informed why their applications for housing assistance had been denied. Men who wanted to appeal an assault verdict. Teens who wanted help with an EU application for a cultural grant for a Palestinian music festival in Norsborg. Women who had been abused, raped, burned with cigarettes. Men who complained of discrimination in the housing market and the job market and when they tried to register the discrimination with the Ombudsman for Discrimination they were discriminated against there too. Women whose shins were kicked in half, whose eyes swelled closed. Women who pointed at the scars on their chins to show where the dog had bitten them. Women who said that when he was driving drunk I wasn't allowed to put on my seatbelt, when I took a second helping he forced me to eat cat food, when my colleagues asked about the bruises he started pulling my hair. Women who said that he had a routine, he locked the security door with a police lock, he put a particular song on the stereo, he whistled along with the melody as he found his gloves. Then he came in and started. The men were lawyers from Jämtland, Finnish-born triathlon medalists, Swedish TV personalities. The men were Syrian fruit sellers, Belgian violinists,

Skåne alcoholics. But the men were unimportant. The men were superfluous. It was the women I wanted to help.

*

We kept working out. I went for upper body, Samuel did push-ups, four regular ones, the rest on his knees (!). He looked over toward the treadmills and suddenly stopped talking.

"What is it?" I asked.

"See the guy in the red tank top? Shit, I think that's Valentin."

"*That's* Valentin?"

I could hardly hold back my laughter. The guy Samuel had described as the terror of the school was as muscular as an earthworm. He had the threatening posture of a croissant. He looked like he might be able to pet a kitten pretty hard.

"Where are you going?" Samuel called.

I wasn't even aware that I was doing it, but I was, I was heading for the guy in the red tank top. I flexed my neck first to the left and then to the right.

"I'll be back in a sec," I said over my shoulder.

I didn't listen to Samuel's objections, I blocked out his cries of "come back!" You remember the people who hurt you, they leave traces that never go away and that was what I wanted to teach him, this guy named Valentin.

*

When I met Zainab for the first time she took off her veil and showed me where she'd been whipped. He'd used an

108

old-fashioned TV antenna, the scars crisscrossed her back like veins, like stings from a jellyfish, but she said it hadn't hurt all that much. It was worse when he degraded her other ways, like when he refused to talk to her because she came home ten minutes late or when he pushed her face into her oatmeal in the morning. The bad part about the TV antenna was that he had waited until the kids came home to do it, it was like he wanted them to watch, her daughters had cried, her son had run out onto the balcony and he just stood there and stared into a corner until it was over. When she found him and carried his stiff body inside, he had round, half-moon fingernail marks in his palms. He was four, almost five.

*

When I came back, Samuel was crouching behind the dumb-bell rack.

"What did he say?" Samuel asked.

"He didn't say much."

I went back to my routine. Samuel was quiet. Then he said:

"How did he manage to hold his breath for so long?"

"He didn't have a choice."

I walked over to the punching bag and slid on my gloves. Samuel followed.

"Did you say hi from me?"

"No, did you want me to?"

"I wouldn't have if you'd asked me. But now it feels like I want him to know who was behind that treatment."

"If he comes back I can tell him you say hi. But something tells me this is the last time he'll show up here."

Samuel looked at me with glistening eyes. He looked sad, but happy too, and I thought it was strange how little things could mean so much to him and big things so little.

"What's with you?"

"Nothing, I just . . . It's such a crazy feeling. To have some-one who . . . I don't know. Is on your side."

"Aw, it was nothing."

"I've never had that."

"Now you do."

A few days later, Laide answered his text. They decided on a time and place for a first date.

*

Zainab didn't want to get divorced, she was also here on her husband's visa, her husband had a work permit and she had to hold out until they could apply for permanent residency. When the girl who worked at the women's shelter asked if she wanted to report him, Zainab explained that her husband was not a monster.

"He has his reasons. He's under a lot of pressure, his boss doesn't pay him the salary that they settled on, he says they had a different agreement, and it's true, my husband didn't know that there was a minimum payment clause, he did everything he could for us to make it here. I don't blame him. I understand. I'm not saying it's okay, but at the same time. Yes. Okay. I love him. But our love is gone. I can't leave him.

I have to leave him. I have nowhere to go, but I'm convinced that Allah, the merciful and compassionate, will find a way."

The representative for the women's shelter cleared her throat and explained that unfortunately, their facility was just as full as all the other shelters. They had a long waitlist.

"I would recommend that you apply for your own work permit. That's the first step toward freedom."

As we stood out on the street, I promised Zainab I would help her with the application. I had helped Nihad and it went well, and now I would help Zainab too. As soon as that was taken care of, we just had to find somewhere for her and the children to live. Then it would all work out. We handed in an application. We were rejected. Even though we had written exactly the same thing as in Nihad's application. We went out to the Migration Board in Hallonbergen to try to find out what had happened.

*

HAHAHA, allow me to laugh my ass off! Who said that Samuel and Laide's first date was "magical"? Who is spreading the rumor that they were "soulmates"? They weren't exactly breakdancing on air, no no no. Their first date was a catastrophe. I wasn't there, of course, but I saw how Samuel looked when he came home. He stood in the hallway looking grim.

"What the hell are you wearing?" I asked.

"Her hoodie. She came straight from the gym."

"Straight from the gym to a date? What did I tell you? This girl is sketchy."

Samuel sank down onto the stool, took off the hoodie, and sniffed it. He gazed ahead emptily.

"No, it wasn't her fault, it was the circumstances. Things kept going wrong all night."

For one thing, it was cold. Unusually cold. Almost below freezing, even though December was still far off. They had decided to meet at the intersection of Vasagatan and Kungsgatan, and he was there on time. He thought it was a poor choice to meet there because cooking smells were pouring from the kebab stand and he didn't want to go around stinking like falafel on their first date. But it seemed that he didn't have to worry, because she didn't show up. It was five past. Ten past. He started to send a text, but just then he saw her coming from up by Hötorget, walking fast. She waved and shouted that she had mixed up Sveavägen and Vasagatan and she had been waiting up there.

"Then she came up to me with her arms sticking out for a hug. But I had already put out my right hand. And by the time I opened my arms for a hug, she had stuck out her right hand. A perfect start."

*

Our application was denied, the guy at the front desk at the Migration Board didn't even want to take our case number. He had a Spanish accent and his breath smelled like bananas and he had the nerve to try to explain to me that "here in Sweden we happen to have an excellent system called 'waiting your turn.'" I admit it, I was a little annoyed, Zainab tried to calm me down, the guards escorted us out. As we stood there in the parking lot and everything seemed hopeless, I heard a discreet throat-clearing and a voice asking us what had happened.

*

There was a bar at a hotel near Norra Bantorget that Samuel had Googled and walked by and stared into for twenty minutes before they met to double check that it looked good, not too full, not too empty, not too flashy, not too anonymous. They started walking along Vasagatan in the direction of the bar, they tried to talk to each other but the conversation limped along. She had a backpack full of her gym clothes and was wearing a purple hat because her hair was wet and she didn't look the way Samuel remembered her. But he thought that if they could only find a place to sit they would have the chance to get to know each other. When they arrived at the hotel bar, Laide said she didn't like the "vibe" there.

"What did she mean by that?" I asked.

"No idea. Instead she suggested that we 'walk around a little.'"

"'Walk around a little'?"

"'Walk around a little'!" Samuel shouted. "Do you know how cold it is out? And how hard it is to keep up a normal conversation when you have to focus on not freezing to death at the same time?"

"Or slipping and falling?"

"Exactly. Thank you."

*

There stood Samuel. His blue-black hair neatly styled. His nose a little crooked. His sideburns grown out. There were two red chili stains on the collar of his wrinkled shirt. His shoes needed a polish. His eyes were kind. His cheeks were downy. He was wearing the biggest smile I'd ever seen.

*

They started walking. A few times, Samuel suggested that they take a seat in a bar or a cafe. But each time, Laide said that bar felt too flashy and that place looked like it was for winos and that cafe reminded her of an ex and that place was closed. So they walked. They walked and walked and walked and walked.

*

A few weeks later we met up downtown. Samuel had texted me, and we took a walk in Vasastan. It was a brisk autumn evening, I had just been swimming at Eriksdal bathhouse so I was a few minutes late. It never felt like a real date. I don't know why. Maybe because it was so easy for us to talk to each other. Maybe because I suspected he was gay. He kept coming back to the fact that he lived with a guy named Vandad and that they had a really great relationship and I remember that when he said that I felt a pang of jealousy, which was a little strange, since we had known each other for about fifteen minutes.

114

*

They walked for an hour. Two hours. Three.

"What did you talk about?" I asked.

"Everything and nothing," said Samuel.

It got late. Their bodies were on the verge of frostbite. Samuel asked questions to avoid awkward silence and Laide answered because she loved the sound of her own voice.

*

For the first hour we mostly talked about work. He told me how he had ended up at the Migration Board, first a degree in political science and then the job on the side that had turned into a full-time position.

"But it's just temporary," he said. "It's really just temporary. I'm not cut out to work for the government."

"So how long have you worked there?"

"Far too long."

I told him about the differences between my job in Brussels and what I was doing in Stockholm. How much easier and, paradoxically, less draining it was to help women than to translate endless contributions about fishing tariffs. He told me that he had chosen political science to change the world, and several of his classmates had gotten jobs at the Ministry of Foreign Affairs or the UN. While he lived in a sublet and worked at the Migration Board's Embassy Division.

"But even if it doesn't pay very well in money, it pays a lot in other ways," he said.

"Like what?"

"That remains to be seen."

*

As the blood in their veins approached freezing point, Samuel suggested they head home.

"And at some point during the evening you borrowed her sweatshirt?"

"Exactly. I was about to freeze to death. Then I forgot about it."

"No sex?"

"Definitely no sex."

"Sounds like a wasted night."

He didn't say anything.

"For real, it sounds like a huge catastrophe of a date," I said, without sounding happy about it.

"Maybe not a catastrophe, but . . . Now that I think about it . . . I don't know. We sort of have different senses of humor. But at the same time, I liked talking to her."

*

We walked in expanding circles but in some magical way, we always came back to Norra Bantorget. The first time, we confirmed that both of us were equally bad at constellations. I pointed at the sky and showed him the stars that made up the Big Wi-Fi Symbol. He pointed out the Little Nike Logo.

"And there's the Curtain Cord!"

"And check out the Big Radiator!"

We laughed and sneaked looks at each other.

As we came back around to Norra Bantorget for the second time, Samuel talked about his grandma. He said she was a strong woman who had always made it on her own, but now, lately, she had started to become addled. She forgot to take her pills, survived on raspberry gummy boats and thumbprint cookies, and had been involved in three car accidents in as many months.

"But she still drives?" I asked.

"Mmhmm. But they're going to revoke her license soon. She's a menace behind the wheel. Last time I visited her it took several minutes for her to remember who I was. It was such a sick feeling. Standing there in front of someone you've known your whole life and they treat you like a stranger."

The third time we approached Norra Bantorget we were talking relationships. I told him about my ex-husband and our marriage and the divorce. For some reason I felt safe telling him those things. Maybe because Samuel asked the right questions. Maybe because it felt so easy to be with him. Undemanding and simple. Neither of us was thinking about anything other than what we were talking about, and I had a hard time figuring out how it could feel so natural. It was like our brains had played music in a former life, they had practiced scales and tuned their neurons in the same key and now that they were finally meeting again they could just jam away, no sheet music necessary.

*

Then a few days went by, the usual daily routine. Samuel showed no signs of having been struck by true love. He didn't walk around with his phone in his hand, freaking out about some text he had written. He didn't sit there with his notebook, writing down things he wanted to tell her. He was his usual self. But now and then, details he hadn't mentioned about the first date slipped out. Like that she had given him a peck-slash-kiss (!). And that he had mentioned his dad (!!!). Both of those things must be considered unusual, because I had known him for a year and a half and could count on the fingers of one hand the number of times he had mentioned his dad.

*

Toward the end of the night I said I had never felt like someone who could be with just one person all my life. Samuel turned to me, cleared his throat, and said:

"But, Laide."

Pause for effect. He batted his eyelashes. In a deep voice:

"Maybe you just haven't met the right person."

For a second I thought he was being serious. Then we started laughing and we laughed until Samuel suggested we head home.

We walked toward the Metro. In the light from Drottninggatan I could see that his lips were purplish-blue, even though I had loaned him my hoodie. I talked about my ex-husband, I said that if there was anything I had learned it was never to stay in a relationship that takes more energy than it gives and that people who are not energy thieves are very rare. We stopped in the red glow from the Skandia movie theater.

"Who do you think you are?" Samuel said suddenly. "A fucking nuclear reactor? Live a little, woman."

He looked surprised, as if the words had come from a place he didn't have total control over.

"Sorry. That talk about energy. It reminded me of my dad. That's the sort of thing he would say to justify the fact that he took off."

We resumed walking toward the Metro. I turned to the side and gave him a peck on the cheek. As my lips touched him, he reacted as if I were trying to brand him. He flew sideways and looked terrified.

"Sorry," he said. "I wasn't prepared."

*

Despite the first date, they kept in contact. They texted each other. Once when I came home, Samuel was talking to her on the phone and I remember I knew it was her because when I walked into the kitchen he was sitting with his feet pulled up under him like a purring cat and his voice was brighter than usual and he glared at me like I was disturbing him even though I was just humming a little tune. When I asked if he wanted coffee he pointed at his headphones as if I should know that you can't talk on the phone and want coffee at the same time. I put on the electric kettle and kept humming and then he stomped off to his room. I sat there with my coffee and wondered what was going on.

*

We went our separate ways in the cold light by the turnstiles. He was going to take the red line, and it was the green for me. We hugged. The hug lasted for quite some time. So long that I wondered if this would be the last time we saw each other. I looked at everything going on around us; two junkies were standing by Åhléns' display window and swaying to inaudible music. A dealer was petting his dog (a collie, strangely enough). A gang of teenagers were trying to nail each other with a shiny silver bag of gum. Two middle-aged ladies were walking into the Pressbyrån with quick steps and hoarse voices. A guy in a hunting vest was talking to two uniformed guards. Samuel kept hugging.

"Okay," I said at last. "I have to go catch my train."

He apologized and let go. We took different escalators down to different tracks and I thought there was a chance that his Norsborg-bound train and my Skarpnäck-bound train might come into the station at the same time. And if that happened, we might end up traveling beside each other on the parallel tracks to Slussen. I told myself that if our trains came in at the same time and we happened to have chosen seats in approximately the same spot in the train and saw each other as the trains crossed the bridge—then it was meant to be. It would be fate's way of saying that we belonged together. When my train left Gamla Stan and sailed toward Slussen, the parallel track was empty, dark and deserted. Fuck fate, I thought.

As the train approached Gullmarsplan, I got a text. Samuel thanked me and said that he would return my hoodie "next time." As if it were perfectly obvious that there would be a next time. I didn't respond until I got off the Metro. I wrote: "That sounds good. Later.." No "xo," no "good night." Short and sweet. Two periods to show that I was writing it so quickly and carelessly that I didn't notice that there were two periods. I walked toward the turnstiles, the little yellow warning sign about deadly voltage was down by the tracks.

*

Later that night, all was forgotten, he came out of his room and walked around the kitchen with the sweeping gestures of a mental patient.

"She's so fine, so fine, so incredibly fine."

"Okay. Do you want coffee now?"

"We have such fucking amazing conversations. It feels like she gets me."

"Okay. Coffee?"

"But we have so much more fun when we chat on the phone than when we meet."

"I'll pour you some coffee. How many times have you seen each other?"

"Once."

"That's all?"

"Both of us have a lot to do at work, with Christmas coming up."

(Brackets: This was in the middle of November.)

Why didn't Samuel want to see Laide? Or was she the one who didn't want to see him? Was she cheating with someone else? Did he have a feeling it would end badly? Was he afraid that she would hurt him? Was he in love with someone else? If I knew the answer, I'd tell you.

Samuel said that Laide had moved home from Brussels, and now she was going around with a lump in her stomach because she had to be here, not that she didn't like it here, but because it felt like the world was still turning without her, somewhere else.

"And that's exactly the way I feel!" Samuel cried as if he had found the answer to the riddle of the universe.

"You do? I've never heard you talk about that before."

"No, but it's obvious, isn't it? That you can long to be somewhere else sometimes."

Then apparently they talked for a long time about how Samuel could possibly work at the Migration Board.

"Why?" I asked.

"I guess she's thinking of my background."

"What about your background?"

"Well, how Dad had political friends who had a rough time, and . . . you know."

"No, I don't know. Are you not allowed to work wherever you

want, just because your dad's friends have a certain history?"

"Well, but, I don't even want to work there."

"That doesn't matter, does it?"

I didn't really know what we were talking about, but we didn't agree. Samuel filled the kettle and asked if I was hungry.

"Cottage-noodles?"

"Cottage-noodles. Want some?"

I nodded.

*

A few days went by after our first meeting. Then Samuel called.

"Everything's fine on my end," I said. "You?"

"Yes, thanks. Everything's fine. Just wanted to see how things were. Later, then."

He hung up and I stood there with my phone in hand, wondering what the hell he was up to. A few days later he called again and this time we talked for longer, at least ten minutes, before I had to go and take a work call. The third conversation lasted twenty minutes, the fourth an hour and a half. When we weren't together in person, we could be much more relaxed with each other. He told me about his background, his childhood, how he had a crush on a girl in the same basketball league in upper secondary school, they hung around at all-night cafes, her religious family suspected they were a couple, she ran away from home to get away from her relatives, they slept in a bunk bed in his room for six months but he couldn't bring himself to confess his feelings. Now she lived in Berlin and was trying to make a living as an artist, even though she seemed to spend most of her time going to art parties. Another time Samuel told me about friends who had died, the guy who drove his motorcycle drunk and crashed into a bridge railing, the guy who overdosed when he was working at a summer camp, the girl who was bitten by a snake when she was in Sri Lanka to visit the woman who had given her up for adoption.

"But that kind of thing happens," Samuel said. "Life goes on."

I sat there on my sofa, feeling empty by comparison. I didn't know anyone my age who had died. My friends had political jobs and talked about the importance of social mobility, they traveled to third-world countries on aid money, they wrote papers about feminist mass media and articles about LGBTQ issues, but hardly any of them came from a background where death was present. For us, death was something that affected old people. Death was something we saw in the movies, or something we read about in articles from war zones. Death wasn't part of real life the way it was for Samuel.

"But that's true for me too," he objected. "Death has never come really close. But for Vandad . . ."

I didn't say anything, waiting for him to finish the sentence. Or at least explain what he meant. In what way had death touched Vandad? In my mind I saw several potential explanations lined up, each as dull and reasonable as the next. Vandad works as an undertaker. He has a second job at a morgue. He's a gardener at a cemetery. But Samuel never finished that sentence.

*

We ate cottage-noodles and drank Castillo and it was like a peace pipe. Cottage-noodles was the dish Samuel made most often. The recipe went like this: pour boiling water (free) over a packet of three-minute noodles (four for ten kronor) and once it's cooled, you put a scoop of cottage cheese (twenty-five kronor for a whole tub) on top. Then sprinkle some herb salt and pepper on it. If you want to be really fancy you can add broccoli, too.

"How often do you actually eat cottage-noodles?" I asked.

"Not that often. No more than three times a week. But I can mix up the flavors, you know. One day you go with beef noodles and red pepper-flavored cottage cheese, the next week it's mushroom noodles with onion cottage cheese. The possibilities are endless."

Samuel raised his glass. We had a toast. I took a portion of cottage-noodles and remembered when I used to go on rounds with Hamza. Five-course dinners to celebrate a good night. The bottles we'd order without even popping them. The drinks, appetizers, the feeling of never having to squash an impulse. Times were different now. In many ways, better. In some ways, worse.

*

Sometimes I wonder what would have happened if we had just kept going on like that. Never seeing each other. Only talking on the phone. Sometimes I wonder if it wouldn't have been for the best. Just imagine if that was the point when we were happiest, when our expectations for the future were greatest and our daily life seemed most distant. Before we started the home, before we started sleeping together, before we turned into that strange couple who might go to bed without making up after a fight about whether or not we should buy organic coffee. Maybe it would have worked out if we'd kept to just talking to each other for several hours and it felt like our words opened up parts of my brain that I hadn't activated for several years.

*

After dinner we watched video clips on his computer. We took turns, he showed me two minutes of Frenchmen climbing up a crane without safety cables, I showed him Japanese monkeys chilling in a hot spring with snow on their heads, he went with a killer whale attacking its trainer, I showed some Eastern bloc workout-fail videos from the early eighties. We were half-lying on the sofa bed in his room, it was full of his clothes, his shirts, his scents. On the table was an ad flyer from Elgiganten, and Mike Tyson was visible on one of the TV screens on it. Samuel pointed at him and said:

"Mike the Rock Tyson."

Which was an odd thing to say because Tyson has been called a lot of things, but never the Rock. Then Samuel yawned and said he needed to sleep. I stood up. On his way to the bathroom he asked if I had plans for New Year's.

"No, not really," I said. "Why?"

"Apparently she has a friend who's having a party."

"Who?"

"Laide. We're all invited."

"What do you mean, 'all'?"

"Didn't I tell you? Panther is coming up to celebrate New Year's with us."

*

I wanted to see him. It didn't feel like our words on the phone were enough. My body wanted its share. But every time I suggested we get together, something got in the way for Samuel. Often he had a lot going on at work, or else he needed to help Vandad with some unspecified matter, or else his sister needed a babysitter. The weeks went by and all we did was talk on the phone. I didn't understand what was going on. Sometimes I suspected he was dating someone else at the same time. There was no neat category I could place my feelings in. Were we friends, siblings, colleagues, soulmates, acquaintances, or moving toward being a couple? It was all so fuzzy. Sometimes I talked to my sister to get advice. She was as blunt as ever.

"Get in a taxi. Go there. Fuck him. See if it was worth the wait. Then we can talk."

"He doesn't live alone."

"Send a taxi to pick him up. Fuck him. Make an assessment."

"It just always feels like he's finding excuses to avoid seeing me."

"Then he's gay."

"He says he's had girlfriends. But I don't know when."

"Then he's not interested."

"He calls like every three days and we have conversations that never end."

"Then who the fuck knows what he's up to. Stop answering and see what happens."

I tried to stop answering. I heard my phone buzz. I saw his name on the screen. I put my phone aside. Ten seconds later I saw my fingers answering. I needed to hear his voice to make it through the day. Not because we talked about anything all that deep. If I were to tell you what we said you would zone out within a few seconds. But at the time those conversations brought some sort of lightness to my body. With him, I became the person I knew I was deep inside but hadn't been in many years. I was quick, funny, smart, imaginative, and above all: curious. His enthusiasm infected me and when he told me about how he had written a list of twenty-three things he wanted to do before he turned twenty-three and then resolutely tackled them one by one (everything from trying cocaine to petting a mountain gorilla to finally reading *The Neverending Story* all the way through), I found myself wanting to do the same thing. Maybe not a list, exactly, and it had been a long time since I was twenty-three, but just that attitude, going out in the world and seeing it as chock-full of possibilities. He took his experiences very seriously, and I was drawn to him, I wanted to be a part of him, I wanted to know him skin to skin, cover his body with my lips, investigate what would happen if we were close. But time passed and we didn't see each other. November turned into December. When I heard that some friends in the neighborhood were going to have a New Year's party, I texted Samuel to see if he wanted to stop by. I was sure he would say no. But his response, just a few minutes later: "Sounds fun. Can I bring two friends?"

*

We had arranged to meet Panther at Skanstull. She was wearing a white jacket and a long turquoise dress with gold patterns and little bells at the hem that made her sound like a miniature cow as she came walking along the platform, waving at us. Around her neck she had a purple scarf worn at an angle like a flight attendant, and we hugged her holding our clinking oblong liquor-store bags and welcomed her home and ten minutes later we were on the train to Bagarmossen.

The closer we got, the more nervous Samuel was. He ripped up the bag handle and dropped small bits of plastic on the floor of the train. He bit his lip. He hmmed and drummed his hand against the windowpane. At first I thought it was because we were heading out of the city, because sometimes when we wound up at the far end of one Metro line or another, where he didn't feel at home, I noticed that Samuel, like other inner-city people, acted strange. They looked at the surroundings and commented on them in an impressed tone.

"Wow, awesome buildings" (about ordinary high-rises).

"Sweet moped" (if someone whizzed by on a moped).

"Mmm, it smells amazing" (about the apple smoke drifting out of a regular old hookah bar).

"Nice, a library!" (as if it were strange that people round here would read books).

"Wow, it really didn't take all that long to get out here" (although we had just taken a 250-krona taxi ride).

But this time there was something else making Samuel nervous. I tried to calm him down by pretending to box him in the stomach, to remind him that no matter what happened, his friends were by his side.

"Girlz up hoez down, right?"

Panther nodded.

"Broz before hoez?"

The bells on Panther's dress agreed.

"But what if it's *her*?" Samuel said.

"What do you mean, 'her'?"

"What if it's her who's the her who's the one?"

Panther looked at me and I shrugged to indicate that he had gone temporarily insane.

*

The New Year's party was in full swing when Samuel walked into the front hall. My body gave a start when it caught sight of him. Within three seconds it decided to become a sweaty dishrag with no spine. I slithered my way out to the hall and hugged him. I felt his hand against my damp back. We smiled at each other, unsure of how well we truly knew each other.

Samuel introduced me to his two friends.

"Panther," said Panther, extending her hand.

Panther? I thought. Did she say Panther? Behind her was Vandad. Tall as a Christmas tree, broad as a wall, round as a sumo wrestler. Wriggling out of his leather coat made him short of breath. His body kept going, beyond the padded shoulders of his jacket. I put out my hand. We shook. He had a clammy, limp handshake. It was like he was dipping his hand into mine. Then he handed his leather coat to me as if I were in charge of the coat check this evening. I looked him in the eye. Then I dropped the coat on the hall floor and went back to the party. It landed as heavily as a clubbed animal.

For the rest of the night, I hung out with my friends and Samuel hung out with his. Ylva was celebrating the fact that she was finally single, Tamara was almost finished with her dissertation, Santiago was on crutches after an encounter with ice and Shahin was Shahin. It was crowded, the dance floor got going, people were drinking, people were smoking up. Samuel made a few attempts to talk to me, but it felt wrong, I didn't recognize him from our phone calls, he was having a hard time focusing, his eyes kept drifting over toward the dance floor.

"Hello?" I said. "Are you listening?"

"Yeah, sorry. I'm just . . . trying to keep track of my friends. Sorry."

I don't know what he was afraid of. His friends were fine on their own. Panther was holding court in the kitchen, she was telling everyone who would listen about the art scene in Berlin, and when no one was listening she kept talking anyway. Vandad was sitting on a barstool in the corner. His glass was constantly in motion, from the bar counter to his mouth, to the box of wine, back to the bar counter, back to his mouth. He was so tall that I didn't realize he was balding until he sat down.

*

The train kept rolling south. When we stood up and got off, Panther said:

"Wow, great vibe—a little like Neukölln."

Samuel agreed and I walked beside them without saying anything. The vibe wasn't great, or different, it was a perfectly normal area, just like everywhere else, and even though I'd never been there before I knew my way around. There was the grocery, there was the pizzeria, there was the alky bar, there was the hot-dog stand, the square, the park benches where the kids sat sneaking cigarettes and scouting everything out, and the path we would take to get to the party. The only thing that was different was that there was an organic cafe on one corner of the square, there was a party going on in there, a bunch of forty-year-olds all dressed up in their going-out clothes were standing out in the snow and smoking and casting nervous glances at the kids on the square.

*

Everyone did the countdown at midnight. TEN-NINE-EIGHT-SEVEN and I felt that obligatory emptiness that everyone feels when the year is about to end,

SIX-FIVE-FOUR-THREE, panic about the passage of time, about the seconds ticking away, about how life will soon be over, TWO, I looked around, trying to find Samuel, ONE, he was suddenly standing beside me, HAPPY-NEW-YEAR, shouting and party poppers and horns. Everyone hugged everyone else and in the tumult that followed we kissed.

*

The occasional rocket flew through the air, it smelled like gunpowder. Samuel took out his phone and called Laide on the way, maybe he wanted to check if we were supposed to bring anything, or check to see if she was there already. He didn't get an answer, but he walked the rest of the way with his phone in his hand like a compass. We met two guys who were going to the same party, I heard Samuel talking to them and I noticed that something changed about his voice. He was walking along that path and talking with an accent. He was rolling his "r"s. He asked the guys if they thought there would be any "sexy chicas" at the party.

The guys replied, "Definitely could be."

They didn't have any accent at all, they just looked at Samuel as if they were wondering why he talked so weird. And why his friend was wearing a dress that sounded like a music box.

*

The kiss convinced me. We were together. Our tongues nudged each other, first softly and gently, then more intensely.

We fell into each other, we danced a slow jam although it was a fast song, we held each other although everyone was looking, we wanted more, I moved against him, he rasped, I rubbed myself against him, he whimpered. It was ten past midnight, it was a new year, we had met each other, we had found someone who made us feel less halved, a person who wasn't perfect but we didn't want perfection, we were tired of perfection, my relationship had been a five-year hunt for perfection and not once had I felt as alive as when I stood there damply at a house party in Bagarmossen.

"Bro."

Vandad's voice.

"Ey, Samuel. Panther wants to talk to you."

Samuel's hand tried to wave Vandad off.

"She says it's important."

We let go of each other, our chests loosened, we awoke from our slumber.

"What is it?" Samuel said.

"Just come on."

Samuel looked at me.

"I'll be right back."

He disappeared into the kitchen. I stayed put. Santiago limped up to me with a glass and whispered: "What an idiot."

To this day I don't know if he meant Vandad, Samuel, or me.

*

It was nine thirty when we got to the New Year's party. We said hi to people, Samuel introduced us to Laide and I said:

"Hey, it's you."

"Excuse me?"

"Yeah, we saw each other at McDonald's. Summer before last."

Laide gave me a suspicious look.

"I moved home this spring. And I don't eat at McDonald's."

"No, I swear, I never forget a face. We had gone out and then we went to McDonald's and you were standing in front of us in line."

"I'm a vegetarian."

"You had two veggie burgers."

"I think you're confusing me with someone else."

"I think you're wrong."

Laide shook her head and walked to the living room. Samuel stayed where he was and didn't seem to know whether or not to follow her.

"Let's turn this around," he said, walking into the party.

*

A few days into the new year, Samuel texted to apologize for what had happened at the New Year's party. Since there were several things to apologize for, I held off on answering.

*

Several times during the evening I tried to remind Laide about our encounter at McDonald's. I mentioned, for

135

example, that she had been wearing a gold owl brooch and she looked at me and said:

"But I don't have an owl brooch. Can we drop this now?"

She shook her head. Samuel gave me a look and flipped his palm to the sky.

"What?" I whispered. "It's not my fault there's something wrong with her memory."

*

In the next text he asked if I was angry. I didn't answer. Then he asked if he could see me, he wanted to explain what had happened. We decided to meet at a cafe on Kungsholmen. I walked there with a clear plan in mind. I had heard what he and his shady friends did at the New Year's party, and now I was going to explain to him that we had no future together. I'm not ready for a relationship, I like you but not like that, it's not you it's me, and so on, insert cliché of choice and repeat until your vocal cords break.

*

Some people have a magical gift. They transform everyone else into idiots. They look at people with eyes that make whatever anyone else says fall dead to the ground. Every joke you utter loses lift and crash-lands. Laide is one of those people. Say someone was standing there at a New Year's party and he wanted to tell a story, people like Laide appear out of nowhere and find fault, they say: "What do you mean Asians are 'super good at studying'? How can you say that women are weaker than men—there are plenty of really strong women. And why do you use 'he' as a general term? It so happens that it's the third person for 'person' but at the same time it only symbolizes people who have penises, so I prefer to use gender-neutral singular 'they.'" Do you know how popular someone like that is at parties? Not popular at all. People were talking about New Year's resolutions and how much time was left before midnight. Laide was talking about how in Sweden there are thirty-six thousand rapes each year. Samuel was listening and trying to appear interested.

"It's a low-level war that no one talks about," Laide said. "It's so sick that mankind doesn't do more to combat it when we totally could."

I leaned toward her and said, "'Mankind' as in 'humans' or 'mankind' as in 'people with penises'?"

It was a joke, I was trying to break the ice. Laide looked at me with eyes full of murder and Samuel tried to defuse the tension by going back to talking about fireworks.

*

Samuel was already at the cafe when I got there. Even though I was ten minutes early. I was surprised, I had pictured myself arriving first, having time to prepare, but he was already at a corner table and he looked up and smiled when he saw me.

"I didn't want to chance not getting a table," he said. "How's it going?"

"Fine. You?"

"I'm a little nervous. But otherwise fine. What do you want?"

And I thought: Why doesn't he protect himself? Doesn't he know what's about to happen? It's one thing to be nervous, or to want to come early to get a good table, but who would admit to that? Who says something like that as if it's perfectly normal? He went up to order and I sat down and when he came back we avoided the New Year's party. Instead we talked about how there were old French newspapers on the walls in the hallway and he said his dad had saved the paper from the day he was born and he had found it not long ago. It was in a box where his parents had kept mementos, there were locks of hair from his first haircut, the plastic bracelet he had worn in the hospital when he was born, and ten baby fingernail clippings.

"Ew," I said. "I hate nostalgia."

"Why?"

"It's sappy. It tries to go backwards. It's fake and inauthentic and . . . cowardly."

"You know where it comes from etmy . . . ethno . . ."

"Etamo . . . What the fuck is the word?"

"Ety . . ."

"Etymologically."

"Right."

"Nostalgia. Something about pain, right?"

"Mmhmm. Like, the pain of never being able to go back."

"Sure you can. All you have to do is remember."

"I have a terrible memory, though. Maybe that's why I need the objects."

"But you remember who I am?"

"Barely."

Both of us smiled and took a sip of our coffees. An expensively dressed family with little kids was sitting at the table next to ours. The son was like five and he was wearing a beige down vest. Samuel leaned forward and lowered his voice.

"You know how to make sure someone will remember you?"

"I guess there are probably several ways. But I guess one good idea is to try to evoke a strong emotion—isn't that right? That what we remember most are the things we have the strongest feelings about?"

"Maybe. But there's an easier way."

"Which is?"

"You should make them associate you with a daily routine."

Samuel started telling me about a memory from when he was ten. He was out in the country with his family, they were sitting in a hammock, it was dark, starry, they had been eating chips and he said to a relative, like, an uncle, "There's something wrong with my teeth because now they're all full of chips," and his uncle said, "Oh no, there's nothing wrong with your teeth, look, I have chips in my teeth too." And he opened his mouth to show Samuel.

"Okay?" I said.

"I thought about it later that night when I was brushing my teeth. And then I thought about it when I brushed my teeth the next morning. And now, fifteen years later, it's lodged in my memory—I'll never forget that perfectly unnecessary conversation. And it was the routine that drummed it into me."

"So if I want you to remember me forever, I should talk nonstop about tooth-brushing?"

"Mmhmm. Or try to associate yourself with something else people do every day."

"Like drinking coffee?"

"Exactly. Coffee is good."

Samuel looked around.

"But water's even better. Just think if I could get you to associate me with drinking water. Then you'd never forget me."

"How would you do that?"

"Like this, maybe?"

Samuel reached for the water glass on the table before us and poured it on himself. Not quickly, it didn't splash, but quite slowly, so it formed a gentle waterfall that ran down his hair, nose, chin. You have no idea how much water a glass can hold until someone pours it onto himself. I was convinced he was only going to fake-pour it, like raise it over his head and then stop right before it came out. But no, he poured that whole glass of water on himself. The well-dressed Kungsholmen couples with their pleasant-smelling dogs and well-manicured nails and well-brought-up sons stared at him.

"Would you like a napkin?"

"Please."

I went to grab a bunch of napkins, he dried himself off,

he shook his head side to side to get the water out of his ear.

"So what do you think?"

"About what?"

"Did it work? Will you think of me the next time you take a sip of water?"

"I suppose we'll find out."

I reached for the other glass of water, closed my eyes, and took a sip. I thought of him, I tried associating the non-taste of water with the person sitting next to me at this cafe. I opened my eyes and was met by his wide smile.

"What do you think?"

"There's a chance I'll remember you tomorrow."

*

Midnight had passed, the party was lame, Laide's friends were boring. A mix of perfumed Iranians, short South Americanos, ugly dykes, tattooed university chicks. Only Panther, Samuel, and I were there to fill up our Experience Banks. I was sitting on a barstool in the kitchen when Panther said:

"This party sucks. But maybe we can do something about it."

She patted her breast pocket.

"I'll get Samuel," I said, heading for the dance floor.

*

We sat at the cafe until the insides of our cups were covered in brown tree-rings of dried coffee. Mostly we talked about memory, how you remember, why you remember, when you remember. He told me he had a friend with a photographic memory.

"It's totally sick. He remembers everything. In perfect chronological order. No wait, you've met him, he came to the New Year's party."

"That big guy?"

"Right. Vandad."

"He does *not* have a photographic memory, I can promise you that."

"What about you—what kind of memory do you have?"

"I don't know. A pretty good memory, I think. I remember what I need to remember. I don't panic when I forget something."

"I do. I don't know why. It's always been that way. That's why I make lists."

Samuel reached into the inner pocket of his jacket, hesitated for a second, and then pulled out a notebook.

"What do you write in that?"

"Everything I need to remember."

"Like today: 'Meet Laide at Petite France'? And then: 'Pour water on myself'?"

"Exactly. For real, I used to do that when I was little. The first time I was going to call someone I had a crush on I had a long list of suggested topics of conversation. I was terrified that we wouldn't have anything to say."

"Do you still have the lists?"

"I save everything. That's why I don't write them in my phone. I still have the lists and the funny thing when you read them is that I had this terrible lack of imagination. Question one: 'Do you have any plans this summer?' Question two: 'What did you do last summer?' Question three: 'Do you like summer?' Question four: 'Any plans for Christmas?'"

"Didn't you ask me that?"

"Sure did. Thank God for the list!"

*

We sneaked into a bedroom, scattered fireworks unfurled in the sky like flowers, occasional volleys of bang-snaps rang out. Panther took out a putty-like lump wrapped in tinfoil paper, she heated it up with a lighter, she divided it into four pieces, stuck the biggest one back in her pocket, gave us each a little ball, and swallowed hers.

"What is it?" Samuel asked.

"A postcard from Berlin," said Panther.

We swallowed them and when we came out the party was one hundred percent more fun. The music was better, the people more beautiful, even Laide seemed pleasant. Panther threw on a bathrobe from the bathroom and let it liven up the dance floor, I put on three songs in a row, Panther instructed the party people to imitate the bathrobe's movements as if the bathrobe were a personal trainer, and no one questioned it, Panther shouted that this was what they should do and people caught on, the Iranians grinded on the university chicks, the university chicks hit on the South Americanos, the South Americanos raised their glasses for *viva la revolución*, the bass vibrated, the floor swayed, Samuel threw himself into the rhythm with that style of dancing that made it difficult to imagine that he worked at the Migration Board by day. He turned his hands into little birdies and pretended to be surprised when their beaks bit him on the nose. He stood perfectly still and tried to wiggle his ears. He waved his hands in the air as if he were directing an airplane to park. Sometimes I saw Laide beside him, she was trying to talk, twice I saw her pull his arm to try to make him stop dancing, but both times a new song he couldn't stand still to came on and ten minutes later Laide was gone. "Did you see where she went?" Samuel asked when the buzz started to wear off and the party was almost over.

"I think she went home," I said, without sounding happy about it.

*

As we left the cafe I felt confused. I had gone there with a clear goal in mind. I was going to be honest and straightforward: I'm sorry, but this isn't working. It's not even an option. You're too young. Your friends are too druggy. Your cohabitant is too creepy. Your job is political, but in exactly the wrong ways. Your clothes are too disheveled. Your cheeks are too smooth. You're too short. You're too skinny. Your head is too big. Your beard is too nonexistent. Your eyes are too naïve. Your hair is too well-trimmed. So thanks but no thanks, I know where this is going so we might as well break it off now, it was short and perfectly fine while it lasted, let's shake hands and say goodbye, goodbye, goodbye. I stopped walking. We kissed. A taxi honked.

*

The guests had gone home, the music had been turned off, the girl whose party it was had come out of her bathroom with her toothbrush and said:

"Listen, you can stay if you want but you have to stop fucking smoking indoors."

We promised. Panther put out her cigarette. But we stayed there, we didn't want the night to end, not yet. Laide had taken off. Samuel checked his phone every five minutes, mumbling:

"I don't get why she took off."

"Maybe she's a psychopath who gets off on making people fall in love with her and then enjoys disappearing?"

"What the hell are you talking about?"

"It's just one theory out of many."

"You don't know anything about her."

"I know her type."

Panther nodded but I don't know if it was because she agreed with me or with Samuel or because she was dancing to the music in her head.

*

We walked along Scheelegatan in silence. We passed Rådhuset, the shoemaker, the bus stop, the pizzeria. We walked arm in arm like an elderly couple and I didn't understand what was happening, how this could feel so right, despite my attempts to come up with reasons why it ought to feel wrong.

Some bellowing soccer fans were outside O'Leary's, cheering at a match that was showing on the TV screens inside. A bus stopped by the hotel and dropped off a group of pensioners who were carrying programs from a musical. We arrived at the escalators at the entrance to Rådhuset Metro stop.

"Did you guys do what you did at that party because you wanted to be remembered?"

"What do you mean?"

"Don't you remember? In the kitchen?"

"Oh, that. No. We just thought it was a good idea in the moment. Something to fill our Experience Banks with. Something that made us remember the night."

We smiled at each other.

"It was nice to see you," he said.

"It sure was."

"I'm going to remember this."

"Me too."

"When will we see each other again?"

"Soon?"

"Soon."

The sun was going down. We went our separate ways. We kissed, we said goodbye, we kissed, we said goodbye, we kissed, we said goodbye, we said that it really was time to say goodbye, we kissed, we thanked each other for the date, it was awesome to see each other, now we have to say goodbye. I have to go home, me too, I have work tomorrow, me too, we said goodbye, we kissed. Forty-five minutes went by before, with a tired tongue and shaky legs, I finally started going down the stairs, into the chilly evening air of the Metro system. Samuel was still standing in the slanting sunlight, with his several-meter-long and thirty-centimeter-wide shadow. He waved when I turned around.

*

There we sat, the kitchen was total carnage. A battlefield of wine-box corpses, piles of plates, mountains of cigarettes, shards of glass, massacred beer bottles, empty liquor bottles, wine bottles full of cigarette butts. Panther had yellow chip crumbs in her downy mustache. It was almost five o'clock in the morning and it was still dark out. Everyone had left but the boyfriend of the girl whose party it was, he was out cold, snoring on the hall floor.

We should have gone home, it was time to go home, we had no choice but to go home. Then Panther looked up from the cigarette she'd just lit and said:

"We should do something insane."

And my first thought was, of course. We should eat up the last of what's in your breast pocket, so I nodded and smiled even before I heard what she said next.

"We should clean the shit out of this kitchen."

We didn't need a reason. We just did it. Samuel found the

Ajax and soap and window cleaner from the cleaning closet, I took out a dustpan, and we had at it. We fixed the clog in the sink, loaded glasses and plates into the dishwasher, emptied the leftover pasta salad into plastic bags. We wiped off tables and swept and mopped and aired things out and I didn't try to stop Panther until we were finished and I noticed that she was sneaking looks at the kitchen fan filter.

"That's plenty," I said.

"We can't make it any better than this," said Samuel.

The kitchen looked like an IKEA catalog, the counters were as sparkling white and bare as the inside of an elbow, the garbage bags were lined up in the hall like an army, next to the sleeping boyfriend.

*

I was sitting on the train on the way home when I got a message from Samuel. "A picture of a water glass." Written out in words. I saw my smile in the reflection in the train window. It was almost as big as his.

*

We were just about to leave, we were finished, we felt proud and satisfied. Panther gave us a thumbs up, took two steps to the side, and puked her guts up into the shiny clean sink. Tiny red specks splashed onto the white tile walls and she threw up one more time and then stood up and said:

"Shit."

Then she puked again and then we just stood there in this

weird kitchen that still could have been in a catalog, as long as the photographer chose the correct angle and ignored the specks and the smell. We looked at each other and headed for the stairwell, left the garbage bags in the hall, stepped over the boyfriend, and ran for the Metro. We just managed to catch a morning train into the city, we sat in an empty group of four seats, as the train approached Gullmarsplan we started laughing, the laughter started way down in our knees and we laughed all the way across the bridge into the city. Some Spanish-speaking ladies turned around and smiled at us and when we said goodbye to Panther at Skanstull I thought that there was no reason to worry. Some friendships can survive anything.

*

I think I loved him. Take out think. I loved him. I loved him in a way I've never loved anyone else. I loved him even though we hadn't slept together yet. I loved him because he whooped like a little boy when he laughed and shed a tear like an old lady when it was windy, because his pointy canine teeth made him look like a cat and because his big head balanced so regally on his thin shoulders and because his shabby clothes made him look like a person who had more important things to think about than laundry or sewing on buttons and because he smelled like a human and not a cologne factory. I loved him because he transformed all my earlier relationships into random asides and sometimes I felt a strong urge to call up my old boyfriends and say that I had to take back a few things: when I said I was in love I wasn't in love and when I said I enjoyed our conversations I was exaggerating and when I said you were funny I was lying and when I said I loved you I didn't know any better and when I ended it and said it wasn't you it was me that wasn't true either, because it wasn't my fault, *I* wasn't the broken one, there was something wrong with *you*. I just hadn't met the right person and once I did it didn't start with a storm of emotions that slowly weakened into a calm breeze that later turned into a stiflingly calm everyday life with nail-clipping in front of the TV and arguments about missing phone chargers. My relationship with Samuel was the exact opposite. We started with daily life, with long conversations between friends, which later, several months later, turned into kisses and closeness and an intimacy that. I don't know how to describe it. But yes. I loved him. I truly did. What's wrong? Are you okay? Yeah, sorry, I just got the sense that you disappeared for a minute there. Should we take a break? Are you hungry?

*

Then it was January. Panther went back to Berlin. During the next few weeks, or months, really, I hardly saw Samuel. We still lived together and our toothbrushes were still next to each other in the mug in the bathroom and Samuel's spring coats and summer sneakers were still in the closet and his notebooks were stacked on his white bookcase. But he himself had vanished.

THE KITCHEN

Are you ready? Shall we continue? I don't remember much
from January to the middle of March. We entered some sort
of fog where it suddenly became inconceivable that we
wouldn't sleep together every night. When we weren't
working, we shared every waking moment. But what did we
talk about? Why did we giggle incessantly? How could a
regular old visit to the laundry room turn into a laugh-fest?
How come everything we touched became so magical? I don't
know. I really don't know. It's all kind of a blur. We explored
each other's bodies with tongues and fingers, we slowly and
methodically inventoried scars and birthmarks, ticklish spots
and pleasure zones. We talked for so long that there was no
time left over for sleeping, which didn't matter because
sleeping was for normal people and we weren't normal, we
didn't need sleep or food, we only needed each other.
Sometimes we went to work with unruly hairstyles and cheek
colors that made our colleagues or clients smile and sometimes

we stood at lunch restaurants waiting to pay and discreetly scratched our cheeks just to smell the scent on our fingers and remember the previous night. Sometimes we went to movies and plays and dance recitals and poetry readings and no matter what we saw it was too long because the time we had to spend sitting there in the dark, unable to talk to each other, went too slowly, but when we finally walked out into the night air whatever we had just seen turned out to be pretty good after all because we had the ability to elevate it, no matter how we had felt at the time, whatever we had experienced became really good, a work of fucking genius whether it was a TV show or a hockey match, because it wasn't thanks to the actors or directors or poets or hockey players, it was thanks to us, we were the ones who imbued everything with meaning, we were the ones who breathed life into corpses. We were the ones who could transform all that was mediocre and ordinary into something else, something greater. We became so dependent upon each other that the very thought of not being together was unthinkable.

*

Things seemed a little empty. I have to admit that. I saw him when he came home to pick up some underwear or drop off dirty laundry, and each time I suggested that we hang out, have a few drinks, go out and take the pulse of the city. But Samuel didn't have time, he always had to take off, he packed plastic bags full of shirts and underwear, shouted bye, and then he was gone again.

*

What do you mean "try being a little more concrete"? What is it you want to know, exactly? How often we fucked? Which positions we used? Whether I had single or multiple orgasms? Even if I wanted to, which I don't, I wouldn't be able to give you many more details. We hung out in bed ninety percent of the time, but we slept like three hours per night because there were endless amounts we had to say. The threads of thought of all those conversations formed a finely meshed net that tied us together and every time we started talking about a new subject there were ten links back to something we'd talked about before breakfast and twenty links to something we would talk about later that evening and even though we shared all these words it feels totally bizarre to realize how little I actually remember of our conversations. One evening we couldn't agree on whether Japp bars and Mars bars were the exact same kind of candy with different names, or different kinds of candy with similar ingredients, so we ran down to the kiosk and bought one of each and arranged a blind taste-test. Why do I remember that in particular? Out of all those first intense conversations about parental conflicts and generational anxiety and childhood fears and sibling envy and hopes for the future, I remember that taste-test, how we sat there naked in my bed with the pieces of chocolate in front of us, immediately unsure which kind was which.

*

No, I didn't feel lonely. I didn't feel deserted. I was glad for Samuel. He seemed happy, and his happiness made me happy. It was just sometimes, if we happened to run into each other at home and I asked how it was going and he replied that it was absolutely fantastic and he had never experienced anything like it in his life and he really hoped I would one day get the chance to feel the power of being really, really in love, of loving someone in a way that made you go completely limp at the thought that something might happen to the other person, sometimes, for a brief moment, I would feel a little bit like an outsider.

*

Yes. There was a difference. One is a little fluffier, the other tastes more of caramel. But I don't remember which is which.

*

Around the time Samuel vanished, I started having trouble getting hours at work. Blomberg said that it had to do with a lack of customers, that there was an economic crisis and fewer people could afford to hire a moving company. But at the same time we figured something was up because the moving trucks were just as busy as usual. There were new last names in the schedule binders, non-Swedish names that weren't listed in the salary binders. The owners of these names came in early and worked late and the only difference between us and them was they didn't have T-shirts with the company logo, they didn't have lifting belts, and they had to bring their own work gloves.

At the end of the day, they received their pay in cash, just like we did.

*

One weekend we were sitting in my courtyard. It was five in the morning, we had flipped day and night, we were wrapped in blankets, everything had that special gray dawn light with haze in the air and frost on the grass and we were whispering so we wouldn't wake the neighbors. We had been talking about our family backgrounds, I told him how my mom fled here, how she and my sister had been given a spot at the camp outside Borås, how they had waited there hoping that my dad would arrive before I was born but everything took a long time, there were papers and political issues that had to be dealt with and when Mom had me my sister stayed with a Nigerian family they had gotten to know at the camp and some kid in that family thought I should be called Adelaide, but I've always used Laide when I'm in Sweden. The only place that nickname doesn't work is in Francophone countries. I was three when Dad finally came to Sweden and he had changed, he wasn't the man Mom had left behind, he had grown thin and hard and they stayed together for several years anyway, they divorced when I was twelve, Dad moved to Malmö and Mom still lives here, she's with a Swedish man now, they live in a terrace house in Tullinge.

Samuel sat quietly and listened. When it was his turn he told me about his parents, his Swedish mom and his North African dad who had met at a bar in Andalusia, his mom was there as an exchange student and his dad worked as an undercover security guard at a mall, they had started talking, they exchanged addresses, a few years later his dad came to Sweden for a visit, they became a couple, they got married, Samuel's sister was born, then came Samuel, his parents were happy at first and then less happy, Sweden changed, Samuel's dad started to worry that he would be fired from his job (Samuel never said what sort of work he did), he got sick (Samuel never said with what, and I didn't want to dig for details), his mom decided she wanted a divorce and Samuel took his mom's side, there was some sort of conflict and even though Samuel didn't specify what it was about I got the feeling it had to do with money, it was something about an insurance policy his mom had through her job that his dad got a lot of money from and then his dad broke off contact with his children and moved back and they hadn't heard from him since, that was many years ago. As we sat there a newspaper delivery guy ran in and out of doors, he had a reflective vest on, a large blue two-wheeled cart full of rolled-up papers. We sat there on the ice-cold outdoor furniture and Samuel nodded toward an apartment on the ground floor where the living room was lit by a string of lights. Out of nowhere he said:

"You know those built-in bookcases? I could never have ones like that."

"Why not?"

"Every time I see them, I think they're going to collapse."

We took the stairs up to my apartment and fell asleep to the sound of the neighbors' kids' footsteps, electric kettles, gurgling pipes, and the mumble of morning TV.

*

The discontent grew stronger among those of us who had worked there longest. Bogdan called the new hires "pack mules" and Luciano said that if he didn't get more hours next month he would have trouble making rent and upkeep. Marre had worked with one of the new guys the week before, apparently he was "a Romanian from Bulgaria or maybe a Bulgarian from Romania," and he had told Blomberg some sob story about how he was here illegally and couldn't work and had to support three children.

"But have you seen his fingers?" said Marre. "No ring anywhere."

"Maybe he has kids without being married," said Bogdan. "Like you do?"

"Hardly," said Marre. "And I don't have three kids. Plus can't you work legally if you come from Romania or Bulgaria? Aren't they part of the EU? I swear they just *choose* to work under the table because they don't give a shit about insurance or retirement. People like him are the reason we're in the shit."

Bogdan and Luciano nodded and I agreed. I felt the same way. But at the same time, I wasn't all that worried. I thought the job was just temporary anyway. I could always find something else. The world was full of possibilities. All you had to do was make use of your strengths, call your contacts, go out into the working world, and help yourself.

*

Another time Samuel told me that he had taken standard Arabic classes for five years and all he remembered were a few random words.

"Like what?" I asked.

"*Mohandis* and *fellah*, for example."

I laughed and asked if his teachers had focused on anything besides occupations.

"Yes, but those were the things that stuck. That and the fruits. I've forgotten everything else. But I can still read and write. It's just the words themselves I need to brush up on."

We were standing down by Söderbysjön, the sun was going down, dogs were swimming in the lake, birds were flitting about. I thought about it as we walked home, that it was typical Samuel somehow, to learn to read and write but not remember any of what he needed to be able to communicate naturally with people.

*

I think we'll take a break there. We're about halfway through. The juiciest stuff is coming up soon. But before we go on, I want to talk financials. How much are you planning to pay me for this? Do you want to go with a percentage of the book sales or a lump sum in advance? It's up to you. I'm flexible.

*

Okay. I understand that you're "super worried about getting bogged down in clichés." But remember, I'm the one describing what happened. It's up to you to rework it so it makes good fiction. We really did stand there in the sunset by Söderbysjön. The colors turned red and then blue. We turned into oblong shadows that wandered home through the dusky forest. We took off our clothes and lay down next to each other. We listened to each other's heartbeats. If you want to write later on that something else happened, I guess that's your prerogative. I'm just telling you the truth.

*

Okay. I understand what you mean. I hear what you're saying. But I didn't agree to meet you because I like charity cases. I'm not free. My time has a price tag. Even if I am stuck in here. I'm giving you my memories, my stories. It's simple logic that you should give me some sort of monetary compensation.

*

For thirty years I had been looking for someone to make me feel like I was one with the world. And then there was Samuel. And I celebrated by building a bubble and keeping the world at a distance. But the world was bigger than us.

*

What the fuck do you mean "a couple thousand in cash"? Do I look like a whore? I want to know here and now what you're prepared to give me to continue this story. There's a lot left to tell. All the important stuff is coming up next and I'm not going to say any more until we have come to an agreement.

*

My friends were curious about Samuel, of course, and the more I withheld the details the more they wanted to know. I hesitated to allow them into our world. My sister, though, explained to my friends that I was hanging around with a guy named Samuel.

"He's young. He's beautiful. He has an extremely large head, very narrow shoulders, and when they first met I called him 'the convert.' Not as in Muslim turned Christian but as in gay turned straight."

But my sister hadn't met him either. I had no reason to show us off. Samuel and I were the couple, it wasn't him and my friends or him and my sister. But now—in retrospect—I wonder if it wasn't some sort of strategy to prolong our happiness. On some level maybe I knew we would become less *us* once we crashed into the outside world.

*

I don't give a shit if "everyone else participated for free." I'm not everyone else. I'm Vandad. And I'm not going to say another word until you come up with an offer that makes this worth my time.

*

One spring evening I had a glass of wine with my sister at Babylon. She had come straight from her job at the Museum of Natural History, she was wearing a T-shirt from a new exhibit under her denim jacket.

"Nice, huh?"

She showed me the print. It was two pandas hugging in a yin-yang type circle. One was smiling, one looked pained.

"I like this one's face—check it out, it looks like he's suffocating."

I went up to the bar to order. The place was full of hipsters in skinny jeans, bearded queers, glitzy PR girls, and tattooed preschool teachers. We were sitting at a small table outside. Two druggies were walking around in the park in front of the place, digging through the grass, it looked like they had buried something and then forgotten where it was.

"Haven't seen you for a while," said my sister.

"You know."

"Is he good?"

"We're great."

"How great?"

"Really great."

"You're glowing, sis."

*

[No one says anything. Vandad looks at me. I look at Vandad.]

*

"This is the first time I've felt this way," I said.

"Super," said my sister. "But you said that about your ex-husband too."

"Did I? But this is different."

"You said that about Emil too."

"Yes, I know. But I've never felt this . . . whole."

"But you said that about Sebbe too."

"Oh, lay off—I'm sure I didn't say that. He was a soccer hooligan, for Chrissake. There was nothing about him that can come close to what Samuel and I have."

"Samuel?"

"Mmhmm."

"Say that again."

"What? Samuel?"

My sister laughed, drops of beer rained across our table.

"What?"

"No, no, it's nothing. Sorry. It's not his name. It's just the way you say it. *Samuel.* I've actually never heard you say someone's name like that before. Try saying it without smiling."

"What are you talking about? I say it normally. Samuel. Samuel?"

My sister laughed some more, the druggies looked up from their digging.

"That's what I'm telling you. This is different."

"What does he do?"

"He works at the Migration Board."

My sister had to hold onto the edge of the table so she wouldn't fall off her chair laughing.

"Stop. It's not like you think. He doesn't deal with asylum cases. He only works on bureaucratic stuff."

My sister managed to calm herself down and wiped a tear of laughter from one eye. Two prim stylist girls at the table next to us were giving us the side-eye.

"What? Haven't you ever seen someone laugh?"

The girls quickly looked down at their glasses and tried not to roll their eyes.

"Ugh, this fucking country."

My sister shook her head and lowered her voice.

"And what's the deal with his roommate?"

"I don't know. But I get a sketchy vibe from him."

*

[Silence. I clear my throat. Vandad sighs.]

*

On the way home from Babylon it felt like I had talked too much. I tried to ask a few questions.

"How's work? What else is up with you? How are your friends?"

But as usual, it was hard to get anything personal out of my sister. She told me that the upcoming exhibit at work was expected to be really good, and that she was looking forward to her vacation.

"And how's the love life?" I asked.

"Oh, fine. The usual. Nothing new. But I really have high hopes for this new exhibit. It's probably going to be even better than the bird exhibit. It's too bad you missed that one."

*

[Silence. I make an offer. Vandad looks out the handle-less window.]

*

A week or so later I met Samuel at a Chinese restaurant by Skanstull. Samuel wanted to "celebrate something" and when I saw him he explained that this "something" was that we had been together for fifteen weeks. Together? I thought. It sounded so final. And fifteen weeks? I felt dizzy—the time had gone by so quickly.

The restaurant was new and it wasn't until we had been seated and I had the menu in my hand that I recognized the name.

"Didn't this place use to be on Fridhemsplan?" I said.

"I don't know. Why?"

"I mean, I recognize the name. I think this place was the target of a union boycott. I'm almost sure of it."

"Oh."

Samuel's finger slid up and down the menu. It didn't seem like he'd heard what I had said.

"The vegetarian appetizers are supposed to be crazy good."

"Hello?" I said. "I think this place paid its employees really horrible wages."

Samuel looked up from the menu. Then he looked over at the waitress.

"Shit, that sucks. Hope they sorted it out."

"What do you mean, 'sorted it out'?"

"I mean, the people who work here look pretty happy. Don't they?"

"But we can't eat at a place that was boycotted."

"Are you serious?"

"Are *you* serious?"

We sat on opposite sides of the dark-wood table, over in the corner a bachelor party was about to go south, the waitress realized something was up and kept her distance. Samuel sighed.

"So what do you want to do?"

"I don't know. What do you say we go somewhere that *doesn't* exploit its employees with slave-wage contracts?"

We stared at each other. Samuel looked around. He stood up and pulled on his coat.

"Do you know of anywhere else nearby?"

*

[Silence. I make another offer. Vandad shakes his head.]

*

We walked down Ringvägen, we found another place that looked cozy, but it was full. The next restaurant was closed. At last we ended up at a spot near a park. We managed to leave our bad moods behind and we talked about other things. I told him that Zainab's request for a work permit had been granted and that she was ready to leave her husband.

"As long as she can find a place to live it will all work out," I said.

"How was your pizza?" Samuel asked.

"Good. Yours?"

"Fine. But I've got to confess, I was pretty hungry for Chinese."

We took the Metro back to my place. It was a little quieter than usual. Or maybe that's just the way I remember it.

*

[Silence. I stand up, walk over to the window, take out my phone, check the balance in my bank account, swallow, think of the power bill, diapers, tenancy fees, loans, preschool tuition, cell phones, food, insurance, office rent. I make a third and final offer. Vandad doesn't say anything. I say that I don't even know if there's going to be any book. I say that I'm awfully grateful for his time. I say that I truly hope we can continue. I promise to bring the money, in cash, to our final meeting. Vandad nods and points at the microphone: are you still recording?]

*

That weekend we talked on the phone. Samuel said he couldn't come over because he had to help Vandad with something.

"Of course," I said. "Sounds good. We'll talk another day."

We hung up. But right after that I felt, like, some sort of itch in my body, the call had been too short, there was more I wanted to say. I called. He didn't answer. Ten minutes later he called back. I waited five, six, seven seconds, then answered. We had a perfectly normal conversation, we talked about how it was still cold and that he still had my hoodie from our first date and how hard it is to find the perfect hoodie, with double fabric in the hood and pockets that aren't too baggy and then we ended up on the most expensive articles of clothing we'd ever bought and I don't know what happened but two hours later my phone warned me that the battery was about to die and my ear was all spongy and warm the way it used to get when you were a teenager lying in front of the TV and talking on your home phone and even though we hadn't been talking about anything in particular it was like we could talk about the simplest, most trivial things and even those things took on value. Sometimes I thought that our conversations, our hanging out together, our entire relationship was like sugar, a quick shot of energy straight to the blood. Before we hung up, Samuel said:

"Listen, one more thing."

"Yes?"

"You know my grandma? It seems she's going to get a spot at a home. She's moving there in a few weeks and her house is going to be empty. My relatives want to make sure she's happy at the home before they move forward with selling it. And if I know my family, that's going to take at least six months."

"Okay," I said because I didn't know what he was getting at.

"So what do you say?"

"What do you mean?"

"If you have anyone who needs emergency housing, just let me know. That Zainab woman, maybe?"

I said I would think about it. We hung up. It wasn't like there was any shortage of people who needed help, the whole city was full of desperate people, students, undocumented immigrants, poor people, the homeless, everyone on the hunt for a safe place. The question was more like who would I contact and whether the house was safe from police-alerting neighbors or people who wanted to peer in. I decided to contact Zainab and Nihad. But first I wanted to see the house.

*

One day Samuel came home and asked if I wanted to hang out. There was no discussion—we slid down to Spicy House. We drank beer, we ate nuts. I told him about the lack of hours at the moving company and how I had started looking at other jobs.

"Like what?" Samuel asked.

"All sorts of things. Hotel receptionist. Insulation fitter. Scaffolder."

"Any good news?"

"Still waiting for a response."

Samuel told me how things were going with Laide. He said he was in love and that it was the greatest thing he'd ever experienced but he couldn't quite explain what made Laide so special. Was it her saggy body, hairy forearms, doughy face, or small breasts? I wondered, but I didn't say anything.

"Plus her taste in music is totally amazing. She loves Erykah, Lauryn, and D'Angelo. Just like me."

"And you're still totally crazy in love? Everything is just as perfect as it was at first?"

"Mmhmm. Or. I don't know. A few things have started to come up. But they always do, right?"

"Like what?"

"Well, we have some differences when it comes to politics. And sometimes she can be a little jealous."

*

We met at the commuter rail station, we walked down the ramp to the construction site. They were blasting an old building to bits, men in yellow hard hats were talking on walkie-talkies, large machines were pounding their way through asphalt, it was dusty and we had to shout to hear each other. In the midst of all this chaos, Samuel pointed at a brick building and shouted:

"There's the library."

We kept walking along the street, the sounds of the construction equipment faded, we passed an Indian restaurant, a secondhand shop, a video rental store, a real-estate agency.

"That's a super cozy place," Samuel said, pointing at a cafe and bakery. "It's been there since like the fifties. The chef's name is August."

We kept walking along the road, we passed a Chinese restaurant, a kebab stand, a deserted gas station with rusty tires and empty soda machines behind a barbed-wire fence.

"There used to be a bike shop there," said Samuel. "But it closed a few years ago."

The house was ten minutes from the commuter rail station, and it wasn't until we approached the mailbox (which Samuel emptied) and started walking up the gravel path (which was full of sticks, plastic toys, bike parts, garden tools, and rotting apples) that I realized that his grandma was still living there. I don't know why I thought she would have moved out already but when we rang the doorbell she was the one who answered, she backed into the hall and cried:

"At last! It's about time, said the watchmaker to the headmaster!"

*

Samuel said that they'd gone on a walk, they had bought soft-serve but forgot to bring napkins and Samuel ran into a cafe and asked if it was okay if he took a few paper napkins. On the way out he ran into a few friends of an ex. When he came back, Laide was furious that he'd taken so long.

"Were they pretty?"

"Who?"

"The girls you were talking to?"

"They were fine. But I mean, we only talked for like two minutes. Five, max."

*

Samuel hugged his grandma. She was half as tall and twice as wide, and as their cheeks touched I saw her close her eyes and smile. It was as if she were filling up on his warmth, the hug must have lasted thirty seconds. I didn't know what to do so I just stood there in the dim light of the hallway, waiting for them to finish. As Samuel freed himself she opened her blue eyes and broke into a wide smile.

"Why ... ? Isn't this Laide? It's been so long. Do you want

coffee? Yes, we'd all like a nice cup of coffee, wouldn't we? Samuel, can you put on some coffee? Here, let's hang up your coat, for goodness' sake, come in from the cold, shall we light a fire? No, I suppose we don't need one, it's so warm in here, no need for a fire, but maybe you'd like one anyway? You're probably used to warmer weather. It's warmer than this in Brussels, isn't it?"

I looked at Samuel but he was already headed for the kitchen to put on some coffee. I wiggled my hands out of his grandma's grip, hung my jacket on a hanger, and took off my shoes.

*

Another night they had been standing by a lake, talking about the differences in their grasp of Arabic, and a dog owner happened to throw a fetch stick pretty close to them. The wet dog came bounding straight for them and the owner apologized and Samuel said it was no problem and petted the wet dog and asked what breed it was and what its name was and Laide kept her distance. On the way home through the darkening woods Laide was angry because she thought he had been flirting with the dog's owner.

"And you want to know the craziest part?" Samuel said. "The owner was like fifty."

"Wow. Even older than Laide."

"Very funny. I don't get why she always thinks I'm flirting."

I didn't say anything.

"Because there is a difference between being nice and being flirty, right?"

He said it like a question, but it was clear that he didn't want an answer.

*

Samuel's grandmother looked at me and squinted.

"When did we last see each other? It must have been several months ago, right? How is everything?"

"Fine," I said, still unsure whether she thought I was someone else or whether she was just pretending that we had met. "How are you?"

"Oh, thanks for asking, still kicking, said the soccer player to the fireworks specialist."

"Why?" said Samuel.

"Excuse me?"

"Why did the soccer player say that to the fireworks specialist?"

"You'll have to ask him."

"Who?"

"The soccer player. Now let's have a little coffee, we certainly deserve some."

She took my hand and led me into the dim house. We passed a fireplace with scorched pieces of plastic among the ashes, a small room with photographs on the walls and a rocking chair on a rug. His grandma stopped to pick up a pink bowl with ornate gold details and a round lid.

"Do you know who made this bowl?" she asked.

"I'm guessing it was Samuel?"

"You're one hundred percent correct."

"I didn't know you could do pottery," I called to Samuel in the kitchen.

"Me neither," he responded.

The smell of urine was stronger in the kitchen. Samuel cleaned the coffeemaker and tried to find the filters. His grandma sat down on a stool and asked who was minding the children.

"But Grandma," said Samuel, "we don't have any children."

"No, that's right, you don't," said his grandma, reaching for a bag of candy. "Raspberry boats?"

"No thanks, that's okay."

"But you do drink coffee, don't you?"

"I drink coffee."

"That's good. And you have a driver's license?"

"Mmhmm."

"Good. A modern woman must have a driver's license. You are nothing without a license. Did you know that they're trying to take away my license?"

I looked at Samuel, he shrugged.

"They say I'm too old. That my eyesight is too poor. I've had my driver's license for over forty years. How old are you?"

"Thirty."

"Can you believe it? I've had my license for longer than you've been alive. And now they have the gall to say that I—*I*—am no longer allowed to drive. Have you ever heard the like?"

"Who said that?" Samuel asked.

"What?"

"Didn't someone say that, like the ear doctor to his patient?"

"No, I said that. Just me."

Samuel turned on the coffeemaker.

"It's a Philips," said his grandma. "That's a Swedish brand."

She took my hand and held it, she looked me deep in the eyes, she had silver rings on one hand, and a silver bracelet around the opposite wrist.

"Do you drink coffee?"

*

One time they went to a Chinese restaurant, but because the girl who showed them to their table was young and cute and Samuel had been a little too nice to her, Laide started bellowing that the restaurant mistreated their employees and threw her glass of water at the owner.

"Did she hit him?"

"I mean, she only threw the water. She set the glass down on the bar before we left the place."

"She sounds unstable as shit," I said. "Not exactly the sort of person you can trust."

"Oh, it's just that there are some things she feels very strongly about. But it is a little trying. Sometimes it's like I have to watch how I'm acting all the time so she won't think I'm doing the wrong thing."

"Sounds unchill."

"Well, it's not as relaxing as hanging here, with you."

I'm not sure if Samuel actually said that last bit, or if he just thought it. On the way home I felt happier. Even though Samuel went to Laide's to sleep there. I knew he would never manage to stay with a person who tried to control him. Soon it would all fall apart. It was only a matter of time.

*

We stayed there for a few hours. Samuel's grandma told us about the house's history, how she and her husband (whom she kept calling "Dad") bought it in the late 1940s from someone named Kuhlmeier, and even though their bid wasn't the highest Kuhlmeier liked them so much that he chose to sell to them anyway. The only condition was that they had to invite Kuhlmeier to dinner once a year. And they did; for eleven years he came over around Ascension Day to eat dinner with her, her husband, and their two, soon to be three, children. Each time, he brought chocolate macaroons. Then Kuhlmeier died and soon the house was too small for three children so they expanded it, she stood up to show us where the new construction started.

"This is where the house stopped when we bought it and this whole side, the parlor, the bedroom upstairs, and the rec room downstairs, is the part we added on."

We walked around the house, she showed us the parlor with its dirty parquet, a decaying terrace, sun-faded curtains. She led us up the creaky stairs, showed us the balcony, the maid's quarters, the bedroom with green jungle wallpaper, and the bathroom with a pink floral pattern on the walls.

"We had a good life here, Dad and me," she said several

times as we walked through the rooms. "And I think you'll be just as happy here as we were."

"Sorry?" I said.

"If you buy it, that is. I know it's a lot of money. You can't just pull that many coins from behind your ear. But there's no rush, go home and talk it over and you can get back to me if you're interested."

"Grandma. It's me, Samuel. I stayed here on the weekends when I was little, don't you remember?"

"Of course. Weren't those the days. It was always fun when you came by and played with Marie and Kerstin and Benke and the little one, what was her name, the little one?"

"No idea."

"Don't you remember her?"

"Those were Mom's friends. My mom. Your daughter. How can you not remember your own daughter?"

We stood in the upstairs bedroom in silence. Samuel picked a bit of dirt off a full-length mirror. His cheeks were glowing red.

"Sorry," he said.

"Anyone want some raspberry boats?"

"Yes please," I said.

We walked down the stairs. I saw a dark shadow across the cracked paint of the ceiling. It must have been an old water-damage stain; it was shaped like a tulip.

*

Then Samuel vanished again. When I didn't get any hours at work and no one responded to my letters of application, I spent most of my time at home in front of the computer. I played strategy games and brainstormed legal ways to earn cash for rent while Samuel and Laide marched in leftist demonstrations and went to luxury spas and ate vegan soup and met each other's families.

*

Later that evening, I called Zainab and told her I'd found a place for her to live.

"It's the perfect house. It will be available in a few weeks. An old woman has been living there. There's room for the children, it's way up on a hill, it almost can't be seen from the street, and there's only one neighbor nearby."

"For how long?" Zainab asked.

"Until further notice. But at least a few months."

"How much?"

"It's free."

"Free?"

"Free."

"Stop kidding around."

"It's free. You can live there for free. It will be your family and a woman named Nihad."

Zainab was silent, she didn't say thanks, she just stopped talking, she didn't say anything for thirty seconds.

"Hello?" I asked. "Are you still there?"

"Yes, I'm still here," she said in a new voice. "I'm still here. I just don't know what to say."

Then she spent five minutes praising Allah most Glorious,

most Gracious, most Merciful, Master of the Day of Judgment, who shows us the straight way, the Powerful and Wonderful and Forgiving. And I have to say that it felt a little weird to hear her praise and thank this God whom I myself didn't believe in. After all, I deserved most of the thanks, and Samuel too. We hung up and I called Nihad, who howled with happiness and kissed the phone until it fell to the floor.

*

Samuel asked more and more frequently how things were going at work. He wondered if I would get more hours next month and how things were going with my job applications. I reminded him that we divide everything up equally and that it would all work out in the end.

"Of course," he said. "But I've covered all the rent for a few months now. And that seems a little wrong since I hardly even live here."

"Come home and live here a little more then," I joked.

*

A few weeks later, Nihad and Zainab moved into Samuel's grandma's house. I got the key from Samuel and met Nihad at the station. She had two suitcases with her, she was wearing make-up, her neck was perfumed, she looked like a human resources director who was going on a conference trip and I don't know why that bothered me. It was like I wanted her to be more desperate than she was. We walked to the house and although it was only the second time in my life I'd walked along that street I heard myself saying the same things Samuel had told me. I pointed out the library, the cafe, and the place where there had been a bike shop up until a few years ago.

Zainab and her children were waiting on the street. They had been dropped off by someone who had already driven away. Zainab and Nihad greeted each other, they had no trouble understanding one another even though they spoke different dialects. The children had their own little suitcases and they looked wide-eyed at the house as we walked up the gravel hill.

"Who else is going to live here?" asked one of the daughters.

"You're going to live here," I said.

"But besides us?" asked the other daughter.

"It's just us," said Zainab.

With a roar, the children ran up the stairs and I reminded Zainab that it was important to keep a low profile so the neighbors wouldn't start to talk. We used the upper entrance, I turned the key, opened the door, and showed them how the alarm worked. It was simple, when you opened the door it started beeping and you had thirty seconds to enter the correct code. If you were to forget the code, there was a piece of paper under the alarm keypad that said "ALARM OFF? PRESS 9915. ALARM ON? PRESS 0" in large print.

Nihad and Zainab looked at the piece of paper and chuckled.

"Perfect for burglars. It's okay if we take it down, isn't it?"

"Of course," I said.

Nihad took the piece of paper with the alarm instructions, ripped it in half, and hid it in the chest of drawers in the hallway. I felt proud when she did it. I thought that it was her way of showing that now she and Zainab and the children lived there. The children had already run into the house, I heard their cries from the parlor.

"There's an echo in here," cried one daughter.

"Where do we sleep?" cried the other.

I still hadn't heard the son's voice, but then he came back and tugged at Zainab's clothes.

"What is it, darling?"

She leaned down and picked him up. He whispered in her ear.

"There's a piano in there."

*

I filled out job applications, placed them in envelopes, and waited for responses. I sat at home. I went out. I came home. Sometimes I called Samuel. Or sent a text. When he didn't answer, I went into his room and looked through his things. I just wanted to remind myself that we still lived together. I paged through his notebooks mostly to help pass the time.

*

The plan was for the house to take care of itself. Samuel had made sure he had all the keys, and if one of his uncles or his mom wanted to go there they would have to contact him. Nihad and Zainab had been living there for a week when the dishwasher broke. Samuel and I went over there together. He showed us where the tools were kept in the basement and we went through the dishwasher, cleaning the filter and adjusting the screws. When we turned the power back on it worked again, and Nihad took Samuel's hand and thanked him sincerely, both for fixing the dishwasher and for letting her live there. She nodded her head until her black curls bounced off her shoulders. She was holding his hand. She didn't let go. Samuel said *tfaddel* with his funny Swedish accent. He looked down at the floor as if he were afraid of what might happen if their eyes met. I realized how beautiful Nihad was.

On the way back to the station, I told Samuel that Nihad had a son who lived with her ex-husband.

"Oh?" he said.

"I just wanted you to know."

"If her son wants to move in it's fine with me," said Samuel.

*

In one of Samuel's notebooks I found a sketch of something that looked like a science-fiction game. I typed Samuel's notes into the computer and tidied them up and thought it might be an idea that could bring Samuel and me back together.

*

What do you mean, "why?" Shouldn't you be asking "why not?" Why wouldn't he jump at the chance to do something meaningful? He spent his days stuck in the straitjacket of bureaucracy. He followed regulations and directives, contacted embassies and booked trips to send people away who wanted to come back. At the same time, his grandma's house was standing empty. And people needed somewhere to live. It's not strange that Samuel wanted to help. The strange thing is that more people don't do the same.

A few weeks later there was a problem with the upstairs toilet. We went out to the house again, Samuel seemed glad for the chance to see Nihad again, when she opened the door he hugged her and did his best to communicate in his sad, Swiss-cheese Arabic. We went upstairs. Samuel showed us how you could remove the lid of the toilet and press a little button to make the water fill up on its own. Then he spent three minutes trying to explain that there were lots of things in the house that needed fixing and that they didn't have to feel too worried if something broke. Nihad smiled and nodded and when Samuel was finally finished she looked at me for an explanation of what all these incomprehensible guttural syllables were supposed to mean. I translated and Nihad leaned forward, pressed her large breasts against him, and kissed Samuel on the cheek.

"Your exceptionally beautiful outside truly matches your soul's incredible inside," she said.

Samuel looked at me questioningly.

"She says you're nice," I said.

Samuel blushed and scratched his ear and as we walked down the stairs he said that the house hadn't been this clean in many years.

"Grandma would have been proud if she knew what was going on here. Tell them that they're welcome to call anytime if there's anything else that needs fixing."

Nihad looked at me questioningly. I explained that she was welcome to call if they needed help with anything else.

"Tell him thanks again," said Nihad. "Tell him my son is coming the day after tomorrow."

On the way back to the train, Samuel said he was jealous that I was so good at Arabic. He said that his dad had always been more eager for him to learn French.

"Why was that?" I wondered.

"He didn't want me to end up in bad company."

*

The rest of that spring just kept going. Time passed so slowly, the way it only does when nothing's going on, and yet, when I think back on that spring, it feels like it was over in a second. Maybe it's always like that, and periods that seem long as you're living them become short in your memory, and vice versa.

*

Sometimes Samuel suggested I come over to his place. But I was only there a few times. I never liked the way things felt at Vandad's. The apartment was dark and impregnated with smoke, Vandad slouched around in sweatpants, drinking ghetto wine from a box and sitting in front of the computer playing war games. I think he was on something, because only someone who was on drugs could live like that without going crazy.

When I asked Samuel what Vandad did for work, I received contradictory answers. Sometimes he was a mover, pretty often he was "between jobs." One time, Samuel said I didn't have to worry because Vandad had always been able to take care of himself.

"He has a thousand ways to support himself," said Samuel.

"Name one."

Samuel said that when Vandad was younger he used to go around Östermalm on the lookout for dogs that were waiting on a leash outside fancy hair salons. He would loosen the leash, take the dog home, and then go back to the same neighborhood a week or so later and put up posters that said he had found a runaway dog. The owners would call, grateful as anything. When they wanted to give him a reward, he would say no at first, and then he would take the money.

"That's sick," I said.

"Why? No one got hurt. The Östermalmers were just reminded of how much they loved their dogs."

I shook my head to show I didn't want to talk about Vandad anymore. It wasn't him I was worried about, it was Samuel. Vandad used him. He let Samuel pay for everything. And I didn't get what he saw in Vandad. When I asked why they were friends, Samuel mumbled something about how Vandad "had his back" and that he could "relax and be himself" with him. Every time he said it, it felt like he was criticizing me.

*

One day I was called in to help a computer company move offices in Kista. The guy who hired us was the sort of customer who had an uneasy conscience because Blomberg's prices were so low. He helped us with the dolly and lifted boxes down from the platform, even though he was some middle-management type with a pale-blue shirt that quickly showed dark rings of sweat under his arms. When we were done he invited us to have coffee in their new conference room. Everyone helped themselves to the fancy coffee and the pastries and I stood there in the bright room thinking that places like that needed employees too.

*

I waited for Samuel by the bus stop and as usual I felt that warm pressure across my chest when I saw him. He looked at me and smiled and even though we kissed, even though he embraced me, even though he whispered in my ear how much he had missed me, I still had the feeling that he was disappointed when he saw me. As if, on the bus ride from Örnsberg to Bagarmossen, he had imagined that I was younger and more beautiful than I actually was. As if, deep down, he wanted me to be someone else.

*

Before we left the conference room, I went up to the middle-management guy and told him that I was putting the finishing touches to the plot of a science-fiction strategy game.

"I see," said the guy, and he sounded like he was really interested.

185

I tried to transform myself into Samuel. I started summarizing the plot of the game the way Samuel would have done. I walked around the conference room, using both hands to make gestures. I explained that the game starts in the future, and the weird thing is that everything is about the same as it is now. Sure, the climate is different and gasoline has run out and countries that had been islands are now underwater museums that you can visit in family-friendly submarines. But people are the same. They cut their nose hairs when no one is looking, they burp when no one is listening. Instead of moving companies, post offices, and airlines, every country has teleporting facilities where you can send yourself and your belongings to foreign places. One day, Genghis Khan shows up in one of those portals. It's the young version of the Khan, a guy who has had a taste of wealth but doesn't live in excess. He walks around wearing gerbil skins and survives week-long raids on the steppe by tapping his horse's blood. The idea of the game is to try to help the Khan take over the world. You have to build up an army of robots and try to outmaneuver other warlords with futuristic weapons like DNA-seeking phosphorus missiles and viral drones. My coworkers had set down their cups. The middle-management guy nodded.

"We primarily work with web-based credit operations," he said.

He signed the hours-worked contract and wished me good luck. He didn't hand me his business card. He didn't ask if I could come in for a meeting later that week.

*

We walked past Konsum on the way home. Samuel picked up milk, ketchup, noodles, cottage cheese, chicken sausage that was like forty percent meat, macaroni, and a bag of oranges on sale. I walked behind him and filled our cart with organic apples, organic lemons, a Tetra Pak of crushed tomatoes, organic black beans, fresh thyme, gluten-free crispbread, and unsweetened soy milk. When the cashier started scanning our groceries at the register, I saw Samuel watching the prices that flickered across the screen.

"Yikes," Samuel said when the cashier read the total.

I took out my card and paid. As usual. We crossed the square, we turned left on my street.

"Thanks for the groceries," he said.

"No problem."

"Damn, they were expensive."

We kept walking. I felt like I needed to justify myself somehow, but I wasn't sure against what.

"I think it's important to be careful about what you consume."

"By buying organic lemons?"

I think he was trying to sound sarcastic. It sort of worked.

"Yes. Or. It's a way for me to say: my goal isn't to maximize my profits. There are things I value more than the three extra kronor it costs to buy organic lemons."

"Nine."

"Nine what?"

"The organic lemons cost nine kronor more than the regular ones."

"So? Isn't that worth it?"

"Yes, but. It's just ... you have to have a certain level of income to be able to be so globally conscious."

"And we do have that level of income. Both of us. Don't we?"

"Not me."

"What do you mean? You earn a good salary, don't you?"

"Yes, but. Quite a bit of it goes on rent," Samuel murmured.

We stepped into my stairwell.

"What? Don't you split the rent equally?"

"Yes, we're supposed to. But things have been a little tight for Vandad lately. So I've been paying it."

"*All* of it?"

"Mmhmm. And for some of the food, too. And some other stuff."

"So what does he pay for?"

"Oh, it will all even out in the long run. It's nothing to get worked up about."

"But how much are you paying per month?"

Samuel told me how much the rent was. My jaw dropped.

"You know he's gouging you, right?"

"What do you mean?"

"There's no chance in hell that apartment costs that much."

"It's a rental. The building's pretty new."

"He's taking your money and using it for something else. I

guarantee it. There's your explanation for why he stopped working."

*

Yes. Okay. I admit it. I missed Samuel. I mean, I didn't miss him as in I thought that our friendship was done for or that someone else was taking over my place in his life. I missed him because he did something to me. And when he wasn't there it was harder for me to be who I was when I was with him, and even though I tried, even though I sometimes went around town and sat at Spicy House and pretended he was there, it didn't work the same way as when he was with me. Something happened between us that made me— I don't know. Strike that. Strike all of that. What I'm trying to say is that when I missed Samuel it was harder not to think of other people who didn't exist and when I did it was harder to sleep and when I wasn't sleeping I had to try to find other ways to fall asleep and when that didn't work I had a harder time doing a good job at the moving company and when I started a shift by falling asleep in the moving truck I got fewer hours and everything turned into a downward spiral that was difficult to get out of.

*

We arrived home to my kitchen. I cooked, he set the table and filled a carafe with water and squeezed lemons. Once we sat down he asked how the week ahead was looking for me. I told him I had a meeting on Wednesday with Maysa, a client who had been living undocumented with four children for three years.

"I'm going to accompany her to a legal consultation."

"Do you get paid for that?"

"What do you think?"

We ate our food, we drank our lemon water.

"What, are you angry because I'm asking if you get paid?"

"I'm not angry. It's just a stupid question."

"Am I supposed to go around being careful not to ask stupid questions? How am I supposed to know—maybe she's a rich undocumented person who can afford to pay her interpreter?"

"Stop."

We ate in silence.

"Let me know if there's anything I can do," he said.

"What would that be?"

"I don't know. Maybe Maysa would like to move into the house too."

He said it as if it were the most obvious thing in the world, as if it didn't take any sacrifice at all on his part to give Nihad, Zainab, and Maysa the security they needed. And I looked at him and thought: If it was so easy for him to help someone, how could he live with not doing more?

*

In late spring, Samuel suggested we go down and visit Panther in Berlin. He said he needed to "get away for a bit" and asked if I wanted to come.

"I'd love to," I said.

"But you'll have to find some way to pay for the trip on your own," said Samuel. "I can't keep supporting you."

He spoke to me in a new, hard voice. I wondered where the old Samuel had gone. But I wasn't upset, I thought it was natural since he had spent so much money on romantic presents and dinners for Laide. I knew her style. She was the sort of feminist who talked herself hoarse about how everything had to be one hundred percent fair but then complained to her friends if her guy didn't have enough cash to treat her when they went out. Or let me put it this way. If the guy didn't pay he was a church mouse, and if he did pay he was a pig who thought he owned his girlfriend. But since it's better to be a pig than a church mouse, Samuel had no choice but to pay for all their dinners and museum visits and the romantic weekends I assumed they were pursuing while I sat at home alone in the apartment.

*

In mid-April, we stopped by the house to make sure that everyone was happy. The children were playing in the parlor, they had lined up their toy animals on the piano. They were taking turns rocking in the rocking chair, and the ping-pong table in the basement was strewn with markers, chalk, and clay. It was great to see how at home they all felt. Even if Zainab whispered that Maysa's kids weren't particularly well-mannered and Maysa thought Zainab's children ate like they had worms.

"Where's Nihad?" Samuel asked.

"She hasn't slept here for several nights," said Zainab, and I translated for Samuel, but I was forced to add a couple words so he would get that Zainab sounded pretty scornful and not very worried.

"This is so awesome," Samuel said as we walked down the gravel hill. "Grandma lived here for how many years, and now I don't even think of it as her house anymore. It's like my memories have been replaced by new ones."

He sounded oddly relieved.

*

What kind of idiot claimed I was "gouging" Samuel on rent? Was it Laide? Don't believe everything you hear. She has no idea how expensive my rent was. She doesn't know how hard I fought to be given more hours. I never wanted to live on Samuel's money. I did everything I could to make my own. Every time Samuel came home from Laide's and told me I really had to "start pulling my weight," I thought: Yeah, but we had a loyalty pact and we were supposed to split everything and I'm trying to pull as much of my own weight as I can but shit, there seems to be a shortage of ways to pull out there, I'm frantically searching for more ways. As a last resort, so I would be able to afford rent and food and the trip to Berlin, I contacted Hamza.

*

We ate at the cafe on the main street. We sat in the sunshine, on the outdoor seating, it smelled like freshly mown grass.

Samuel asked about my teenage years and I told him about my Kafé 44 days, my involvement with the syndicalists, my first boyfriend, who was ten years older than me and spent two years in prison after the Gothenburg riots but currently works as a guidance counselor in Sätra. I told him about the demonstrations we organized on May Day, the Reclaim the Streets years, the fights with skinheads in the nineties, the anti-Nazi demonstrations in Salem. I told him about the time several hundred of us gathered outside the Iranian embassy in support of the Green Movement and the police used pepper spray and some of us got bitten by dogs and others were injured by the sharp points of the fence and when they called for a doctor like fifty people raised their hands. I said that sometimes I miss that fervor, the feeling that it really was possible to bring about change. Samuel nodded and looked like he understood.

*

Hamza sounded happy to hear my voice.

"Did you finally crawl out of your pussy shell?" was his friendly greeting when I asked how things were.

"Since when does a pussy have a shell?" I asked.

"It's a figure of speech," Hamza said. "What do you want?"

"Got anything for me?"

"What do you mean, got anything?"

"You know. A round? A job?"

"Do you think the world stands still while you're sleeping? Hell no. The world keeps turning. Money changes hands. People are replaced."

"Nothing?"

"Nothing."

"I need money."

"Me too."

"I'm serious. I have to get my hands on some cash. Fast."

"You want a loan?"

I didn't say anything. Hamza laughed and his tone changed.

"It's no problem," he said. "I'll drop by. I'll give you the friends and family interest rate. Do you still live in the same place?"

He hung up before I could say thanks.

*

The sun was going down, the cafe was about to close, we were still sitting in the outdoor seating. I told him about when we blockaded a police escort that was supposed to transport a family who had been threatened with deportation away from the detention unit in Märsta. We arrived around four in the morning, we had brought Thermoses and ridiculously fancy pastries because one of us had a second job at a posh cafe in Östermalm. Saffron croissants and truffle biscuits and piping hot, quickly cooling herbal tea. We held out in the winter cold for six hours. By the end we had no feeling in our toes, it hurt to breathe through our nostrils, we had ice crystals in our eyelashes. But we stood there and felt like we were making a difference. Every time a car approached we linked our arms tight together, we were a human chain that would never be broken. Then a police car approached us, the window rolled down, the police lady in the passenger seat told us that the family was already at Arlanda airport, they had taken them out the back way, the family was already on the plane, they were already up in the air, and she said it with a tiny smile that made us explode, fancy pastries rained down on their windshield and the police officers just looked at each other, shook their heads, and turned on the wipers. We made our way to the railway station in Märsta and after a while we found out that the passengers on the plane had revolted, they saw the family's tears and the upset mom who begged for compassion and they refused to put on their seatbelts, the plane couldn't take off, the family was removed from the plane and taken back to Märsta and that created a tiny gap: hope that we would be able to make a difference.

"Then what happened?" Samuel asked.

"They appealed."

"And were they allowed to stay?"

"No. They were sent home."

*

Hamza rang my doorbell and when I answered I noticed his foot sliding through the gap.

"Sorry," he said, pulling his foot back. "Old habit."

He had brought with him a mountain of a person who had to duck to walk through the door. When we said hello his voice was as high as a little boy's.

"Is it okay if I use your bathroom?" he asked.

"Be my guest," I said, pointing him in the right direction.

All the while I hoped that he wouldn't sit on the toilet because he looked like a person who could break porcelain just by sitting on it.

"How is he?" I asked Hamza, who was wiggling an envelope out of his inner pocket.

"Okay. Not like you, of course. But perfectly fine. He's learning. The only problem is he has a ridiculously tiny bladder. It's hard to make the right impression on people when you come over to demand your money back and then you have to ask to use their bathroom."

We smiled at each other. I asked if there was something I had to sign. We smiled even more. Both of us knew that there are some things you don't write down. I gave him my word that I would pay it back. He gave me his word that the interest wouldn't be any higher than usual. Then the giant with the baby voice returned from the bathroom and thanked me for letting him use it.

*

We were still sitting at the outdoor cafe. The sun had vanished. When I asked Samuel about his political engagement, he went quiet and gazed over at the tray cart.

"I mean, I don't know. I'm not a conservative or anything, but . . . I've always been skeptical of political movements."

"What do you mean by that?"

"My dad always warned me about politics. I've sure seen how much his friends sacrificed for their struggles and how it always ended with disappointment and broken friendships and ... I don't know ... I've only demonstrated once in my entire life."

"Seriously?"

"Yes. Against the Iraq war. Two thousand three. But then the war started anyway and it all felt pointless."

"But what about the Gaza bombings? When the Sweden Democrats won seats in parliament? REVA? Don't any of those things make you react strongly enough to take your body and walk a few hundred meters?"

"No, but I don't know why ... It's like it's ... Every time I think of joining a demonstration I see the signs and I wonder if I really agree one hundred percent. Then everyone starts shouting their slogans and I don't know what to do."

"But what do you do on May Day? If you don't demonstrate?"

"Chill out. Hang with Vandad. Fill up the Experience Bank."

He tried to smile his way out of the situation but I could tell he felt uncomfortable.

"Speaking of," he said. "I'm going to Berlin soon. We're planning to visit Panther."

"Who's we?"

"Me and Vandad."

"Are you paying for it?"

"No, actually, I'm not. Not this time."

We finished our food in silence.

*

A few weeks later we went to Berlin. It felt major, it was major, it was the first time we were traveling abroad together. When we met at Central Station, Samuel walked up to me with a smile as radiant as a nuclear power plant and a hug as big as a sumo wrestler.

"This is going to be so fucking fun!" he said, hugging me.

"Totally," I said, giving him a friendly punch on the shoulder.

"Ow, dammit. Take it easy. We're taking the bus, right? It's cheaper."

*

The next weekend, the Sweden Democrats were having a rally in Farsta. The whole gang was going down there to protest, except for Santiago, who was away on a work trip. But Ylva and Shahin and Tamara and her new girlfriend Charlie were there. Charlie who had a narrow mouth and taught special needs kids in Södertälje. We realized right away that she was used to demonstrations, when we met at the barricade she handed out various instruments she'd borrowed from her school, maracas and whistles, and she herself had a big drum hanging from her shoulders by polka-dotted suspenders. We walked onto the square and stood there in the sunshine. There must have been two hundred of us, although the local paper believed the police, as usual, and wrote that there were "around seventy" of us. The usual mix of people. The anti-fascist action kids, old hippies, multi-colored families, hand-holding queers.

*

The plane took off and Samuel sat next to me, in high spirits.

"Holy shit, it's crazy how much we have to catch up on," he said.

And we did. As the flight attendants passed out menus he told me that Laide had worked at McDonald's after upper secondary school and the rumor that they wash the toilet seats in the same dishwasher as they wash the fry cages—it's true.

"Okay," I said.

We ordered wine and nuts.

"Laide is allergic to nuts. But not all nuts, peanuts are worst. She has to make sure they know every time she flies."

We received our little bottles of wine, I paid for both of them.

"Thanks. I'll get it next time."

"Cheers! To the Experience Bank! To immortality!"

"To love!"

We toasted with our fridge-chilled red wine and at last I felt like our trip could start.

"You know what Laide's doing this weekend? She's going to a demonstration and then she's going to grab dinner with two friends."

*

When the Sweden Democrat cars approached, the police stood between us and them, the police horses whinnied, the police dogs seemed unfazed by our instruments and roars. Charlie started chanting slogans, at first the classic ones ("No racists on our streets," "What are we gonna do? Stamp out racism! When are we gonna do it? NOW!") and soon enough slightly more specific ones to fit that day in particular ("Farsta says: FUCK SD, Farsta says: FUCK RACISM!"). Tamara was standing next to her and smiling, and even though she wasn't singing along it was obvious that she was proud. I felt young that day on the square, I felt like I had in the past, it wasn't until the SD representative had given his barely audible talk about the importance of closed borders and a return to the classic values that made this country what it is that Ylva looked at me and asked where Samuel was.

"Samuel?" I said.

"Yeah. Isn't he coming?"

"He's in Berlin."

But once I'd said it, I realized that he wouldn't have been there even if he had been in Stockholm.

*

It was like that all the way down to Berlin. He described (and imitated!) how cute she sounded when she snored. He told me that she had an older sister who worked at the Museum of Natural History. He said that what made Laide's particular version of Arabic so special was that it was pretty similar to that dialect in all the Egyptian soaps. When the flight attendant approached to collect money for the next round of wine bottles he let me pay again.

"Sorry, my wallet is up in my bag. I'll get the next one—I swear."

I picked up the seat-back magazine as the plane descended to land in Berlin. I read an article about Venice. Samuel leaned over my shoulder, pointing at the black-haired model who was on a boat with an umbrella.

"Foxy," he said. "But not as foxy as . . ."

And I thought: Is he messing with me? I've *seen* Laide. I know how old she is, how worn out she looks, I've seen her bitten nails, her hunted expression, that is not a person at peace, that is a person who is always prepared to be left and always has to keep her hand on the emergency brake so she can leave first. But did I say that? No. I kept it to myself, like an idiot.

*

I came home from the demonstration. I stood in my empty hallway. I want to say I enjoyed my time alone. That Samuel's absence meant I could completely be myself. That I could let my body relax and pick my nose and masturbate and fart and burp and definitely not feel any sort of emptiness. Because that's the way it always had been before. But I missed him. And that annoyed me.

*

We landed at the airport and it was like traveling back in time. It was still 1995 there, everyone who worked there looked like pale bartenders in old music videos, their hair was moussed and their faces were either heavily made up or well-mustached and their jeans were so unmodern that they were either seriously unmodern or extremely modern. Samuel looked around and exclaimed:

"Berlin here we come!"

Then he stopped and turned on his phone.

"I'm just going to say we landed."

*

Then the texts started coming. He sent one when he landed, and the next fifteen minutes later: "Now we're getting in *ein taxi bitte*!" He sent a picture of a trampoline in a park, he took a photo of a table full of drinks and wrote: "*Aufwiedersehn.*" But not once did he write that he missed me. Instead my phone filled up with proof that he seemed to be doing at least as well without me. I took a bath, I read a book, I sat quietly and listened to the murmur of my neighbors' TV, they were watching *Let's Dance*. I tried to convince myself that I was happy. Serene. Free. But in my mind I could see a car crashing into Samuel's taxi. He got out of the taxi and was kicked down by a Nazi. He was at a club and someone offered him candy that wasn't candy. He got drunk and fell into the river. He was at a roof party and climbed over the parapet.

The final text came at 11.30, he asked how I was, he said that he was about to go to bed but that he'd had an epic night and signed off by sending "*ein godenachte* kiss." I didn't know how to respond. His text felt like an attempt to reassure me, and a person who has no intention of betraying someone doesn't need to reassure said someone. I lay awake until it started to get light out.

*

The line for taxis was long but the creamy white taxicabs were standing at the ready and everything went smoothly, we jumped into the backseat and gave the address and the guy behind the wheel was a Turk and laughed at Samuel's terrible German. Samuel tried to give the address again, the driver corrected him. We headed into the city, Samuel tried to make small talk, it didn't go very well, the Turk's English was German, Samuel's school German was Swedish. The roads were narrow, the neighborhood looked Polish, we drove through a forest, past a few brick buildings, the taxi driver pointed proudly at a few blocks and said:

"All this new, before: nothing!"

And we gave impressed nods at the new buildings, which already looked shabby. We passed a train station, we turned right and nearly collided with a yellow streetcar. We were getting closer to Panther's neighborhood, it wasn't too far, the driver slowed down, he looked at the street names.

"It should be here."

We turned right, onto a street as wide as a soccer field and perfectly empty, no trees, no stores, just long rows of cars parked at an angle and buildings that looked like forgotten embassies. We stopped outside the door to Panther's building.

"Can you ..." I said, pointing at the horn.

He looked at me like I was nuts.

"This is Berlin."

I'm not quite sure if he understood that I meant the horn or thought it was something else, but we thanked him for the ride and I paid because Samuel was already at the door, using the intercom. It cost twenty-three forty and I gave him twenty-five euros and he thanked me for the tip, surprised. At first I thought he was being sarcastic, but he seemed truly happy as he zoomed off over the cobblestones.

*

The day after Samuel left, Maysa contacted me to ask if it was okay for her sister to move into the house for a little bit, because she needed refuge as well.

"Of course," I said. "That shouldn't be a problem. Will she be by herself?"

"Mmhmm. With her daughter."

*

The street was quiet again, I looked up at the building. It was the only one on the whole street that was flaking, it looked like a fire had damaged it, the plaster had fallen off long ago, the door was darkened by decades of dirt, two large parts of the façade had come loose and were lying on the sidewalk. On the first floor I saw a big red flower and a few pieces of paper with words I couldn't make out. On the second floor the white curtains were drawn. On the third: Panther's happy face.

"I'll come down," she signaled, and soon the door was open.

We hugged each other in the darkness under the broken porch lamp. She looked just as I remembered, except that her skin was paler.

"Sweet glasses," Samuel said. "Are they real?"

"Of course," Panther said, sticking her finger through the empty frame. "When in Rome."

*

Later that same evening, Nihad called. She said she'd met an older, female Persian poet whose application for a residence permit had just been denied.

"Is it okay if she stays here for a few nights? Just until she finds somewhere else?"

"Of course," I answered.

It didn't cross my mind to check with Samuel. What would he say? "No, sorry. This house is just standing here empty but I really must okay everyone who moves in?" In fact, I thought the more women who lived there, the better. I thought it made the place safer. My only worry was that one of the neighbors might become suspicious.

*

We walked up the stairs together, it smelled like coal and wood, the graffiti made it hard to tell what color the stairwell was supposed to be. The apartment had white walls and an old wooden floor, there was a yellow-tiled igloo in each bedroom, one was warm and the other was cold. One of the walls in the bathroom was covered in a five-meter-long strip of wallpaper with Alps on it, and in the kitchen was a gas stove and a fridge that closed with a rope.

"Cool, huh?" said Panther. "A genuine Berlin apartment."

"Definitely," said Samuel.

I nodded because it's easier to lie with a gesture than with your voice. Sure, I thought the place was cool. But not so cool that I wanted to live there, more like cool as in, okay, places like this exist in the world too, but please keep driving until we get to my hotel with functioning heating, a big-screen TV, a mini-bar, and not two rooms that are heated by coal. Because that was why there were sacks of coal in the bedrooms. The two yellow igloos were coal stoves.

"But I didn't have to use them all that much this past winter," said Panther. "And there's electric heat too."

"But isn't that pretty expensive?" Samuel asked, and I looked at him and wondered what was up with him. I'd never heard him talking about money like that. And I thought that it couldn't be his fault—it had to be someone else's.

*

On the third day, Nihad called and said that they'd had some problems with the electricity in the house, now and then it would sort of turn off and on. They had tried changing all the fuses, but nothing helped. I said I would come over, and that afternoon I was sitting on the commuter train again. The garden looked like it usually did, the same plastic toys, the same piles of rotting apples, and that was good, I had been careful to tell them that they couldn't change too many things that were visible from the outside. The inside, on the other hand, was very lively. About ten kids were playing with a Frisbee in the part of the yard that didn't face the street. Two men were smoking on the terrace, they said hi to me and one asked if I was Rojda's lawyer.

"No," I said. "Who's Rojda?"

"Never mind."

I walked into the house. The spider webs and urine smell were gone, it smelled like fresh bread, an old lady about Samuel's grandma's age was sitting in the living room and watching a children's show with two toddlers. Zainab was in the kitchen, cooking, she explained that Maysa and her family lived on the bottom floor and that the new arrivals without children took sleeping bags up and slept in the attic.

"But there's only women living here, right?" I asked.

"Of course," she said. "Women and children."

"Who are those people out there?"

"They're leaving soon."

Zainab explained that she only cooked for her own family. At first they'd tried making common meals but she ended up buying all the food and after a while she got sick of it.

"It's nice that you came," she said. "But the electricity seems to be working now—we found another fuse box in the basement and there haven't been any problems since we fixed the wires in there."

I stood there in the kitchen. I wanted someone to say thanks, point out how great it was of us to organize all of this. But people were wrapped up in their own lives, the lady in the

TV room waved goodbye as I left, and Nihad wasn't home, but I assumed her son was the one playing Frisbee, he had her dark curls and beautiful dimples and the same kind of sparkling brown eyes that made it hard to look away.

*

That first evening we hung around the neighborhood, which was totally deserted, hardly a person in sight, even though it was five in the afternoon.

"Where is everyone?" I asked.

"Well, they're definitely not at work," Panther said. "There's, like, no one in Berlin who has a job."

"So what do people do?"

"In my building there are two Danish designers, an unemployed Portuguese architect, a schizophrenic war veteran, and a Swedish author. He's half Tunisian, by the way," she added.

"Who is?"

"The author."

This was the first and only time I ever heard Panther mention you. Samuel seemed uninterested. We walked toward a water tower, we passed a restaurant that was closed, a few abandoned ping-pong tables, an empty bar on a corner. Still zero people.

"It's like Östermalm-empty here," I said.

"Like a ghost town," said Samuel.

"Mmhmm. But it's this part of the city, too, they've gentrified the shit out of it. It's kind of a shame. But this is sick."

Panther ran over to the playground, she took aim and

jumped onto a little mound and suddenly she was bouncing on a trampoline, her black hair became a waterfall in the wind, she bounced higher and higher.

"Whooo! Cool, huh?"

And I twisted toward Samuel to say "What is she doing?" But I didn't have time to finish my sentence because Samuel was already on his way to the next mound, suddenly both of them were jumping up and down in the playground and shouting "wheee" like two lunatics and I stood there for a few seconds and didn't know what to do. Then I looked around and thought, Fuck it—Experience Bank, and ran toward the third trampoline mound.

*

Samuel was gone for five days, and every night I imagined he had met someone new. The first night it was a South African circus artist who had recently gone in a new direction and become a union-representative nurse. They talked for hours about the societal consequences of living with memory loss in a post-Apartheid system. Then they went home and fucked. The second night it was an Indonesian political scientist, they talked for hours about how they were so much more than their boring careers. Then they went home and fucked. The third night it was a half-Jordanian performance artist. They talked for hours about the importance of frequently adding to your Experience Bank. Then they went home and fucked. Deep down I knew that Samuel lacked the willpower to resist. An experience like that was impossible to say no to, he turned to

Vandad and Panther who locked their lips with invisible keys, and to avoid being eaten up by his guilty conscience he bombarded me with texts in which he wrote everything except that he missed me.

*

The next day we rented orange bikes and went to the Stasi Museum. We looked at cases full of historical agent technology, there were scent-capturing mushroom chairs, hidden cameras, eyeglass-walkie-talkies. Then we biked to Neukölln and ate tortillas and drank beer. Panther wanted to introduce us to her friends and I nodded and thought that it might be fun to meet some Germans. Unfortunately, none of them were German. There was a Thai-American author, his Irish artist girlfriend, a red-haired British language teacher, a Polish girl who was dating a Hungarian director of short films. And later, after midnight, you showed up on a rickety black women's bike. I watched you and Panther nod at one another. Samuel and I put out our right hands. We said hi, but as soon as you realized we were from Sweden all the interest drained from your face. You quickly moved on, and Samuel said:

"Do you know that idiot?"

"No," said Panther. "We're just neighbors. I don't hang out with other Swedes much here."

Panther introduced us to more and more people and all her friends said they lived in Berlin and loved the city "despite the Germans," but no one could speak German, aside from a few polite phrases. Time and again, Panther said that she didn't miss anything in Stockholm, and every time she did it was like Samuel's neck stiffened.

*

On the last night, I pictured Samuel realizing it was Panther he loved. She was the one he was meant to be with. His memory of me disappeared, dissolving like a dream. *She* was the one he'd been in love with since he was a teenager and now that they were both in the same foreign city, they had rediscovered one another. They went into Panther's bedroom and didn't come out until it was time for him to go home. Samuel gave his phone to Vandad and assigned him the task of walking around the streets of Berlin and sending three texts per day. Then they swore never to tell anyone what had happened. Then they returned home.

*

The day after that we biked to a big field with lots of sculptures that were supposed to make people remember the Holocaust. We walked around among the gray rectangles and lost each other and found each other and as we biked home, Panther told us she had met someone. She was in love (!). With a guy (!!!). From Baltimore. An artist who was putting up shadow boxes in a warehouse in Potsdam. Samuel's jaw clenched. A basketball game was underway in a park. Samuel braked his bike.

"What do you say? Should we hop in?"

"I'll sit this one out," I said, but the question had been for Panther.

"Aw, let's go home and have lunch instead," said Panther.

"Feeling like a wuss, huh? Afraid I'll beat you? Don't want to rip open old loser wounds?"

Panther and Samuel joined opposite teams as I watched the bikes. They started out playing for fun but it quickly turned into something else. Samuel and Panther were guarding each other and their newfound teammates seemed surprised that they were playing so seriously. When no one was covering Panther, Samuel shouted "LOOK OUT!" and pretended to stick his hand in her stomach so she missed the shot. The next time Panther took aim for a three-pointer, Samuel leaped into the air with a roar to block her. Too late, he realized it had been a feint and he landed hard on the asphalt, his cheek scraped up and his pinky finger almost broken. Panther's team creamed Samuel's.

Afterwards they sat on their bikes, panting.

"Well played," I said.

No one responded. Samuel rubbed the mark on his cheek. Then he took out his phone and mumbled:

"How hard is it to answer a goddamn text?"

*

I hardly slept at all. I realized I didn't trust Samuel. I wondered if I ever would.

*

The last night, we ate at a Vietnamese restaurant near a square in Kreuzberg. We took the U-Bahn there because it was raining. We walked through the yellow tunnels, we passed the junkies and the homeless people and the dogs. The place was tiny and Samuel looked at the menu before we sat down.

"Really nice prices."

Panther and I exchanged glances. I wondered if she too had noticed that something was off. Was she also thinking about how Samuel hadn't bought a single round this whole trip? Had she noticed that Samuel had changed? The person who was usually ready to do anything for a new experience had started acting like an accountant. The guy who used to say that money is there to be spent was sitting there reading the menu right to left before he ordered.

*

Samuel came straight to my place from the airport. When I got home from work I found him sleeping in my stairwell. He had sunk down on the floor with one hand resting up on his suitcase handle like a patient with an IV. He had a red mark on one cheek, it looked like the trace of a violent kiss. Or maybe a bite mark. He woke up, stretched, and said:

"I can't find my keys."

*

During dessert, Panther asked:

"So what's going on in Stockholm?"

Both Samuel and I were a bit taken aback, because up to then we had only talked about Panther's art, her gallery-owner contacts, her friends. She had told us where to find the best döner and which neighborhoods were best for drugs and what tricks you could use to avoid being turned away by the tattooed bouncer at Berghain. But she'd hardly shown any curiosity about us, not even once. I said I was still working at the moving company, but it was harder and harder to get enough hours, so I was looking for another job, among other things I had contacted a computer company with an idea for a science-fiction game. Samuel checked his phone. Panther stuck a toothpick in her mouth.

"What about you, Samuel?" Panther asked. "What are you up to, besides being in love?"

"I don't know," Samuel said, spinning his phone like a roulette wheel. "I don't know what I'm doing."

"Isn't she texting back? Maybe she lost her phone," Panther said.

"Maybe she met someone else," I joked.

"I don't know if I'm in love," Samuel said. "I feel more ... sick. Nauseous. Like, a little dizzy."

"But you love her?" Panther said.

"Yeah, I guess I do," Samuel said, shaking his head.

We sat there in silence, the waitress brought the check, Panther reached for it.

"No, I'll get it," I said.

And I did it in slow motion so Samuel would have time to grab my arm and say, "No, you've paid for far too much, allow me!" But he didn't, he just sat there staring straight ahead. I paid and when the waitress came back with the change he got a text. As fast as if he were drawing a pistol in a duel, he picked up his phone to check the number. He shook his head.

"Mom."

*

We went into my apartment. He put down his suitcase in my hall. He found his keys in an inner pocket. He placed his toothbrush in my medicine cabinet. I thought he tasted and acted and looked just like normal. Except for the mark on his cheek. There was nothing about his mouth or his tongue to suggest he had kissed anyone else. But he seemed a little tense. And when he told me about their nights out it felt like he was hiding something.

"I mean the clubs in Berlin are total madness. One night we were at a party in an abandoned bathhouse, can you believe that? You went in through the changing room and the pool itself was empty and then you climbed down through a long passageway and there, in the middle of like a big cave, was a gigantic dance floor and there was condensation running down the walls and there were sound systems in the halls and the party didn't start until six in the morning and it stopped at ten the next night and it was so crazy, it was so awesome, shit, we should go there, we should try living there together, you and me, it would be so great to just up and leave, wouldn't it?"

I didn't respond.

*

After dinner we dropped by a Northern Soul party where Panther was supposed to meet her Baltimore guy. The people there had a different style than the rest of the city. Here they were rocking pressed suits and lots of make-up, everyone seemed to be dreaming of being young in the sixties, their shoes were nicely polished and several of them had brought a white powder they poured onto the dance floor so their soles would slide better. We sat around a table, the DJ was on the stage, he was dressed like everyone else, a too-small jacket and a minimal mustache and even his headphones seemed to be from a different age, they were big and round and he only played vinyl and he handled his records like jewels, every time he took one off the turntable he blew on it carefully before he placed it in his oddly modern DJ bag. We drank and waited and tried to find our way back to the mood we'd had at the New Year's party in Bagarmossen. But something was missing, something was different, none of us seemed to know what it was. Samuel checked his phone for the hundredth time in fifteen minutes. Panther glanced toward the entrance. I was lost in my own thoughts.

"It feels kind of perfect to be going home tomorrow," Samuel said. "There's a lot to do on the house."

"The house?" said Panther.

"Yeah, sorry, maybe I didn't mention it. Laide and I turned Grandma's place into a safe house for women."

I took a sip and nodded to make it look like I knew exactly what he was talking about.

"That's awesome," said Panther.

Then we were quiet again. After a few minutes Samuel stood up to go outside and check his signal.

"Have you noticed anything weird about him?" I said.

"What do you mean, weird?" said Panther.

"Is it just me or is he a little . . . different?"

"I don't know. He hasn't talked about his bad memory even once—maybe that's new. But otherwise, no. Or. He *is* madly in love. That'll make you weird."

Samuel returned with his phone.

"Can one of you text me? Maybe there's something wrong with the network."

I sent a text from my Swedish phone. His phone beeped right away.

"DAMMIT!" he yelled.

And then, a little more softly:

"Fucking shit."

*

He said that Berlin's official slogan is "poor but sexy" and that it's still possible to find cheap housing and that furthermore there is a strong anti-capitalist movement. There are squatters, and they're left alone, and near Panther's apartment there was a store full of free stuff.

"Isn't that crazy? You can just go in and take whatever you want and if you wanted you could leave something in return, but you didn't have to, either. Just think, what if that's the way to start, to take a little place and make it into an example of an alternative, say, 'Look, this way could work too, what if this world is within reach? Things don't have to be the way they've always been.' And that's true not only on a societal level, but also on a more personal level, do you know what I mean?"

I tried to nod, I tried to smile.

*

It was starting to get late, it was the last night, Panther's guy didn't show up and something had to happen. Samuel came back from the bar with a pen and paper, he looked decisive.

"Let's turn this around," he said.

The plan was to have a competition. The goal: to make the night as memorable as possible. The strategy: everyone writes three challenges on a piece of paper. The pieces of paper are put in a bowl. Whoever completes the most tasks in the shortest time wins.

"Wins what?" said Panther.

"I don't know—just wins," said Samuel.

"What kind of challenges should they be?" I asked.

"It can be anything. But it has to be possible to complete, on a practical level."

I wrote, more or less:

1. Go up to the DJ, request *The Macarena*, do the Macarena dance, and when he says he doesn't have it, say "Then any song by Phil Collins will do."

2. Go up to any table with more than three people and take a sip of each drink on the table.

3. Slide out on the dance floor and pull someone's hair.

*

EVERYTHING I DON'T REMEMBER

Samuel said that on the last night they had Vietnamese and then they went to a soul club and all in all, it was an awesome trip.

"But—"

He paused.

"There was something about being away from you that made me . . . I don't know . . . I really had time to think while I was there. I thought about us, about you, about me, about this thing we're trying to build up, this thing that's on its way to being *us*. And you need to understand how awful I feel when you don't answer my texts. You just go silent. Like a fucking parent. And then I'm sitting there, in a foreign country, terrified that something happened."

*

Then we folded up the scraps of paper and placed them in the tea-light holder on the table. Panther got Samuel's list, Samuel got mine, and I got Panther's. And I hardly had time to read what Panther had written before Samuel was off and running. He went straight up to the table next to ours and said *änshylldigung* and explained that he was so terribly *"törstich* is it okay if I . . ."* And then he started drinking from their bottles of beer. Then he slid out to the dance floor and grabbed a blond girl by the hair. Then he went up on the stage, tapped the DJ on the shoulder, and stuck his arms out in a daring sort of Macarena dance. The DJ just looked at Samuel, his surprised eyes as round as his headphones. When Samuel received no response, he smiled and leaned over and whispered something in the DJ's ear. Then he left the stage and came back to our table. Panther and I applauded, but then I discovered that it was just me because Panther was missing, she wasn't in her spot, when I glanced toward the entrance there she was, standing on tiptoe and hugging a tall guy with dreads. Samuel looked at Panther.

"Vandad. I love her. I want to be with her always."

"Which one?" I said.

*

I wanted to respond, I tried to explain what happens inside me when someone leaves and how hard it is for me to trust people and that I had gotten the feeling that his texts weren't honest, that they were written only to reassure me, so that I wouldn't worry, and for that very reason I started worrying, and— He cut me off.

"But Laide. Don't you know that I love you?"

*

On the last day we woke up around lunchtime. Samuel and I were lying under the blanket in the cold bedroom. We were wearing the same clothes as the day before, we smelled like cigarette smoke and yesterday's beer. Samuel gave a start and quickly rose from the mattress.

"Everything okay?"

I nodded. Noises from the bathroom told us that Panther was awake—first the sound of puking and then an electric toothbrush. Samuel started tossing his belongings into his suitcase.

"When does the plane leave? We're not going to miss it, are we? Should we take a taxi or are there any buses to the airport?"

"We're going to take a taxi and you're going to pay for it," I jokingly said.

"Sure. Of course. I just have to make sure I have enough euros."

Panther came out of the bathroom, stretched, and asked if we wanted breakfast.

"Is this the way you live here?" Samuel asked.

"Pretty much. When I'm not working."

"When do you work?" I asked.

"When I need to. Should I call a taxi?"

The last sounds we heard after we'd hugged goodbye and gathered our bags to head down to the street were a few gags and the mechanical buzz of the electric toothbrush, like a battery-driven bumblebee.

*

Samuel said it like he wasn't even thinking about what would happen if I didn't say it back. He said it like he'd just realized it himself. He said it like he was overjoyed at the realization. He said it and then he smiled that brilliant, yellow-toothed smile that made girl cashiers postpone their breaks and made bouncers become suspicious. He said it like he didn't give a single fuck that the balance of power between us would be forever shaken if I didn't respond in kind.

"I love you too," I said.

An abyss opened up beneath us. We clung to each other and persuaded ourselves that we could fly.

*

Then we came home. I applied for more jobs. I applied to be a fish farmer, a fire-damage cleaner, a car re-conditioner. Always the same response. Or the same non-response. I borrowed Samuel's bike instead of buying a Metro pass. I returned bottles so I could afford food. All throughout, I kept thinking that things would work themselves out. But I wasn't sure how. Hamza started calling with updates about compounding interest.

*

Are you okay? Should we take a break? Should we stop there and continue another day? You look tired. Do you have allergies? We're nearly there, so I'd prefer to keep going. Would you like more coffee? Should we go sit out on the balcony?

*

In early July, Samuel called and his voice sounded like he'd been running.

"Are you at home?"

I was about to say "of course." But instead I said:

"Yes. What's going on?"

"We need your help."

I had my shoes on before he had even told me what was up. I ran down the stairs just as he was saying that there had been "trouble at the house."

222

"The house?" I asked.

"Yeah, Grandma's house."

Apparently someone who shouldn't have been there had been there and the women were frightened, so Samuel and Laide were on their way over and he said it would be really great if I could come by too.

I was already on my way, I knew the deal, they couldn't call the police so instead they called me, they needed some muscle for backup, they needed an extra brain to handle the situation. Samuel texted me the address and I started running toward the house, then I saw on the map how far it was, turned back to the apartment, and grabbed Samuel's bike.

THE BALCONY

It was our rule from the start that the house had to be kept a secret. I had told this to everyone who moved in.

"This is a temporary refuge and there are several people here who are under threat, so be careful who you give the address to."

But one day Bill contacted Nihad and claimed that he knew where she was. He included the address of the house and described in great detail what he would do to her once he found her. We went over. Samuel wanted us to call Vandad right away.

"Why?" I asked.

"For safety reasons."

I don't really know how sumo-sized Vandad was supposed to make the women any safer, but I let Samuel call him. I thought it couldn't hurt to have more than two of us. And Samuel guaranteed we could trust Vandad.

*

I whizzed toward Hägerstensvägen, I fought my way up Personnevägen, I flew across the E4 bridge. I tilted like a motorcycle through the curve onto Älvsjövägen. When I arrived, Samuel and Laide were still on the commuter train.

"Wait down by the mailbox," said Samuel. "Don't go in by yourself, we don't know whether he's still in the house or not."

I waited by the mailbox, I planted my legs wide between the two stone pillars at the bottom of the hill. I gazed up at the house that wasn't a house. It was a palace. It had three stories and a large yard and a separate garage. Even if it was painted brown and the curtains were drawn, it wouldn't have been totally out of the question to make a hip-hop video here. The honeys in bikinis could chill on the terrace, the guest rappers could park their Lexuses on the gravel hill, you could put the grill full of steaks and the coolers of frosty forties over there by the bushes. I stood there lost in my thoughts until I noticed Laide and Samuel running toward me from the station.

They were holding hands. Their hair was the same shade of black. They ran in perfect rhythm, although one was running with knees as high as a gazelle (Laide) and the other was running as if he didn't want his body to leave the ground (Samuel). There are few things as difficult as running while holding hands, and I remember that when I saw them I thought: Okay. Maybe they are meant for each other. Maybe I just have to accept it. Maybe I was wrong.

Although their faces were clouded with worry, they looked happy. Samuel hugged me and thanked me for coming. Laide nodded and headed up the hill.

"Wait here," said Samuel. "We'll go up and check it out. Keep an eye out."

"For what?"

"A blue Saab station wagon," Laide called.

I stayed put. I laid Samuel's bike down across the gravel path like a roadblock. I imagined that there was a hip-hop video shoot taking place behind my back and that I was in charge of security, I liked the feeling, I was in the right place at the right time and I kept an eye on every car that approached. They were mostly Volvos and Audis and BMWs and Mercedes, and the occasional Toyota Prius. Fifteen minutes passed. Half an hour. Samuel called and said that they were almost finished.

"Is everything okay? Do you want anything?"

"No, I'm fine," I replied. "I have everything I need."

No blue Saab station wagon ever appeared. When Samuel and Laide came back down the hill, they thanked me for my help, they said everything had gone just fine, but I don't know exactly what they meant by that. "Fine" as in they had learned that the guy had been apprehended? "Fine" as in the girl he had threatened was going to move somewhere else?

"Can I buy you lunch as thanks?" said Samuel.

We went to a lunch place that was further down the same street. We filled our plates at the buffet. We sat down at a table.

Samuel and I next to each other, Laide alone on the other side. We were supposed to talk, we were supposed to get to know each other, we were supposed to become friends. But Laide seemed absolutely uninterested. She spent lunch with her phone out, looking up different women's shelters, she had a chat with a person who I think was someone's lawyer. Between her calls I tried to ask questions, but she would only respond with one word at a time, two at the max.

When we stood up to leave and Samuel went up to the register to pay, she said:

"THANKS for buying us lunch, Samuel."

Then she glanced at me as if she wanted me to repeat after her like a trained monkey. I didn't say thanks. I had nothing to thank him for. Samuel and I had a different kind of friendship, one that was independent of money. So it had always been and so it would continue until the very end.

*

I never felt safe with Vandad. It didn't matter how much Samuel talked about his loyalty. There was a darkness to Vandad. I couldn't trust him. Every time we met he did his utmost to make me feel like an outsider. In the middle of a sentence he would start laughing and elbow Samuel in the side.

"That reminds me of Berlin. Do you remember . . . ?"

Samuel nodded. Or:

"Shit, do you remember the night at East?"

Samuel smiled.

"Girlz up hoez down, right? Broz before hoez!"

Vandad raised his hand in a give-me-five and Samuel looked self-conscious as he returned it. I sat there like an idiot. Later, when I asked Samuel what was so funny about the night at East or Berlin, he said you probably had to be there to get it.

One time, all three of us ate lunch together. Vandad cracked his knuckles and eyed me. Samuel was struggling to keep up a conversation. He asked if we had any plans for the weekend and what we had done last weekend and the more I watched him struggle, the more forced the whole situation felt. At last Samuel went to the bathroom and Vandad and I were left behind in a tense silence you could have cut with a knife. He looked at me and said:

"So . . . Samuel told me you had an abortion?"

"Excuse me?"

"Samuel told me you used to live in Brussels?"

"Did you just ask me if I had an abortion?"

Vandad looked at me like I was nuts.

"No, Brussels, I wondered if you used to live in Brussels."

But I heard what he said the first time. And I couldn't believe that things I had told Samuel in confidence had trickled down to Vandad.

*

The second time they needed help in the house, I had just been called in to work, to empty a five-room place in Brandbergen and move everything to a house in Skärmarbrink. Samuel asked if I could drop by the house again, apparently it was urgent, and this time I took the truck. I swung by on my way to the office, Blomberg would never notice and Bogdan would never snitch. He stayed in the passenger seat as I ran up the hill with Samuel.

"What happened?"

"He was here last night. Nihad's ex."

*

When I brought it up with Samuel, he dodged the question. He couldn't say what he had and hadn't told Vandad, and when I asked him again he got annoyed and said it was impossible for him to remember all the conversations they'd ever had.

"Vandad is my friend. I share stuff with him. The same way you share stuff with your sister. You just have to accept that."

But I wasn't going to let him get off that easy. We kept talking, and a few hours later Samuel said:

"Laide. Please. It's two thirty in the morning. I have to go to sleep. Please realize that the world is not out to get you. Let it go."

I thought: You don't know what you're doing. You are going to regret those words.

*

I had no idea who Nihad or the guy were, but when we approached the door I saw that the glass was broken. The first woman who saw us jumped, she had a knife in her apron, I didn't know whether it was for cooking or protection.

"Is Laide here?" Samuel asked in English.

"Yes," said the woman, giving me a suspicious look.

"A friend," said Samuel.

"Why big car?"

She pointed at the moving truck that was parked down on the street.

"Friendly car," said Samuel. "No problem, nice car, nice friend."

We walked to the kitchen, the house was even flashier on the inside. When you stood in the kitchen and looked out at the yard, it felt like you ruled the world. All you could see were the apple trees and the wind and the clouds, and far, far away, down the hill, the white cube that was our fifteen-footer. I thought: How could she have noticed the truck from way up here?

*

We tried to go back to normal. But I sensed that something had changed. One evening in early autumn, I took him along to a birthday dinner at Lisa and Santiago's. We arrived early, I wanted Samuel to get to know everyone gradually, I got that it could be nerve-racking to walk into a brand new situation like that. But Samuel didn't seem nervous at all, he was psyched to get to know my friends and when we met up at the Systembolaget at Fridhemsplan he had already selected a three-liter box of ghetto wine. I informed him that it was probably a better idea to buy wine in bottles, since it was Santiago's birthday. And Samuel wasn't offended, he just switched out the box for a few bottles and on the way to the register he pointed at one of the labels, which read *Vino ecológico*, and smiled. We got in line, the cashier looked at us and asked Samuel for ID.

*

Laide was standing in the kitchen, the woman on the stool had a face but it was hard to tell eyes from mouth from cheeks because all of them were black and blue and swollen except for her mouth and lips, which were a mix of purple and red. I tried not to look at her. It was hard, because my gaze kept being sucked back, my brain couldn't grasp how someone with that face could be sitting up and answering questions from Laide, who was speaking Arabic with her as she spoke Swedish into a telephone.

"Yes, I understand that, I'm not a complete idiot," said Laide. "But what you don't seem to understand is that this is an emergency."

I left the kitchen, I wanted to look around, I walked through an adjoining room and into a dining room and then on into a gigantic room that looked out onto the terrace, which I had seen from the street. It must have been the living room once, because there was a brown piano and a crystal chandelier and the people who lived there now had stacked the furniture that used to be there in the corner, chairs and tables in an old rococo style, like the kind of furniture you see on *Antiques Roadshow* and that the experts say is worth a hundred thousand even though it looks like it'd go for twenty kronor at a flea market. I wanted to go all the way to the terrace but I couldn't, because the floor was full of sleeping mats, sleeping bags, plastic bags, IKEA bags. Suitcases lined the walls, none of them had four wheels, several didn't even have extendable handles, they were just plain, ordinary suitcases, made of hard, thick plastic. The room was full of objects but empty of people, except for two sleeping bodies, I didn't see their faces, their hair was sticking out from under an army-green blanket.

*

Santiago and Lisa lived in a brightly lit four-room apartment with a view of the water in one direction and the highway in the other. Their daughters were with Santiago's mom, and as we entered the hall we were hugged by a perfumed Lisa and a red-spattered Santiago, who excused himself by saying that he was in the middle of the lasagna and there had been a "tomato-related incident." I introduced Samuel and they embraced him even though it was the first time they had met and I stood there in the hall feeling proud of my friends, that they were so welcoming and kind and didn't show any signs of thinking that he was too young or smelled funny.

The next to arrive were Tamara and Charlie (who seemed annoyed at each other) and Ylva and Rickard (who were apparently back together again although no one understood why). We sat around the oval table and waited for a lasagna that would soon, soon be ready.

"There was a small incident," Santiago said again. "A tomato-related incident."

"We have all the time in the world," said Rickard.

"I can only cook one thing," said Samuel. "It's called cottage-noodles."

I heard myself laugh, a little too loud. Samuel explained how you make the dish. Two-minute noodles. Cottage cheese. Herb salt. Done.

"Hold on a second, I have to write this down," said Santiago, and everyone laughed.

*

On the way back to the kitchen I heard one of the women crying, and someone comforting her. As I came in I realized that it was Nihad, the beaten woman, comforting the woman with the knife, Zainab. Even though it should have been the other way around.

"How many people are actually living here?" I whispered to Samuel.

"What do you mean? Two or three families."

I laughed.

"What?" Samuel asked.

"Have you seen the living room?"

We walked over together. Samuel's hand flew to his head.

"Three very large families," I joked.

We went up to the second floor, the same thing there, piles of sleeping mats, bags, banana boxes. There was a balcony up there, and two guys were having a smoke on it. They nodded at us and smiled, and one of them opened the door and asked in English if we were "Rojda's lawyer."

"No," we responded.

"Okay," they said, closing the door.

Samuel went from room to room, his hands clenching and unclenching, he took out his phone as if he wanted to call someone, but who could he call? Who could help him out of the bind he had gotten himself into by trusting Laide?

*

The lasagna had been eaten, the wine glasses had lip prints and were cloudy with grease spots, they had left round red footprints on the table. We had talked about the health risks of plastic toys (Lisa), criticism of Montessori preschools (Santiago), the art fair in Basel (Tamara), the poor financial situation of the municipality of Södertälje (Charlie), the proof that homeopathy really works (Ylva), and how good the dessert was (Rickard). Toward the end of the evening, I started to relax, Samuel could handle this. I went to the bathroom and when I came back I heard him say:

"... and everyone has their own personal definition of love—don't they?"

I sat down beside him and patted his arm so he would understand that this wasn't the time, not here, not now. We could talk about topics like that at recess when we were thirteen, but now we were adults. There was a short silence after Samuel posed the question. Tamara, who had hardly smiled once since arriving, maintained that love had to be linked to humor, that you had to be able to laugh together. Charlie said that for her, love is when you have an unfortunate urge to want to own the person you're with and control everything they do. Ylva said that love is accepting everyday life, lowering your expectations and forgiving your partner for being human. Rickard didn't say anything. Lisa said that love involves addiction somehow— daring to let yourself become maximally dependent. Santiago talked about the role of love in the capitalistic world order, how a couple's solidarity is the key to constantly increasing consumption. Then everyone turned to me.

"How about you, Laide?" said Samuel. "What is your definition?"

"I don't know. But I know that the few times I have been in love, I have never had to ask myself whether I am or not."

Ylva let go of Rickard's hand. Santiago cleared his throat. Samuel took a sip from an already-empty glass.

*

We went back down to the kitchen, Laide was finished making her call, she still hadn't said hi to me. She was treating me like air, like someone even more unimportant than air, because after all there are still those short moments when you are reminded that air exists and that it can be useful to have. Nothing like that happened for Laide when she looked at me.

"There might be a spot in Bergshamra," she said. "They're going to call later this afternoon."

"Have you been upstairs?" Samuel asked.

Laide didn't answer.

"There are like fifty people living here."

"More," I said.

"You're exaggerating."

"Did they ask you for permission to bring in more people?"

Laide fixed her eyes on Samuel as if he were the one who had done something wrong.

"What was I supposed to say? 'No. This house is empty but

you can't let anyone else in even if they're going to die without shelter'?"

"The guys on the balcony don't exactly look like they're dying," I said.

"What do you mean, 'guys'?" said Laide.

It was the first time that day she looked me in the eye.

"The guys who are smoking on the balcony."

Laide darted from the kitchen. It was quiet. The women at the kitchen table couldn't talk to us. We couldn't talk to them. Outside the window was a birch tree whose sad branches were moving in the wind. The house creaked with small noises, and coming from the basement we could hear footsteps and children's laughter.

Another woman came up from the basement with a bucket, she nodded at us and started filling it in the kitchen sink.

"No water downstairs?" Samuel asked in English.

"No water—broken," said the woman.

Laide returned to the kitchen. She started speaking Arabic with the women at the table. It sounded like she was telling them off. She must have been telling them off. Laide shouted and waved her fist and slammed it on the table, but it didn't make a very impressive sound. Nihad and Zainab mostly just sat there without saying anything. When she was finished, Laide shook her head and said that we should go.

"What did you say?" Samuel asked as we were walking toward the hall.

Laide didn't answer. We left the house. Somewhere inside me I started to realize that it was up to me to help Samuel.

*

The taxi zoomed across Central Bridge, dark water, heavy sky, red lamps swinging from boats. Samuel held my hand, he touched it, he stroked my arm up and down, at first it tickled, then it just felt creepy. I pulled my hand back.

"They were nice," said Samuel.

"Mmhmm," I said.

"Are you mad?"

"No."

"You seem mad."

"But I'm not mad."

"Okay. But why are you being so quiet?"

I didn't answer, but I met the taxi driver's gaze in the rear-view mirror. He was thinking: Shouldn't you be with someone your own age? Someone who's ready for something serious? Someone who doesn't think that life is just drinking box wine, eating cottage-noodles, and filling up your Experience Bank? Someone you can trust? I nodded, I agreed with him. Samuel broke into my thoughts.

"All your friends seemed to know about the house."

"So?"

"I was just a little surprised."

The taxi driver turned up the volume on the radio.

"They're my friends. They just think it's really awesome that we—"

"I get it. But didn't we agree not to tell anyone outside of us about it? Because that's not why we're doing it, is it? So we can tell people about it?"

The taxi drove on. We didn't say much more before it pulled up outside my door. I had my card out, out of old habit.

"I'll get it," Samuel said, handing over his card.

We snuck up the stairs and fell asleep on opposite sides of the bed.

*

It was Samuel's idea for me to take over running the house. He was worried that more and more people would show up, and he asked me to stop by once a day and keep an eye on things so it wouldn't get out of control.

"Maybe you can make up a list of everyone who sleeps there. Like, write down their names and where they're from and how long they're planning to stay."

He repeated several times that the most important thing was that everyone understood that it was a temporary place to stay, and it could end any day.

"We can't give them false hope. If my relatives want to get into the house, they all have to be out with a few hours' notice."

"It's going to be a little hard for me to keep an eye on the house and still get in all my hours with the moving company," I said.

"Don't worry about that. We'll figure it out. We'll keep splitting what I make."

And sure, it was generous of Samuel. But it wasn't enough for me to start paying off my debt to Hamza. He was contacting me more and more often to inform me of how the interest had grown. Sometimes he texted pictures that showed what would happen if I didn't pay up soon. It might be a hand without fingernails. A hockey pro who'd taken a puck to the eye. A cartoon character, tarred and feathered. A cute lamb that had been gutted on a strip of gray asphalt.

*

Then it started. And it was impossible to stop. First it was his voice. I started thinking that Samuel sounded fake. I noticed that he always adjusted his manner of speaking. If we were at a flea market and he wanted to buy a cigarette case from an old woman, he talked like an old woman.

"My, what miserable luck!" he might say when the old lady said that she didn't take cards.

When we walked by the square to buy fruit, he would start speaking in an Arabic accent. He haggled over oranges by calling the seller alternately "*brushan*" and "*habibi*."

"*Baraka'Allah Oufik*," he said, winking, when he received his change, totally unaware that the guy was a Kurd.

When we went to the library he would walk among the shelves and talk about how much he longed to read a "present-day political novel with a contextual framework that problematizes the formats of its contemporary peers but simultaneously takes a critical stance on modernistic history." And the sick thing was that it worked. Not always, but pretty often. The librarians and the old lady at the flea market loved him. But I noticed that the guy on the square looked at him with squinting eyes, as if he could tell that something was wrong. As if he knew: this guy has an accent because I have an accent. I started wondering who Samuel really was. Did he talk like me when he was with me? Who was he when I wasn't there? Did I even know his true self?

One day we said goodbye in the hall, he had to run to the Metro to make it to work on time, I kissed him goodbye and locked the door behind him. Then I watched him through the peephole, as he entered the stairwell and started going down the steps. I wanted to see what he looked like when I wasn't there. I wondered if he would speak Finland-Swedish with the one neighbor and southern Swedish with the other. Because I noticed how quickly he switched from one personality to the next, and the more I noticed it the more obvious it became that the version I knew was just one of many.

*

Every morning I biked over to the house and made the rounds. I checked off the residents against my list, I explained to new arrivals that the house was primarily for women and children but that in exceptional cases and on a short-term basis there might be a chance that men could sleep there too. Often there were practical items that had to be purchased, toilet paper and soap and dish detergent wouldn't last forever, and I started collecting an administrative fee from people who wanted to stay in the house so that Samuel or I wouldn't have to pay for those things. It was a small, symbolic fee that really didn't cover very much more than those practical items.

I knew that Samuel wouldn't have anything against it, so I didn't tell him about it.

*

Later on it was his impatience. It started to bother me that Samuel could never relax in the present, he was always looking ahead to his next experience. There was something self-absorbed about him, because he was always focused on his own experiences and his own memories. Never anyone else's.

And then it was his blackheads. At first I thought they were cute. But then they started to grow. I couldn't sit on the couch next to Samuel without noticing them, thinking about them, wanting to squeeze them or just get rid of them. On two evenings I suggested that he wash his face with my soap, and he just looked at me and shook his head.

And then it was his body odor. Samuel might wear the exact same clothes five days in a row. Sure, it's super that you're not walking around smelling like a perfume counter, but there's something to be said for being able to sit down on the subway next to someone and they *don't* start to look at you sideways and then switch seats as soon as they get the chance.

And then it was that I felt all this stuff and he didn't seem to notice a thing. He just kept living his life as if he had no idea what was about to happen.

*

At first it seemed weird for Samuel to pay me for taking care of the house. But then I realized how much time it took up. Something happened almost every day. A woman claimed that two men had stolen her gold watch. I came in as an arbitrator, I convinced the men to open their luggage and there were quite a few things that weren't typically masculine, several gold rings and some jewelry, but the watch the woman had described wasn't among them. Two nights later, the men had disappeared and the small, broken TV that had been on the second floor was missing too. One woman was pregnant and feverish and terrified of going to the hospital, I called the medical advice hotline to make sure she could seek care risk-free, then drove her to Huddinge in a borrowed car. I left her at the emergency room and drove back, I didn't want to take any chances. Her suitcase was still in the attic, and it was one of the things that was destroyed in the fire.

*

Everything just kept escalating. We were at a restaurant and I noticed that Samuel smacked his food. I saw his gums, the bits of food, his big, yellow teeth slowly grinding the food into a grotesquely chunky sludge which he then swallowed in large, greedy gulps. I said I had to cruise on home. He thought he would be coming along. I said I needed to do some prep for work.

"Laide," he said. "You have to remember to live a little. You. Only. Have. One. Life."

And he really said it like that. Slowly. With. Philosophical. Pauses. I had the urge to lean over and bite him on the nose. Who the hell was he, to sit there talking like some fucking life coach? What did he know about my story, my life, my choices? I shook my head. He smiled. There was green stuff stuck between his teeth.

On the way to the Metro he ran into someone he knew and I noticed him stiffen, he backed away when the girl wanted to hug him and he rapidly brought the conversation to an end. We kept walking. I thought he was trying to be the person he thought I wanted him to be, but instead he was transformed into a shell of what he was.

"Who was that?" I asked once we had gone through the turnstiles.

"No idea."

He turned toward me for a kiss, I twisted my head away and pretended to check my phone. I knew what I had to do, but I was putting it off, I didn't want to do it, I knew how bad I would feel afterwards. But I had no choice. Neither of us was happy that way. If I just did it quickly, at least we would still have the memories of what we had once been.

*

One time I answered when Hamza called and he was so surprised he didn't know what to say. I had ignored so many of his calls, and now we could suddenly hear each other's voices.

Instead of hissing all those things I'd heard him say in the voicemails, that he would do this and that to my earlobes and shatter my kneecaps and fuck my mom and kill my pets, he told me how big the loan was and that I would regret it if I didn't pay up soon.

"Is that all?" I said.

"I don't want to have to do this," Hamza said, sounding sad.

"Then don't," I said.

"I have to do it."

"Give me a month."

"One month?"

"Two months."

He hung up.

*

The autumn grew colder, the days shorter, the darkness more intense, and I couldn't look at Samuel without thinking of how stingy he was. How he automatically let me pay when we went to the movies, or ate at a restaurant, or had coffee or bought flowers. When he paid, I thanked him. When I paid, he merrily picked up the goods and walked out of the store. He didn't seem to think about money at all. And the less he focused on money, the more I was forced to do so. In the end, it wasn't his stinginess that bothered me, but my own—his casual attitude to money made me seem uptight, his mantra that everything would work out in the end transformed me into the stingiest person I'd ever met. I started to hate myself when we hung out, and I despised myself for noticing that he frequently chose cheap filter coffee when he was paying and expensive flavored lattes when it was my turn to pay. Everything seemed like a countdown.

*

Right after that, Samuel called and I could tell from his voice that something had happened.

"Spicy House in twenty," I said.

I was sitting at a window table, I saw him walking up. He had a plastic bag full of swimming gear. But his hair was dry. His body was moving like he had dumbbells in his hands. He hugged me.

"It's over," he said.

His body seemed to be pulsing with strange twitches.

*

In September, Samuel talked about how incredibly happy he was with me and how he couldn't manage without me. In October he wanted us to start planning a trip abroad for the next summer. In November he asked if I wanted to have kids, and if so when. I thought: The only reason that you're saying and feeling all these things right now is because you can tell I'm about to leave.

*

I went up to the bar, bought two drinks, and came back.

"I love her," Samuel murmured.

"No, you don't love her."

"It hurts so bad."

"Soon it won't hurt as much, here, chug this."

"I don't get it."

"There's nothing to get, she was a betraying cunt, you just have to realize that."

"What did you call her?"

"Sorry, I mean . . . It's like this. You can't trust girls. That's just the way it is. Hamza has a saying. He likes to say, 'Girls are fat, smell like strawberries, and can't be trusted.'"

"Who the hell is Hamza?"

"Never mind."

"And what experience do you even have with girls?"

The question hung blankly in the air. Instead of responding, I raised my glass and we toasted and downed our drinks.

*

In late November, I did it. I hadn't even been planning to do it. Not there. Not then. We met at the Eriksdal bathhouse, we were going to go swimming but before we changed we grabbed coffee in the cafeteria and right there, just after we ordered and found a seat in a secluded corner with our respective trays, I said it. I told him how I felt. I said that I loved him and I wanted to be with him but I couldn't because I didn't trust him and I said that if we didn't do something about it now we wouldn't remember the good times we really have had and I said I've tried to ignore these feelings, tried to work through them, tried to remind myself that I'm the broken one, not you. But it doesn't work. It doesn't help. I turn into a person I hate when I'm like this and it's not cool, the way I've treated you, and every time I'm not with you I feel so awful that the times when we're together can never balance it out and I know you get what I mean because I can tell that you've started to close off, you're not yourself anymore, you've started to act the way you think I want you to act when we go out, I'm saying this with love, you can't take it as criticism, I just have such a hell of a hard time trusting people and I wish I were different, I wish I didn't feel so guilty for not feeling enough, I wish I could be a hundred percent honest when I say that I love you, but I don't know if I am and knowing that makes me crazy and I hope you can forgive me because I wish I were different, that everything was different, that we were different, and that and that . . .

Though to be perfectly honest I'm not sure how much of this I actually got out, because I started crying after a minute or so. Samuel held me and comforted me.

"There, there," he said, getting up to find some more napkins.

*

Because these were special circumstances, I went straight to the bar and bought two more.

"It hurts so bad. I can hardly breathe."

"It will feel better soon."

"Should I call her?"

"No."

"I shouldn't just call her up? Just real quick?"

"Give me the phone."

"For real?"

"Yes, hand over your phone and drink up. You can have it back when we get home."

"I love her so goddamn much."

"You've known each other for like a year."

"Exactly. And now it's over—I can't believe it."

"You just have to accept it and move on."

I turned away as Samuel started to cry. It wasn't that I was ashamed, but I knew how he would feel the next day. It was for his own sake. I slid on over to the gambling machines. Once he had calmed down I came back to my seat. We took a few sips. Toasted.

"Sorry. Aw, shit. I feel better now."

He wiped his nose and tossed back his drink.

"I'll get the next round, what do you want?"

I smiled and thought: He's back.

*

When I looked at him sitting there with his big mouth and his kind eyes, I knew that I would regret it. But I had no other choice.

"We can't keep going like this, can we?"

"I thought we were happy," said Samuel.

In one instant my irritation was back. It bugged me that he

sounded so naïve when he said that, and at the same time it bothered me that he didn't look sad enough. We left the bathhouse and walked to the Metro. It bugged me that he walked too slowly. I was annoyed when he checked the time on his phone on our way through the tunnel under Ringvägen. As we stood and waited for the train and I was shuddering from all the crying, a beggar came up with a picture of his two kids and even though he must have seen I was fragile he didn't give up, he rattled his coffee cup, he pointed at his mouth, he said "please please" and at first I was irritated that Samuel was too stingy to give him money. But then he dug out a gold ten-krona coin and gave it to the beggar and then I was irritated that he was so gullible.

When my train finally rolled in, we hugged goodbye. It was the last time I touched him. The doors closed. He was still standing on the platform. The train moved through the tunnel, out onto the bridge. I tried to focus on the view. Årstaviken. The treetops. The roads. The badminton hall. And the bathhouse where we could have been swimming that moment if I weren't broken. As we departed Gullmarsplan I started crying again, I saw my contorted face in the reflection in the window and realized that Samuel hadn't shed a single tear.

*

A few hours later. Last call. We were fine sitting down, but had a harder time standing up.

"What do you want?" I asked.

"My phone," Samuel said.

"Fuck your phone. Fuck Laide, fuck Sting." (I only said that because a Sting song happened to be playing on the bar speakers—I don't have anything in particular against Sting.)

I returned to the table with two to four drinks. Four Samuels looked up and smiled, I sat on one of five chairs and thought, the battle to help him find his way back to being himself starts now.

"Shouldn't I call her?"

"No, you shouldn't call her."

"Just to see how things are?"

"Give me your phone."

"You already took it."

"Oh right. I have your phone and you are not going to call her."

Even though last call had come and gone they let us stay there and soon it was last last call and it was Samuel's turn to buy. He walked a crooked line to the bar, he grabbed it like a lifebuoy, the bartender smiled as he placed his order. Then he came back with just one beer.

"I felt like I had enough," said Samuel.

I sat there with my single beer. I asked if Samuel wanted a taste.

"No, I'm good."

I tossed back half the beer, put down the glass, and went to the bathroom. When I came back, Samuel was by the door with his coat on. We walked out onto the square, the night wind was icy cold, a very fit couple was working out side by side on the Stairmasters in the gym, they were staring at their reflections and looking pleased. On the way out I noticed that the half-full beer I'd left on the table had been drunk. And I don't know why I noticed that or what it changed, but I remember thinking that Laide was still there inside Samuel, even though they had broken up and would never be together again, she would be a part of him forever. I hoped I was wrong.

*

I was convinced he would call. I waited for the phone to ring. If only he had called I would have taken it all back. But he never called.

*

Samuel was back. He was himself, and yet not. One night I heard him talking to someone in his room. The same song had been playing on repeat for several hours, I recognized it but couldn't place it, when the song ended I could hear a few seconds of the next song and then a few seconds' pause and then the song started over again. Every time it happened I thought that he should either turn on the repeat function so the same song would play over and over again automatically, or else he should let the disc or the playlist play. But instead, the same song and two seconds of the next one, for one hour, two hours, three hours. At last I knocked on his door and asked how he was feeling. He didn't respond, but I heard him mumbling.

251

"Come on now. You can fix this, you will fix it, come on now, come on."

My first thought was that he was talking to someone on the phone. Or that he was playing some sort of game.

"Samuel?" I called. "Is everything okay?"

For a few seconds, there was silence. From inside his room I heard the song end and the next song begin.

"Definitely. Sorry. Everything's fine."

His voice sounded like it was coming from a pressure cooker, as if he had to use all of his abdominal muscles just to say those words. I stood by the door, I rested my hand on it, I thought that I ought to help him, but I didn't know how.

*

I couldn't work, I couldn't breathe, I couldn't sleep, I couldn't see friends, I couldn't read the paper, I couldn't watch TV, I couldn't listen to music, I couldn't check my email, I couldn't shower, I couldn't look out the window, I couldn't hide under my blankets, I couldn't think, I couldn't dream, I couldn't do laundry, I couldn't do dishes, I couldn't live, I couldn't answer the phone and I couldn't call him, no matter how much I wanted to. At last my sister came over and when I opened the door she looked at me and said:

"Smart choice. Looks like you feel terrific."

She shook her head and took a big step across the pile of newspapers on the hall floor.

*

Samuel took off work sick for a week or so. He sat at home in sweatpants, in the kitchen, surrounded by notebooks full of scribbles. Unshaven, he read through the notes from their year together, he mumbled to himself and when I asked what he was up to he claimed he was "on the trail of something."

"Of what?" I asked.

"I don't know. But it's here somewhere."

He picked up another notebook and read through the tiny letters.

*

I imagined that Samuel was sad for a few days. Then he moved on. By the weekend after we broke up he was back out on the town. He and Vandad were standing at the bar at East, they were shaking their skulls in time with basslines, they were nodding at mixed beats, they were flirting with yoga instructors and organizing druggy after-parties. It only took a few weeks for Samuel to meet someone new, she was like me, only prettier, smarter, richer, simpler. Samuel suggested coffee at Petite France and when she arrived he was already in his usual spot, they hugged and when he returned with the coffee he used the newspaper clippings on the walls as a pretext to start talking about memories and nostalgia. He told her about the chips getting stuck in his teeth. Then he reached for the glass and poured water on himself, slowly and deliberately, secure in the knowledge that she would never be able to forget him.

*

One time Samuel asked if I thought he was fake.

"What do you mean by fake?" I asked.

"Well, I mean, Laide insinuated that I was. Several times. That there is something wrong with the way I act around other people. She thought I conformed so much that I erased myself."

"I've never thought about it," I said, being almost completely honest.

"I think she has a point. Before her I never thought about the way I acted. I just was. Blissfully unaware, somehow. But now—the more I do it—the more fake I feel."

He drank cup after cup of tea. He walked around at home like a pale, smelly ghost. I tried to tell him that the only way to get over an old love was with a new love. But he just looked at me and said he felt tired, terribly tired. I let him sleep for ages, I hoped he would find his way back to himself soon. After a few weeks had passed I suggested that I go over and have a talk with Laide. I thought I could mediate, get them back together. Better a Samuel who's himself for short periods than a Samuel who has completely lost himself.

"Talk as in talk or talk as in 'talk'?"

"What do you mean?"

"Well, we can always ask Valentin how he felt after your 'conversation.'"

"Aw, that was forever ago. I meant that I would talk talk with her."

"What would you say?"

"That she should apologize to you and reconsider."

"I'd prefer it if you didn't contact her."

"Are you sure?"

"A thousand percent."

*

A few weeks went by. I tried to find my way back to my daily routine. My sister moved in with me and I went back to work. Since I didn't hear from anyone at the house, I thought everything had worked out. I hoped that Samuel's family had decided not to sell it right away. Maybe they had even opted to keep it once they saw the good it did as a place of refuge. I thought, if that was the case, then Samuel's and my relationship had been worth something. Or. That sounds weird. Of course it was worth something, no matter what happened to the house. But if the house were to live on as a refuge, then maybe the value of our relationship was more permanent. Ugh. That sounded wrong too. Get rid of that.

*

Since it's a sign of good health when you start doing things you actually hate, I was happy when I noticed that Samuel started going back to the Migration Board. But he was still coming straight home after work. He didn't want to find fun things to do on the weekends. He was moving strangely, he walked as if all his body parts were heavier than normal. I saw him stop abruptly in front of the mirror in the hall several times. He smiled, he looked angry, he scrutinized his face like it contained the answer to a riddle he had forgotten.

When several months had passed and Samuel was still acting odd, I took the bus to Bagarmossen. The same bus Samuel always took when he was with Laide. I crossed the square we had passed that New Year's Eve that felt like a hundred years ago. I found the street and the front door. I pressed the light button and stood in the stairwell for a moment to gather my thoughts. Laide's last name was on the list of occupants. I mostly wanted to get her to understand that she couldn't treat people any way she pleased. I wanted to talk some sense into her. I wanted to explain to her that if Samuel shared her secrets with me it didn't mean that Samuel didn't love her, it meant that he loved her so much that he couldn't stop talking about her. That everything that happened to him could be linked back to her and that it was impossible for him not to pass it on to me or write it down in one of his notebooks. I readied the words, I didn't want to stumble over them, I was breathing calmly, I pressed the light button again. I was just about to walk up the stairs and ring her bell when Laide came through the door. She was carrying two grocery bags and the sight of me startled her.

*

My sister was going to go grocery shopping. I said I could take care of it. My sister refused, she insisted on going. I wanted to make sure to pay for it, at least. I found some bills and stuffed them in her jacket pocket. She took them out and put them on the bureau in the hall. They would stay there for several weeks, every time I saw them I shuddered and yet I couldn't move them. Blood money, I thought when I saw them.

*

She looked the way she usually did, maybe just a little older. She was wearing her owl brooch and when I tried to talk to her she walked straight past me like I was invisible.

"Hey there, hold on a sec," I said.

"What the fuck do you want?" she said in a voice that sounded harder than I remembered. She kept walking up the stairs briskly, and I walked behind her. I said that she ought to learn that there's a difference between empty air and people and that everyone is worth listening to and when she didn't listen, and instead walked even faster up the stairs, I ran to catch up with her and grabbed her wrist. Her grocery bags fell to the floor. Her self-confident smile vanished. Finally, she understood that I was serious. I never wanted to hurt her, I just wanted her to listen, but she yanked herself free and started screaming, and to make her be quiet I put one hand over her mouth and told her to calm down. Then she bit me and I adjusted my grip and told her that if she bit me one more time she would regret it.

"Just be quiet and listen, and everything will go fine, okay?"

But instead of listening she struggled and kicked me in the shin and I pushed her up against the wall to get a little distance. I wanted to say what I had come to say, that Samuel was unhappy and that she ought to reconsider, but I didn't have time because she bit me again and this time her sharp teeth punctured my skin and the lights on the ceiling went out and for a few short seconds I lost control, I didn't hit her but I shoved her, once against the wall and once against the railing. That was all. Two tiny shoves. Then I left the stairwell.

*

My sister didn't come back from the store. After twenty minutes I was worried. I called her phone, and at first I thought she had forgotten it because I could hear it ringing, it was ringing somewhere in the apartment. I went from room to room and finally I realized that it was coming from the stairwell. I opened the door and hit the light button. She was lying on the second floor, the first thing I saw was her left arm lying at a strange angle from the rest of her body, the white shaft of bone was sticking out from the tear in her denim jacket, her face was turned toward the floor, there was blood on the wall, blood on the railing, her mouth was a gaping hole of broken teeth and split lip, she woke up when I touched her, she started crying when she saw me, she mewled, I held her, I said that everything would be fine, I screamed and kicked on doors until the neighbors came out into the stairwell.

*

I took the Metro so I wouldn't be seen by any bus drivers. I hadn't wanted to hurt anyone. But she had gone on the attack and bitten up my hands and the lining of my jacket was wet with blood and it stiffened in the cold as I walked home from the Metro. I washed my hands and used paper towels to dry off so the towels wouldn't turn red. Samuel was in his room. I went to my own room. I thought, if anything had gone wrong, it was Laide's fault.

*

The police labeled it an attempted rape, but my sister said it felt more like a junkie looking for easy money. She put up a fight. He never got hold of her wallet.

*

Yes. Of course I regret it. But you have to understand, we're talking about two shoves. Two tiny shoves. That was all.

*

After the attack I decided to leave the country. I couldn't bear to stay. I couldn't handle walking through that stairwell every day and thinking about my sister's motionless body. I had promised myself not to stay for too long, and I wanted to keep my promise. In March of two thousand twelve I left Stockholm and moved to Paris. It felt like a weight was lifted from my body when I landed at Charles de Gaulle. Five days later I had picked up enough interpreting jobs to brave signing a lease on an apartment.

*

And it's not like Laide was so innocent. Sure, I shoved her. But she had crushed Samuel. She got into his brain and rearranged the furniture until he started doubting himself. Some things heal faster than others.

*

It took a few weeks before I heard what had happened. And yes, of course I was sad. I thought about his family. His mom and sister. His friends and acquaintances. But you want to know something strange? I really didn't feel guilty. That chapter of my life was over. We hadn't spoken since we broke up. There were other people who were closer to him. And I suppose part of me was grateful that we weren't together when it happened. I don't know how I would have survived that.

*

She made him believe that he could trust her and then she betrayed him and he never got over it.

*

Why did he do it? Do we know for sure that he *did* do it? That he did it on purpose, I mean? I heard he lost control of the car. His mom said that the brakes were bad. I think he was simply driving too fast. I can picture it, how he's sitting there behind the wheel in his grandma's car, revving the engine and deciding to push the envelope and see how fast he can take a curve. He probably wanted to see what would happen if he brushed up against death. Maybe he was curious about the light at the end of the tunnel. He wanted to experience something that no one else had seen.

*

She killed him.

*

Thank *you*. I have to confess, I was a little nervous but it was nice to get it off my chest. Do you have a plan for how you're going to make it into a coherent narrative? Just as long as you don't try to write Samuel in the first person it will probably work. I don't think it's possible to capture the voice of another person, it would be foolish to even try. Should I call a taxi? This neighborhood can be a little sketchy at night. My husband always takes a cab when he comes home late from the firm. But then again, that's because he looks the way he does, people react when they see him, they don't believe that he lives here. I'll call a car.

[A long silence as we wait for a taxi that never comes.]

I'm convinced it wasn't deliberate.

[A long silence, she occasionally gets up to see if the taxi has arrived, it hasn't.]

Samuel loved his experiences far too much to ... I think he was just driving too fast.
  [Short silence. Still no taxi. Laide pours water from a carafe.]

Because, I mean. If it had been deliberate—how do you explain the seatbelt and the skid marks? Because there were skid marks, weren't there?
  [Laide reaches for her water glass.]

*

Everyone I've talked to says there were skid marks.

[Laide takes a sip, looks at the water, puts the glass down with a trembling hand.]

Here it comes.

PART III

PM

THE SELF (I)

It's a few minutes past one and I'm sitting in yet another waiting room. Grandma's handbag is resting in my lap, the fake white leather leaves small flakes on my jeans. I open and close the zipper, then I open it again and let my hands explore its contents. There's her wallet with its five-hundred-krona bills, her notebook, the bag of old candy all stuck together, the throat lozenges (Emser), the bottle of Vademecum mouthwash (its label worn), and her cell phone of course, the one she never learned to use. Grandma's house is burned, Laide has moved, Vandad has betrayed me, and I have five hours left to live.

*

I was at the house that morning and everything was perfectly normal. The kids were playing in the basement, the moms were mopping the floor in the kitchen, young men were sitting on the terrace and scraping away at their Triss lottery scratch cards. It was a sunny day, the geothermal heating was working, there was no reason to use the fireplace or have lights on inside.

*

I take out Grandma's yellowed notebook with coffee stains on the front. It's almost unused. Her wobbly handwriting, the crooked "r"s. On the first page it says "What sort of Christian am I? Am I—" On the lines beneath, the same cell number, written twelve separate times. On the last line, the same cell number, but only the first four digits.

*

I was on my way home when my phone rang. Nihad bellowed:

"Fire! FIRE!"

I made a U-turn and biked back to the house. I hurried, but I didn't think it could be that serious. Maybe someone had left something on the stove, maybe some kid had been playing with a lighter in the yard. I couldn't imagine what had happened.

*

I rub my eyes. I yawn. Over the past few weeks, Grandma has started calling me at odd times. Two thirty in the morning. Three thirty, ten to five, my phone wakes me up and I see her name on the screen. Sometimes I answer, sometimes I let it ring. When I answer I hear her delighted voice:

"Why, hello there! Are you awake?"

Usually she just wants to make sure that this is really my number. She recites all ten digits. I confirm that the number is correct. She gives a sigh of relief and can go back to sleep.

*

When I reached the house I saw that the entire parlor area was full of smoke. It looked like all the windows were covered in black curtains. I jumped off my bike and dropped it onto the gravel just as a windowpane broke, I thought it was because of the heat, shards of glass fell onto the bushes like snow. Nihad, Maysa, and Zainab had gathered with their children and a few suitcases down by the street. Maysa was holding a rolling pin in her hand and there was flour on her face, Nihad was sobbing.

"Where is everyone?" I asked in English.

"Gone."

"Afraid of police."

"Is everyone out?" I asked.

"Yes," said Nihad. "Everyone is out, right?"

Maysa and Zainab looked around and nodded. Another window broke, this time it was a small round one up in the attic. The smoke came shooting out like a laser beam and at first I thought it was an optical illusion, but then I saw something moving.

*

Everything has taken longer than planned. The plan was for me to be back at work after lunch, but first they wanted to test

267

Grandma's vision and then her cognitive capacity and at last they let her into the simulator room. She looked nervous as she walked in. Her cheeks were rosy when she came out.

"How did it go?" I asked.

"Absolutely wonderful."

The doctor showed us into a separate room and explained that it was over. There was no chance that she could get her license back. She had crashed into motorcycles, driven straight through roundabouts, she had backed into a lake, and even though the doctor had reminded her that she was in a simulator she repeatedly tried to roll down the windows.

"It was so warm," Grandma murmured.

No one said anything.

"When can I try again?"

"There isn't going to be a next time," said the doctor. "You have to accept that."

*

A taxi stopped and Samuel vaulted out of the front seat. He was wearing his work clothes, but his hair was going every which way, it looked like he had slept in the taxi.

"What happened?"

"No idea."

"Is everyone out?"

"Think so."

"Yes, everyone is out," Nihad said again, although she didn't sound as sure this time. Then we heard the voice. Someone was screaming, it sounded like it was coming from the attic, the women gathered their children close, some of the children were crying, Zainab and Maysa counted the children again and again as if they couldn't believe that everyone was really there. Samuel looked at me with wild eyes.

"Are you ready?"

*

I'm ashamed that I didn't figure it out, the thought didn't even occur to me. Sure, there was a smell as we drove here and I could see that she was limping, of course, but she'd been limping for a long time. I thought that the rustling noise was from her adult diaper. We had to hold her down in the chair and make her take off her shoe to see what was wrong. It was hard to tell toenail, flesh, and pus apart. The worst was her big toenail, which had grown out and then in again in an arc, it looked like the yellowed talon of a bird. The plastic bags she had wrapped around her foot fell to the floor with a wet sound.

"How long have you been walking around like this?" the doctor asked.

Grandma didn't answer.

"We have to do something about this," said the doctor.

*

We ran up the gravel path, Samuel first, me behind him. We took the stone steps up to the upper entrance, the door was open, smoke was rushing out, we could feel the heat even from the terrace, we heard sirens in the distance.

"We can't," I said. "It's too hot."

Samuel looked at me and smiled.

"Experience Bank?"

He tore off his jacket, held it up to his face, took a deep breath, and threw himself into the smoke. His back vanished. I counted to three, then I buried my nose in my elbow and followed him.

*

When they roll her out of the examination room her foot is wrapped in a white bandage. They used an electric saw to cut off her toenails and the nurse pushing the wheelchair says that she's extremely lucky that the infection hadn't spread.

"Thanks for your help," I say.

"Let's go eat lunch," says Grandma.

*

The fire roared at us to turn back, it laughed at us as we tried to go up the stairs, I kept close to the wall because I saw Samuel do so. We made it to the second floor and it felt cooler there, we searched the office, the children's room, and the bedroom. No one there. But the wardrobe in the bedroom was open and there, among the shards from the broken window, lay a boy, he looked about fifteen, he had splinters of glass in his downy mustache, and his face was gray. Samuel looked at me, I shrugged. I had never seen him before. We lifted him up. He didn't weigh a thing. Samuel took his legs, I got his upper body. We headed for the stairs but the air was hotter now, the stairs creaked as we tried to walk down them,

270

when I brushed against the metal railing it felt like the hair on my forearms caught fire. We fell headlong down the last few steps, we lay in a pile on the hall floor, the whole parlor was in flames, I could see the fire consuming the piano, the paintings, the parquet, the rug. It popped and crackled and I mustered my last bit of strength to crawl toward the sunlight, I dragged the boy's body behind me, his head came over the doorstep, Samuel came behind him on all fours. He was coughing himself blue, he had black streaks of soot on his face.

"Hold on a second."

He turned around and crawled into the heat. I reached for him, but I didn't have the strength to hold him back.

*

We sit in the hospital cafeteria and wait for our food. We're surrounded by exhausted patriarchs, trembling elderly people, children with the tops of their snowsuits knotted around their waists, hospital employees absorbed in evening papers, taxi drivers talking on cell phones, and then there's Grandma, sitting at our table and observing everyone and everything. She leans forward and asks if we are in Sweden.

"Yes, we're in Sweden."

"You'd never believe it."

I don't say anything, I don't want to go there, not now. Our food is ready, I go get it, Grandma is ready with her fork and smiles when I put down the tray, salmon quiche and a slice of lemon for her, a chicken wrap for me. The receipt tells me that it is twenty-seven minutes past one on the fifth of April, two thousand twelve.

*

Samuel couldn't have been gone for more than thirty seconds. But it felt like a lifetime. At last I saw his crawling body. He fell forward and gasped for air, a pink porcelain bowl with gold details fell out of his jacket.

"I couldn't find the lid," he croaked.

*

We're still in the cafeteria. Grandma looks at her food. She hasn't touched it.

"Aren't you hungry?" I ask.

She is sitting there with her fork at the ready, looking at the food like it's a crossword puzzle. At last she reaches for the lemon slice and swallows it whole.

"I'm full now."

"Do you want coffee?" I ask.

"Please. Half a cup. Black, said the homeowner to the painter, and regretted it. And I think we deserve something sweet after a day like this. Check and see if they have raspberry boats."

She takes out her wallet and hands me yet another bill. The receipt tells me that it is fourteen minutes past two when I come back with the coffee and sweets.

"Look, Grandma. Chocolate macaroons. Who was it that used to bring macaroons when he came to visit you?"

Grandma sips her coffee and ignores the question.

"What was his name again? The man you bought the house from? K something?"

Grandma turns to gaze at the people walking by in the corridor. She makes a comment about each person, just loud enough so they can hear.

"My, that's a yellow skirt. Well, I suppose it takes all kinds. Don't you think she's freezing? Is that how you're supposed to look these days? Is that sort of metal jewelry really modern? Well, I suppose that's one way to do it!" (This last was about a woman who was talking loudly on a cell phone that was secured in place by her veil.)

Then Grandma's head falls forward and she dozes off.

*

The first fire truck had a hard time getting up the gravel drive. It stopped halfway up and the firemen put on their helmets and unspooled their hoses. They entered the house without taking any notice of us. Only later, once the fire was under control and the ambulance crew had seen to the boy did two firemen approach us.

"Where are the heroes?" they said, shaking their heads. "Or should we say, the idiots?"

But they said it in an impressed way that still made us feel like heroes. Samuel's hair was kinkier than usual. We were leaning against one of the stone pillars down by the street and watching as the firemen put out the last pockets of fire.

"Is it done for?" he asked one of the firemen.

"That depends on your definition. But it's safe to say it will be a while before you can celebrate Christmas here."

The ambulance crew said that the boy up in the attic was going to make it and when they asked what his name was everyone looked at each other in confusion. No one recognized him. Neither Nihad, Maysa, nor Zainab could remember ever seeing him in the house.

"Was it Rojda's son?" Nihad asked.

"Who was Rojda?" asked Maysa.

"He must have come on his own," said Zainab. "Otherwise we would have noticed him."

Maysa and Zainab had found temporary housing. Nihad would go home to her ex-husband. I looked at Samuel. The flames had been extinguished, the yard stank, the bushes were full of black soot and fluffy foam. Half the parlor area had been destroyed. Several of the nearby trees had burned down. I thought that Samuel would be absolutely crushed. In just a short time he had lost his girlfriend and his grandma's house. But there was a peculiar look on his face. It was almost like he was smiling.

*

Suddenly she snorts and wakes up, her eyes are wide open and she's flailing her hands.

"No no no no. There will be none of that. How many times do I have to tell you? Let me go, let me go, I don't want to, do you hear me, I don't want to, let me out of here."

People are looking up from their phones, the security guards over by the information desk take a few steps in our direction. I meet their gazes, I try to calm her down, I take the photos out of the plastic bag, graduation parties, family reunions, weddings, funerals. I remind her where we are, I say my name, I say her name, I say Mom's name, I say her sons' names. When she finally calms down, she says:

"I want to go home now."

*

The day after the fire, Samuel's phone rang nonstop. After he put it on silent, the apartment kept buzzing with vibrations.

"Who is it?" I asked.

"Guess," said Samuel.

But I didn't have to guess, because soon the answer was standing in our stairwell. Samuel's mom rang the doorbell and banged on the door and when I opened it she walked straight in without removing her red down coat with the logo of the preschool where she worked.

Before I could respond she had walked into Samuel's room and started chewing him out for making her worry needlessly. I stayed in the hall; her voice, which was usually shy and gentle as a whisper, had taken on a new harshness. She said that the police had investigated what they were calling "the crime scene."

"And apparently there were signs of a break-in," she said. "It seems that someone, or several someones, got into Mom's house and were living there. And according to the neighbors it's been going on for quite some time. Do you know anything about this, Samuel? It's very, very important that you answer me honestly."

Silence. If Samuel said anything in reply I didn't hear what it was. Samuel's mom went on.

"They say it's going to cost around a million kronor to restore the house—that is, not renovate it, just to clean it up enough to sell it. I don't know where we're going to get that kind of money from, I suppose we'll have to try to take out another loan on the house. If that's even possible. Svante might have some money saved up, but Kjell is Kjell . . ."

Without knowing how Kjell was, I understood that these were her two brothers. Samuel walked into the kitchen, and his mom followed.

"What's going to happen, my God, what are we supposed to do?"

As Samuel's mom spoke, she walked around and around our apartment, sometimes she stopped to fold a T-shirt that was hanging on a chair or to throw away an apple core that had fallen onto the kitchen floor. She did it without thinking, like a robot who had been performing certain motions for so many years that it couldn't stop.

"We just have to cross our fingers that the homeowners' insurance will cover something like this, do you think it will? Does this count as a break-in or something else?"

Samuel shrugged.

"If anyone from the insurance company calls it's very important to make it clear that you didn't know anything about this. Because you didn't, right, Samuel? Tell me you didn't know anything about what was going on at Grandma's house?"

And I watched as Samuel—who usually couldn't lie without scratching his earlobe while he picked at his upper lip—looked his mom in the eye.

"I had no idea whatsoever."

They looked at each other. Mother and son. For a long time. And it was like his mom understood something her son couldn't put into words. She nodded. Samuel nodded. Then she left, and Samuel said:

"Money, money, money, that's all anyone thinks about."

The coin doesn't fall far from the vault, I thought.

*

We are sitting in the car. According to the parking receipt, the time is three minutes past three.

"Drive me home," Grandma says.

"Your house is still there, just as you left it."

"Please drive me home. That's all I want."

I start the engine and drive out of the parking lot.

"Are we going home now?"

"Mmhmm. Home to the home," I say, putting on the Lars Roos CD. As we drive onto the highway I reach for the plastic bag in the back seat and take out the pink candy bowl that is sometimes an antique and sometimes a project I made in school.

"Thanks," she says, petting the bowl like a cat. "Where's the lid?"

"You can have that next time."

Grandma looks out the car window. A darkening sky, the faint silhouettes of a few birds.

"You have to understand that I don't like it at the home. The windows are far too small. The bathroom is too close to the hall. The kitchen is an unpleasant color. The balcony makes me dizzy. But still, the worst thing of all is the bed. It's far too soft. I can hardly sleep in it."

"But Grandma," I say. "You brought the bed from home. It's the same bed you used back in your house, isn't it?"

"It's still too soft."

*

I told Samuel that there was a soul club night at East. DJ Taro was playing at Reisen. Tony Zoulias was spinning at Spy. Or should we swing by the pool in Bredäng? Go up to the top of Kaknäs Tower? Do something, anything? But Samuel didn't want to. He had a sore throat. He had to get up early. He didn't have any money. Instead of doing things he went to see his grandma at the dementia home. It was like the loss of the house reminded him that she existed.

"Is she happy there?" I asked.

"She hates it. More than ever. But she puts so much energy into hating it that I almost think it's good for her."

His grandma spent her days writing long, muddled letters to the editor in which the main idea was that she should be allowed to move back home and that her driver's license ought to be restored immediately and that school policy needed to be rewritten. Samuel sat beside her, agreeing with her monologues about how everything was wrong with immigration policy and the school system and the EU. Only when she dissed his dad did Samuel contradict her, and that in itself was strange, because the things she said about his dad (that he had betrayed them, that he ought to be there for his children, that no real man deserts his family) were things Samuel had said to me any number of times. But his grandma always added, "that's what happens when you marry a Muslim," and Samuel couldn't get on board with that because his dad was the least Muslim man he had ever met.

*

Out on the highway, Grandma asks how things are going with Vandad.

"Don't you mean Laide? Laide is fine. She says hello."

"And how is Vandad?"

"He's fine too."

We approach the city, we don't say anything for a few minutes. Then Grandma turns to me and asks how things are with Vandad. I say that he's still fine. On the way into town, Grandma suddenly needs to pee. We stop at "Korv and Go" in Årsta, park the car, Grandma uses their bathroom, we pay five kronor and I stick the receipt in the car door. It's twenty-seven minutes past three and I have less than an hour left to live.

"Now where are we going?" Grandma asks.

"We have to go back now," I say.

"Home?"

"Home. To the home."

"What a shame."

"Mmhmm."

"But do you know what?"

"No."

"We can do this tomorrow too, can't we?"

"Mmhmm."

"And the day after?"

"Mmhmm."

"And do you know who will drive next time? Me."

"No."

"Oh yes. If I can only get the chance to take that test, why, I'll show them what's what. Easy as pie, said the baker to the baker's son."

"Why?"

"What?"

"Why did the baker say 'easy as pie' to his son?"

"How should I know? That's just something we said when we were little."

"More and more of them keep turning up."

"What do?"

"Those expressions."

"The older I get, the more I remember. That's just one of the advantages of aging."

She smiles, there are so many folds in her eyelids that she has to squint to see. As we approach the Liljeholmen bridge I pass three cars on the left.

"Now that's more like it," says Grandma.

*

Then there was some liar who thought it was important to tell Samuel about the fuss in Laide's stairwell. This person changed two tiny shoves into an aggressive robbery. This person said that it was Laide's sister who was attacked, not Laide. Samuel came into my room and asked, his jaw tight, if I knew anything about this. I said no. Samuel asked again. I explained that rumors were lies. I said that I had gone there to talk to Laide and then she pretended not to recognize me and then she attacked me, biting and kicking, and all I did was give her two fairly puny shoves.

"It's not my fault she tripped down the stairs."

Samuel just looked at me. Then he went to his room and started packing his things into moving boxes.

"I just wanted to talk to her," I said.

He didn't respond.

"She started it."

Samuel went to the bathroom to get his toothbrush.

"I don't know what you heard—but it really wasn't anything serious."

Samuel said he'd heard other things as well, like that I had exaggerated my rent to get him to pay more (untrue). And that I had started extorting money from people in the house (also not entirely true).

"Who told you that?" I said.

"Laide was fucking right," Samuel mumbled. "You can't trust anyone."

When he wanted to leave, I stood in his way. He looked at me. The light in his eyes had gone out. I stepped aside. We parted. Not as enemies, but not as best friends either.

*

I speed up, cross the bridge, and zoom up to the home. All the parking spots are full, so I drive up to the entrance and help Grandma out of the passenger seat.

"You can't park here," Grandma says.

"It's fine. We'll be quick."

I empty the plastic bag into her suitcase. The photos and perfume bottles, Grandpa's fur cap and the Lars Roos CD with the see-through grand piano. Then I follow her to the front door. I remember the mnemonic and enter the code.

"Did everything go well?" asks an aide I don't recognize.

"Not too bad," Grandma says.

"Oh my, what happened?"

"It's not a big deal," Grandma says, waving her foot.

"Ingrown nails," I say.

We hug, I kiss her on the cheek, it's rough and full of liver spots, she smells like Grandma, she will always smell like Grandma, which is adult diapers and old-lady perfume and Emser lozenges and a faint hint of Vademecum.

"Thanks for our day," I say.

"That's nothing to thank me for."

I leave. I take the elevator down. Then I discover her suitcase and turn back. When I walk into the TV room she looks at me, throws out her arms, and cries:

"At last! I've been waiting so long!"

I hand over her suitcase, stand there for a few seconds. She wrinkles up her face.

"Well? If you're waiting for a tip you're wasting your time. I don't have any change."

When I get back to the car there's a parking ticket on the windshield. It was written at five minutes to four. I curse, stuff the ticket into my wallet, and start the car.

*

That was the last time I saw Samuel. Although after the funeral I still saw him. Everywhere. I mean, not people who look like him, but *him*, I saw Samuel. For real. The real Samuel was walking around the streets of Stockholm. He was sitting at a cafe on Götgatan wearing a turquoise tank top, he was rushing by on an escalator and carrying a large kite, he was driving a silvery Citroën with rusty back tires as he spoke into one of those old-fashioned Bluetooth headsets that sits on your ear. And if it had been a movie I would have walked up and discovered that it wasn't him at all, that it was someone else, an actor with similar features, but here, every time, I noticed that I looked away until the person had disappeared. I had no choice, it was like my body wanted to let me believe that he was still alive, that he was walking around with kites and driving Citroëns and sitting in cafes in turquoise tank tops.

*

I approach the place where it will happen, I exit the round-about, I pass the gas station, the superstore, the McDonald's drive-in. I'm not going terribly fast. I don't recklessly try to pass any other cars. No one sees me, no one notices me. None of the oncoming cars have gone past the tree and thought, soon, right here, a car will go flying as if its driver has decided that the road should keep going straight ahead even though it curves to the left.

*

A few weeks after the funeral I heard Samuel's voice. I was walking by Medborgarplatsen, I passed the lawn with the drummers and the drunks and the junkies and the class-cutting students and it's not a place that has any link to Samuel at all. I had made it to, like, the fountain, and a few Roma were washing their clothes in the water, it was soapy, a couple of kids were cooling their feet, their mom was trying to get them to come back to their double stroller, the air smelled like grilled eggplant, a dog owner was sitting on a bench eating a popsicle with its paper peeled down like a banana, it was very normal, nothing was special, and suddenly I heard Samuel call my name. It's true, I heard his voice, it sounded part happy, part annoyed, as if he had noticed me ages ago and was grumpy because he thought I had walked right by him, playing blind, as if we had decided to meet in this very spot and I had shown up twenty minutes late without calling.

*

I stop at the red light, I wait, I rev the engine, I think about Vandad, I think about Laide, I think about the house, I think about Grandma, I try to figure out how I feel, I tell myself I'm sad, I look at myself in the rear-view mirror, I try to cry, I try to squeeze out a few tears, but all I see is that blank face, that false body that has never felt a genuine emotion, that has never burst out in rage without considering it first, that has never kissed someone without thinking about how the kiss will look to outsiders, that is still waiting for emotion to win out over control someday, and when the red light turns green I put the pedal to the metal, I drive far too fast through the intersection, I pass the crosswalk going seventy, I take the first curve at ninety, whatever's going to happen it has to happen now, I have to feel something, something has to make it in, it all can't just keep trickling through, and when the road curves left I go straight, I didn't plan it, it just happens, as the road stops and the car approaches the tree I'm still thinking, it's fine, there's no problem, my seatbelt must be good enough, the airbag will fix this, the hood of the car is hard, the tree is skinny, I don't have any last thoughts, no last wishes, no flood of memories from my childhood, all I see is Panther putting on a turquoise turban and asking if I can tell it's a towel, Grandma putting out her right hand and introducing herself, Laide looking up from the editorial page of *Dagens Nyheter* and roaring, "Have you read this piece of shit?" Vandad eating up the last slice of his two pizzas and asking if I've ever been in love with someone for real.

*

Even though my brain knew that Samuel was dead, my body spun around, my eyes searched for him, it was like my body wanted to show my brain that it still had hope that Samuel would one day call my name. I heard his voice, crystal-clear. I am one hundred percent sure of it. You don't have to believe me, but I know that he called out for me. It was him. I know it.

*

I'm sure that this isn't the end, the tree is getting closer, soon it will plow its way through the hood of the car, the rotational forces will crush my brain, my internal organs will be ripped apart, but for now I have all the time in the world, there are the clouds, and further off the tunnel and the gravel pit and the soccer field and the highway and I think about the noise, I wonder what it will sound like, if it will echo, explode, crash, rumble, squeal, how far the sound will travel, will the people standing at the bus stop be the first ones to reach me, will the kids on the soccer field notice what has happened before the ambulance arrives, how loud does a crash have to be for it to be heard all the way into the future, how fast do you have to go to survive in someone's memory, how close to death do you have to come to be worth being turned into history? I move my foot from the gas to the brake, I ought to brake, I have to brake, at the same time as the tree the tires the windshield the shards of glass the smash and then the silence. They say it happens quickly but they're lying. It lasts forever. I'm still there. Waiting for the tree. And afterwards, as if there is an afterwards, there are no sirens. No voices. No explosion. Just the hissing sound of steam from the crumpled engine that has been shoved all the way into the front seat. The squeal of bent windshield wipers moving back and forth, back and forth. Running steps. Voices. Chirping birds. Sirens. From far off: the chimes of an ice-cream truck. The click of a phone taking pictures. The wind whistling through what was so recently a car and what was so recently a person. Now it is happening. Now it is happening. I smile when it happens.

THE SELF (2)

The first time I ever hear of Samuel I'm living in Berlin.

*

This is the last time we'll see each other. Before we're done I want you to show me the money. Put it on the table. I want to see it before I tell you the end.

*

I have just walked down to the cobblestone street. I'm bending over to unlock my bike when I hear a mewling sound behind me. I turn around to find my neighbor. Not the schizophrenic German war veteran who puts up signs all over the stairwell about how together we can "drive the talking dildos out of the walls." Not the unemployed Portuguese architect. But that girl, the Swedish artist, who for some reason wants to be called Panther.

*

288

Here are my memories from the last day. Samuel and I hadn't spoken in a month or so. After he moved, I went out to Kungens Kurva now and then. I didn't do anything in particular. I walked around the parking lot. I grabbed a coffee. Sometimes I stood in the place where it happened and thought about how much better it would have been if it had been me and not my brother. There was a note outside the transport school that said that the museum at Skansen was hiring new train drivers. I smuggled the note into my pocket and called the manager later that same day.

*

My neighbor is huddled outside the door, she has dark streaks of make-up on her cheeks. Several minutes pass before she manages to tell me what happened. She was standing at a market in Kreuzberg, someone called to say that her childhood friend had died in a car crash. Then she walked all the way home. Why didn't you take the U-Bahn? I wonder. And why does the name Samuel sound familiar? Did I meet him? Was he the one who visited you last summer, the guy who was sitting at that outdoor restaurant with a friend as big as a bodyguard?

*

The train looked like a toy train but it went on tires instead of rails and it had a steering wheel and a stick shift, just like a bus. Three cars and one locomotive. The tourists loved it. The manager said that it was hard to maneuver the train, especially when it was packed full of tourists, because then it weighed over three tons. But for me, a person used to parallel parking fifteen-foot trucks at rush hour, it was a piece of cake.

"You're a little older than the people we usually hire," said the manager, but he said it as a compliment.

*

Three months later I move home from Berlin. I give up the novel project with the working title *The Genderless Love Story*, which I have spent four years not finishing. I return home to Stockholm with fewer pages than I had when I moved down.

*

But still I was nervous when it was time to drive my first circuit. I was wearing the red coverall. The nametag showed everyone my name. I had driven it a few times without any tourists so I could learn to time the guide voice. I knew how slowly I needed to drive for the English-speaking voice to say "Stockholm. Look at her. Isn't she beautiful?" as we crossed the Djurgården bridge. I knew how quickly I needed to drive down Strandvägen for the voice to say "To the right we see the prestigious Royal Dramatic Theater" as we passed Dramaten. I knew I had to zoom past Kungsträdgården so we didn't end up stuck on the bridge as the guide voice started talking about the palace and Gamla Stan. The manager explained that this part of the route was new, an experiment, but if all went well and I did a good job they would continue to run the tours through the city and it wasn't out of the question that my short-term employment for this project could turn into a full-time job.

*

Then Grandma gets a blood clot. M's dad has a heart attack. D's aunt dies of lung cancer. A friend's son sniffs glue and dies of cardiac arrest. B and P are run down by a drunk driver on Birger Jarlsgatan.

And then E, who—

E, who—

I try to write it, but it doesn't work, I can't write it, it's too soon. *Too soon? It's too late, when will you understand that it is too late?*

*

Up on Katarinavägen you could choose whichever speed you liked, because the voice went on and on about the view and the cobblestones and the historical buildings. On Fjällgatan we made a stop for coffee and ice cream and photos.

*

I ought to write it, I try to write it.

And then E, who—

E, who—

But I can't, I can't, if I write it it's like it really happened. *It did happen, when will you realize that it happened? It happened it happened it happened it happened.*

*

Fifteen minutes later I was driving back toward Skansen. The voice coming from the speakers was automatic, all I had to do was drive at the correct speed and ignore the teenagers who were laughing and pointing.

*

After E's funeral I start doing research on Samuel. I contact people who lived in his grandma's house, I email his mom and sister, I call up the girl who rented her apartment to him, I have coffee with his old basketball coach. I convince myself that I am a part of the real world, that words are not more important than people, that all I want is to try to understand what happened. *But is that really true?*

*

After a few days at my new job I felt confident behind the wheel. I joked around with my coworkers, I brought my lunch in a lunchbox. I was finally on the right track. Soon I would be able to start paying back the loan from Hamza. I thought about reaching out to Samuel pretty often. But I didn't do it. I didn't call him and he didn't call me.

*

I record voices and ask follow-up questions, I listen and nod as people say that it was an accident, he lost control, he ran into a tree, he fell asleep at the wheel, it wasn't anyone's fault, it really wasn't anyone's fault. The only one at fault would be Samuel, if he had been driving too fast. And maybe his uncles, if there was something wrong with the car.

*

It happened on a Thursday afternoon in April, two thousand twelve. I was up on Fjällgatan with the train. The group of tourists were a white-toothed American family, a few British girls, three young people from Japan, and two middle-aged guys, Italians or maybe Croatians, suntanned with expensive shoes. Everyone had been impressed by the view, had taken their photos, drunk their coffee, eaten their ice cream. Soon we would go back downtown. My phone vibrated. It was a foreign number. I answered.

*

People say that if it was anyone's fault, it was the fault of the home. They ought to have taken better care of his grandma, if they had discovered her infected foot maybe she would have passed the simulator test and then maybe Samuel would have been in a better mood when he drove off.

*

Panther's breathless voice told me what had happened. Sometimes I think about that phone call. What would have

293

happened if I hadn't answered. How long it would have been before I found out. I wouldn't have gotten fired. I would have driven back downtown, waved goodbye to the tourists, parked the train, and gone home. But I answered the phone.

*

People say that the dementia home had nothing to do with it. It wasn't the nursing staff's fault, and it wasn't the parking lot attendant's fault, either. It was no one's fault. But it never would have happened if Panther hadn't moved away. She left him and stopped calling and her betrayal reminded him of other betrayals and that was what made him drive off the road.

*

Panther told me that someone had called her from the scene of the accident, they had found Samuel's phone and dialed the most recently called number.

"It must have just happened, it was close to a gas station in Solberga. Apparently they're waiting for the fire department."

*

People say that's a load of crap, he and Panther kept in touch, she called him on the last day, the last text he sent was to her. The only one who has any blame in this is Laide, because she said she loved him but she was never brave enough to let him in for real. She was terrified of the feelings he awoke in her and when he got too close she made him start doubting himself, he started to see himself through her critical gaze, and that was what made it impossible for him to keep living.

*

The line went dead, I thought: The fire department? Why do they need the fire department? Is the car on fire? Do they have to cut him out? My hands turned the key, my foot slammed on the accelerator.

"Woohoo!" shouted the American dad as the train leaped into action.

*

People say that's not true. Laide had nothing to do with it. Their relationship lasted for a year and when it ended Samuel moved on, it took a month or two but then he started seeing other people and that was really what made him feel desperate, that he realized that it was possible to move on, that none of what had seemed so major was major enough for him to truly remember it, and that was why he aimed for the tree.

*

The train whizzed down toward Katarinavägen, the tires squealed as I skidded onto Hornsgatan, the cars rattled, the wind howled, I just wanted to get there, I had nothing to lose, or what I had to lose was nothing compared to what I risked losing.

*

People say it all hinged on the house. It was those undocumented people's fault, there were too many of them, it was the smokers' fault, they threw their cigarette butts on the terrace, it was the neighbor's fault, he set the fire, it was his family's fault, they wouldn't talk about anything but money.

*

The tourists were holding on tight, the children were crying, the pre-recorded guide voice kept speaking as if we were headed back to Skansen. As we passed the pool hall in Zinkensdamm the guide voice said, "To the left we can catch a glimpse of the famous restaurant where the Swedish Academy have their weekly meetings" and as we crossed Ringvägen and were honked at by a bus and passed the Chinese pub that did the Asian buffet the voice said, "After the Swedish Castle you will see the Swedish Government building, or as the Swedes call it: the Riksdag." As we zoomed out of town across the Liljeholm bridge the voice said, "We are now returning to Östermalm—one of Stockholm's most affluent areas."

*

People say that's a load of crap. It was only one person's fault, and that person is Vandad.

*

We passed cars on the left, people pointed and laughed, one of the tourists shouted:

"Hello please where are we going please?"

But I thought, to hell with them, I didn't have time, I just had to get there, it wasn't too much farther. As we came out of the roundabout in Västberga and passed the industrial area and the gas station I heard the guide voice saying, "Honestly—have you ever seen a more beautiful view? This is why Stockholm is called the Venice of the North."

*

People say Vandad would do anything for cash. He was emotionally disturbed. He would have sold his own mom for a thousand kronor.

*

As we got closer, I heard sirens and an ambulance sped by in the other direction. There were only fire trucks still at the scene. I was too late. They had had to cut off the roof to get him out, his grandma's Opel looked like a convertible. I stopped at a distance. The recorded voice was silent, the tourists didn't know what to do, someone left the train to approach the wrecked car, someone took out a phone and took pictures, someone spoke comfortingly to their children. I wanted to go over there but I couldn't. From a distance I could see that the car looked pretty okay, except for the skinny tree growing out of the hood. Sure, there was smoke coming from the engine and the windshield wipers were bent out of all shape, but I didn't want to believe that it was so serious.

*

People say Vandad let Samuel pay for everything. When they moved in together he collected an insane amount of rent just so he wouldn't have to work. When he took over responsibility for Samuel's grandma's house he started extorting money from the people who lived there, he raised the rent every week, he confiscated their passports, he threatened to call the police on those who couldn't pay.

*

After a while, the guy who had called Panther came up and asked if I was the one he had spoken to. He said that the phone was lying there undamaged and he didn't know who to call, he just dialed the most recent number. He asked several times how I felt and offered me a ride to the hospital. I didn't respond, I couldn't respond, I just kept squatting there and looking down at the grass, there were dirt and ants and a few pinecones farther off, the guy asked again if I was okay, the tourists started going back to the train cars, it was time for me to drive back to Skansen but the guy didn't want to stop talking, he said he had been a medic in Cambodia and had seen some things. He put his arm around me and said:

"Listen, don't worry, it's going to be all right, there there, take it easy, don't worry."

It felt good to have his arm there, I felt his warmth, smelled his sweat smell, in the background I heard the guide voice starting over, the actor's voice welcoming the tourists to this guided tour and when the train was meant to be crossing the Djurgården bridge instead of sitting at the edge of the road in Solberga, the voice said "Stockholm. Look at her. Isn't she beautiful?"

*

People say that it was because of Vandad that the boy had hidden in the wardrobe.

*

What are you talking about? Who told you that?

*

People say that Samuel's internal organs were pulverized, his aorta was severed, his heart collapsed, he was crushed by the engine. He died instantly or on the way to the hospital. Because he did die, right? Yes, everyone is in agreement, at least, that he did die. He was born, he lived, he died.

*

Who? I want names.

*

People say that after Samuel's death, an author started asking questions. He met Samuel's acquaintances, he said that he had lost someone too and now he wanted to map out what had happened with the people who knew Samuel, he wanted to understand how people had moved on, he wanted to put the feelings of guilt behind him, and every time he heard that it wasn't planned, that it was only an accident, that Samuel was not at all the type to do something like that and thus he hadn't done it, the author felt a little better. His feelings of guilt disappeared, he convinced himself that Samuel's story was his friend's story, and if the people Samuel knew could move on then he could too. *But you can't move on because deep down you know Samuel's story isn't E's and what might have been an accident was no accident and no matter where you look you see traces of E, in kneecaps, in dimples, in flat rocks, in backseats of cars, in stick shifts, in windshield wipers, in dryers, in laundry rooms, in courtyards, in sunsets, in neon signs, in farewell letters, in regular letters, in missed calls, in unanswered texts, in the name of Grandma's throat lozenges, in E-major, in em-dashes, in scents, in sugar-free gum, in too-strong perfumes, in water glasses, in jean cuffs, in hoarse laughs, in the backs of park benches, in poached eggs, in American angels, in Berlin dance floors, in Parisian subways, in hotel bars, in made-up constellations, in memories that will soon vanish, in unchanged unending words that can never be erased.*

*

They're lying. Everyone is lying.

*

People say that that's a lie too, because the author didn't feel as guilty as he wanted to make it seem. He had other feelings too, he felt furious about being fooled and relieved about avoiding responsibility and happy that his theories checked out because once again here was proof that people could not be trusted, they say they will be there but then they disappear and all that survives is the words and the naïve hope that the next sentence, no the next one, no the next one, will change everything. The crazy thing is that not even his words could be trusted because as he neared the end he realized that every time a hole appeared in Samuel's story he had used his own memories and it was too late by the time he realized who it was that wrote lists of conversation topics and who collected definitions of love and who panicked over his crappy memory and whose dad had disappeared and whose friend no longer existed.

*

You're lying.

*

One evening I go back to the dementia home. Guppe shows me into the TV room where Samuel's grandma is sitting in front of a muted screen with a remote in her hand.

*

You've got to understand, it was a symbolic administrative fee. It got bigger because the household expenses grew as more people moved in.

*

Guppe cautiously touches Samuel's grandma's shoulder.
    "You have a visitor."
    She looks up and smiles.
    "At last! I've been waiting so long!"
    She hugs me and I hug her back, unsure of who she thinks I am.

*

I never betrayed Samuel. I never cheated him out of money.

*

Samuel's grandma tells me what they had for lunch and asks three times if I'm hungry.

"No, I'm fine," I say. "I ate before I came over."

"Wouldn't know to look at you."

She asks if my sister is well and how my mom is. I try to explain that I don't have a sister, and that my mom is fine, but my mom isn't her daughter and I'm not Samuel, I'm me. *Are you sure of that?*

*

I never confiscated any passports. I never threatened to call the police.

*

I explain that I was neighbors with a Swedish artist in Berlin who called herself Panther, and that was how I met her grandson Samuel.

"Even though we didn't know each other very well I'd like to ask you about the last time you saw him."

"The last time?" she says, her eyes opening wide.

It looks like something is breaking loose inside her.

*

I had no connection at all to that boy in the wardrobe.

*

Once she has calmed down and taken her medicine, we sit without talking.

"Oh dear, oh dear," she says.

The news is on TV. I want to ask if she remembers anything about the last day. Does she recall what they talked about that afternoon? Did Samuel seem sad? Unbalanced? Was he himself, or someone else? But I don't ask her any questions. We just sit there. In front of the muted TV.

*

None of it was my fault. Everyone is lying. Just like Hamza lied to the police when he was arrested and the prosecutor lied to the judge when he said that I was behind everything that happened on our rounds. Just like my lawyer lied when she said it could be worse and the prison chaplain lied when he said time heals all wounds.

*

After a while she takes my hand, she hums a tune, her hand is warm, she has elephant-wrinkly skin and brown liver spots that look like they're about to fall off. Her hands look like Grandma's.

*

Are we almost done? Do you want to ask one last question?

*

"Vandad," she suddenly says. "How is Vandad?"

303

"I don't know," I say. "But I'm going to see him soon. Did Samuel talk about Vandad the last time you saw each other?"

"Oh, did he ever. Samuel always talked about Vandad. Vandad this and Vandad that."

*

Oh yeah? And what do you want me to do with that information?

*

"Is Vandad a man or a woman?" Samuel's grandma asks.

"A man."

"'Well, look at that,' said the optician to the fly."

*

Listen. We were friends. We were brothers. We shared everything equally and we were loyal unto death.

*

"But I'm sure Samuel talked a lot about Laide, too?" I ask.

"Who?"

*

But it was never anything more than friendship.

*

"Vandad," she says again. "Samuel went on and on about that Vandad. And the way he said that name, I knew it was something more than friendship. You can't hide that sort of thing. Not from your grandma."

*

You can decide for yourself who to believe—me or an old lady. The guy with a photographic memory or the woman who can barely remember her own name.

*

"His betrayal hurt him more than hers did."

*

Why would I feel guilty? Don't project your feelings onto me. I'm not you. Samuel isn't you. Your actions are your own, don't expect me to help you deal with them.

*

"I think he loved him."

*

Stop. I don't want to hear any more.

*

She dozes off. I sit beside her. Her breathing is calm. Sometimes a snore comes out. Sometimes she becomes perfectly quiet and doesn't take a breath for five or six seconds. I look at her, I lean forward, I almost have time to believe that she is . . . when the next breath comes.

*

I'm done with this.

*

As the time nears eight thirty I rise, liberate my hand, and sneak out toward the elevators.

*

I have nothing more to say.

*

I stand there watching her through the pane of glass. And once again it's as if she is ... Surely she hasn't?

*

[Silence.]

*

I go back in to check, I place my hand in front of her mouth, I feel her breath. Warm and damp, like a child's.

*

Take your money and go.

Acknowledgments

Diane (for everything)
Lotfi, Hamadi, Gudrun
Babak, Soledad, Ignacio, Mohamed
Joel, Karl, Rebecka, Shang
Daniel Sandström, Albert Bonniers förlag
Astri von Arbin Ahlander, Ahlander Agency